Jane and the Damned

Also by Janet Mullany

THE RULES OF GENTILITY

Jane and the Damned

JANET MULLANY

AVON

An Imprint of HarperCollinsPublishers

JANE AND THE DAMNED. Copyright © 2010 by Janet Mullany. All rights reserved. Printed in the United States of America. No part of this book may be used or reproduced in any manner whatsoever without written permission except in the case of brief quotations embodied in critical articles and reviews. For information address HarperCollins Publishers, 10 East 53rd Street, New York, NY 10022.

HarperCollins books may be purchased for educational, business, or sales promotional use. For information please write: Special Markets Department, HarperCollins Publishers, 10 East 53rd Street, New York, NY 10022.

FIRST EDITION

Designed by Diahann Sturge

Library of Congress Cataloging-in-Publication Data is available upon request.

ISBN 978-0-06-195830-4 4357 9464 10/10

10 11 12 13 14 OV/RRD 10 9 8 7 6 5 4 3 2 1

*In memory of my aunts Phyl and Nell Dowling,
who introduced me to Bath and the novels of Georgette Heyer.*

acknowledgments

Thanks to my brother Martin for helping me come up with the original idea (and for the suggested titles of *Austen Powers* and *Blood Bath*); to May Chen for suggesting I try a paranormal starring Jane Austen, and for her firm, smart editorial hand; and to Lucienne Diver for her firm, smart agently hand.

Chapter 1

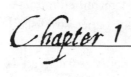

Steventon, Hampshire, England.
November 1797.

Declined by Return of Post.

Jane stared at the words scrawled across the top page of the stack of papers. She patted the manuscript as though the pages were disordered, although they were piled neatly together, tied carefully with string. Undisturbed, untouched, unwanted.

"Do not be downhearted, my dear." The Reverend Mr. Austen reached out his hand to his daughter. "We shall try another publisher."

"Thank you for sending the book to them, sir. It is not your fault they did not like it; it is mine. I beg you, do not send it to another publisher."

"Jane, you cannot give up after your hard work. Another publisher may think better of it. Your mother and I, the whole family, believe in your talent."

"Of course you do, sir, and I am most grateful, as a daughter should be. But this gentleman"—she flicked a fingertip at the devastating statement—"does not care about my feelings and knows that he shall not have to eat dinner with me and suffer my reproachful glances across the table. Perhaps he is right. I am not giving up, sir. On the contrary, I am determined to make this book a better one. I trust we can afford the paper, sir? I shall need a quantity."

"My dear, of course you may have as much paper as you need— all the pens and ink in the world, too." He gestured around his study. "All of this is at your disposal, unless you are still determined to write in your parlor upstairs?"

She glanced around her father's room, with its book-lined shelves and shabby, comfortable furniture, its air of masculine privilege and privacy. A half-written sermon lay on the battered leather of the desk, along with a feather—blue and bright, a jay's feather that he must have picked up on one of his walks around the parish.

"It is very good of you, sir, and I thank you," she said. "But I prefer my little table; and besides, I can see who comes to visit and keep an eye on the great world."

"But the interruptions. Surely they distract you?"

"Not at all, sir. I need interruptions, else I should become a poor creature lost in her own thoughts, which, I am assured, are of little import." She picked up the manuscript and cradled it in her arms. "I shall get to work immediately. No, not immediately. It is Thursday, sir, and today Catherine Bigg and Cassandra and I make merry at Basingstoke Assembly Rooms. We leave for Manydown Park this afternoon."

"Promise me, dear Jane, you will put nothing of this in any of your books."

Jane smiled at her sister sitting opposite her in the carriage that carried them to the Angel Inn in Basingstoke. "As if I should do such a thing!"

"But that is the best part of an assembly—to talk about our neighbors after," cried Catherine Bigg. "Why, Jane has so wicked a tongue, and there is nothing I like better than to hear her recount what she has observed but which we have merely allowed to pass us by unnoticed."

Mrs. Bigg frowned. "I know Miss Jane would not be unkind, my dear, but do you not think such frivolous behavior unbecoming?"

"Oh, Mama, you are such an excellent chaperone!" Catherine squeezed her mother's arms.

"But what place better to behave frivolously than at an assembly room?" Jane said. "Would it not be a different sort of frivolity, ma'am, to not behave appropriately at such an event—to stand at the side of the room all gloom and seriousness? Besides, I expect we shall meet no one new, and as usual there will not be nearly enough gentlemen. No, do not smile, Catherine. It is a very serious matter. We shall be abandoned at the side of the room, listening to elderly ladies whisper that the Austen girls, who never had any money in the first place, are now losing their bloom. Yet I assure you it will happen."

"Nonsense," said Mrs. Bigg. "Still raining, I fear. I shall go first with Catherine and Cassandra and send William back with the umbrella for you, Jane."

Jane helped her sister and friend gather fans and gloves. Here she was, twenty-one years of age, attending a ball at some provincial assembly rooms where possibly the shopkeepers would not outnumber the gentlemen and the ladies would almost certainly outnumber the gentlemen. Every day, the newspapers brought dire news of England's failures at sea against the French; in

London the Damned of the *ton* gambled and whored and scan-
dalized decent folk (they said already the Prince of Wales was
in their thrall), and in the country all the talk was of militia and
a possible French invasion. It was certainly not a time for trivial
pursuits and merriment; or possibly it was the time for pleasure,
because it was almost certainly the worst of times, and none of
them knew what the future might bring.

And such dreadful weather for it, the small ironic voice in her
head murmured. She must remember that.

She watched Catherine and Cassandra avoid the puddles and
the worst of the dung and straw that littered the street while the
Biggs' footman held the umbrella over their heads. Mrs. Bigg,
beneath her own umbrella, flitted between Catherine and Cassandra, lifting delicate muslin hems out of harm's way.

It was absurd to be so excited about a provincial assembly. She
had been trapped in a girlhood that once seemed infinite, Miss
Jane, the youngest and brightest daughter of the Austen family,
the one who wrote and read and played the pianoforte with dash
and flair, and was always ready with a witty comment. But now,
with her twenty-second birthday occurring the next month,
childhood was falling away. How many years would it be before
the matrons at assemblies and balls murmured about poor Miss
Jane, who almost certainly would not marry now, for she was
sadly faded and had too sharp a tongue for her own good?

How long before she sat behind the matrons, a spinster's cap
on her faded hair, and listened to the malice and gossip, herself
an object of pity and mild derision—the gentlewoman of limited
means with a small talent for music and writing.

There would never be any malicious gossip about Cassandra,
only sighs and gentle comments that it was a pity the eldest Austen
daughter would never marry now poor Tom Fowle was dead; as
though her status imposed upon her some sort of honorable dis-

charge from husband-hunting. Unkind, Jane. Unkind. Cassandra had been so sad, and she and Jane had wept together, all of the Austens mourning the loss. Jane's tears had been real.

She was being unkind because a day or so ago an unknown clerk in a publisher's office had been instructed that polite novels by ladies were of no interest and he should take care of the stack of paper forthwith. On receiving the bad news she had put a good face on her disappointment. She had smiled and joked, and proclaimed that she would write more and better. If necessary, she would tear the book apart with a ruthless hand and eye and begin again; she could not let her family down. But inside, resentment and anger burned, forcing its way to the surface in uncharitable thoughts, angry actions—like clenching her hands so hard that even in this dim light she could see the deep crease in her gloves.

"Are you ready, Miss Jane?" The door opened to reveal William, the shoulders of his livery already darkened by rain, his nose red with cold.

She nodded and pulled the hood of her cloak over her head and fixed a polite, agreeable smile on her face. Publishers' minions could go to the devil. She had her fan, her gloves, her pretty gown, and her reputation as a bright-witted, pretty girl; a dashing, high-spirited girl who tossed her chestnut curls, picked up her skirts, and skipped away from the footman and his umbrella to weave between the puddles and dirt as though performing a particularly complex and pleasurable dance step. She arrived inside the door of the Angel Inn with a few dark spots of rain on her muslin, some specks of mud on her stockings, and, she knew, a becoming pinkness in her cheeks.

Mrs. Bigg tut-tutted and, murmuring of finding others who would enjoy a hand of whist, directed the young women to the ladies' retiring room and ascended the staircase that led to the

Assembly Room. Bright candlelight glowed at the top of the stairs, and a small ensemble played a country dance with great vigor. The hum of lively conversation indicated that festivities were well under way.

"Jane! I do not think that muslin will clean well," Cassandra said. She leaned forward to whisper, "Some of the gentlemen remarked upon your behavior. You must be careful."

"Indeed? Which ones?"

Cassandra slid her eyes sideways with a small tilt of the head as Jane slipped her cloak from her shoulders and handed it to William.

"Those ones? I did not expect to see any of *their* kind here."

"I fear so. We must be very careful."

"But—here? Does London prove too tedious? Oh, how foolish I am. Doubtless they wish to make the acquaintance of the famous authoress Miss Jane Austen and her beautiful, virtuous sister and their most elegant friend Miss Catherine Bigg." She rubbed at a speck of mud on her skirts. "But it is still the same, is it not? Too many ladies and not enough gentlemen."

"Jane!" Cassandra giggled. "Oh, pray, do not say such things. Catherine, that is such a pretty ribbon. Did you buy it in Basingstoke?"

As Catherine and Cassandra chatted of fashion, Jane pretended to listen while observing the crowd of women engaged in putting the finishing touches to their appearances, jostling to see themselves in the large mirror propped against the wall. The room rang with the patter of leather-soled dancing shoes on the plank floor, the chatter and giggles of feminine voices, the rustle of muslin and silk. A young woman exclaimed as her wreath of silk flowers slipped over one ear and she reached behind her head to twist the wire into a more secure shape. Another, her back to the mirror, turned her head to view the back of her skirts, doubtless concerned about a scorchmark from an iron in the hands of an overenthusiastic maid.

Jane licked her fingers and reached to squeeze into shape a descending curl that brushed Catherine's neck. "More spontaneity to the curl, my dear Catherine. You must look as though you care not a jot for your appearance, but look like this always with the slightest of effort, not after an hour and a quarter with a curling iron and both you and your maid close to tears."

"Oh, heavens, this damp weather." Catherine sighed. "By the end of the evening I shall look like a furze bush, I know it."

"But a pretty furze bush," Jane said. She took a quick glance at her reflection in the mirror—she was tall enough to see over most of the other heads in the room and did not have to squeeze herself forward or stand on tiptoe. Adequate, she decided. But— she looked again.

How odd. The lady—the very fashionably dressed lady who stood at the back of the room, smoothing her silk gloves—did not appear in the reflection. It had to be a trick of the light, although the room was remarkably well lit with an oil lamp and several candlesticks embellished with hanging crystals to reflect the light.

"Cassandra." She touched her sister's arm. "Tell me I do not imagine things. The lady at the back of the room—the one with the silver fillet on her hair and the cream gown with the Greek pattern along the hem—"

"Oh, most elegant," Cassandra said. "Surely she did not have that gown made here. It must be a London dressmaker. And the fabric—what a beautiful drape. It cannot be a cotton, surely. I suspect it is a silk, or even, do you think, a very fine wool? I think—"

"The mirror. Now look in the mirror."

"Oh." Casssandra gripped Jane's arm. "So it is true."

The woman moved toward the two sisters, bowing her head in acknowledgment, a faint smile on her red lips. Her feet, clad in the briefest and most delicate of red leather Grecian sandals, whispered on the floorboards as she passed them and walked toward the doorway. She left in her wake a hint of a heavy, exotic perfume, and the train of her gown lifted, floated, and caressed Jane's muslin skirt as she passed by.

"'Pon my word, Miss Austen, you're as cool as a cucumber, whereas I . . ." Her dance partner produced a handkerchief with which he mopped his sweaty brow. "I beg your pardon, ma'am."

Jane made a polite curtsy in reply and looked for Cassandra and Catherine. Ah, there they were, laughing and chatting with the gentlemen who'd partnered them in the lively country dance that had caused her own partner such discomfort. She might well look as cool as a cucumber, but she was a cucumber in need of refreshment. The musicians, engaged in tuning their instruments and drinking tankards of ale—playing must be as enervating as dancing—seemed inclined to linger before they began the next dance. It was the perfect opportunity to drink some tea or punch and then hope for a partner, preferably a more athletic gentleman than the last, for the next dance.

Double doors at one side of the room led to the card tables; a set of double doors opposite them led to the refreshments room, an excellent arrangement for Mrs. Bigg and the other chaperones, who could play cards and gossip, yet keep an eye on their charges.

It might be considered fast, certainly unusual, for a young woman to approach the refreshment room alone, but fetching a drink for her chaperone was surely an act of kindness, of duty even. She would pay no heed to wagging tongues—after all, if she wished to cause talk, there were plenty of other ways to do so, many of them far more gratifying and pleasurable.

At that thought her gaze alighted on the group from London, who stood at the side of the room. She wasn't the only one who cast surreptitious or openly curious glances at them, for they were certainly well worth observing. The fashions of the ladies alone made Jane, in her best muslin, feel dowdy and provincial, but she could not carry off the exotic silks and glorious Kashmir shawls flung over bare shoulders with such dashing elegance. No, even Miss Jane, one of the sophisticated and learned Austens, would appear a country mouse dressed beyond her means and station, an object of ridicule. And the jewels that winked and flashed at wrist and throat—of course, at the throat—put her own modest pearl bobs to shame.

But it was the gentlemen she found most fascinating, even if there were not enough of them and so far none of them had made a move to dance, not even with the ladies who accompanied them. They stood among the Hampshire shopkeepers and local gentry like thoroughbred horses in a field of donkeys, beautiful and dangerous, stilled power in their limbs, mystery in their eyes.

She had dawdled as long as she dared without making herself an object of ridicule and she broke into her usual brisk walk. Arriving at the punch bowl, she instructed the servant there to pour her two glasses, and turned away to find herself face to face with the lady without the reflection. They both smiled and dipped their heads in acknowledgment, the meeting of two women a degree shy of being perfect strangers.

"Pardon me, ma'am," the woman said. Her voice was deep and husky. She touched a gloved hand to Jane's shoulder.

Enveloped in a sudden wave of warmth—oh, she hoped the woman did not know how unsettled she felt; could her kind not read minds?—Jane stepped away, spilling a little punch onto one glove.

"A pin is loose. I fear you may lose the sleeve. You danced with such energy—my brother and I were most struck by your grace—but I fear your gown has paid the price."

"Oh!" Jane put the glasses down onto the table. She looked around for Cassandra or Catherine, ready for a hasty retreat into the retiring room. They were nowhere in sight. If only she had allowed Cassandra to sew in the short sleeves in preparation for the evening, but no, she had assured her sister a few pins would do as well, and be less trouble when she restored the long sleeves the next day.

"Do not move." The woman stripped off her gloves, laying them on the table. "I shall make all well. It will take but a few seconds and no one will notice. Or would you rather I introduce myself so we may observe the proprieties? I am Sybil Smith."

"Jane Austen." She dipped a stilted curtsy, afraid the sleeve would thoroughly disengage. "It is most kind of you, Miss Smith."

"My pleasure, Miss Austen." Miss Smith's nostrils flared slightly. She moved closer to Jane, enveloping her in perfume, as though the two of them were wrapped in a shawl lifted from a chest of exotic, fragrant wood. Her fingers tugged and straightened the muslin at Jane's shoulder, twisting the fabric so she could adjust the pin to its rightful position.

"It has scratched you, I fear." The fabric settled at Jane's shoulder.

"No matter. I am much obliged, ma'am . . ." Jane's voice faded into a gasp as Miss Smith raised a finger to her mouth.

"Ah," she breathed. The small smear of scarlet had disappeared from her fingertip when she lowered her hand with a smile and a sigh.

Jane recognized it as sacrilege, decadence, as she had been

taught; a parody of Holy Communion. Yet she wondered, looking at the expression on the woman's face, what the equivalent would be for her: something rare and delicious, sweet . . .

"Apricots," the woman murmured. "Sun-warmed apricots from a tree splayed against a stone wall. The first of the summer, the juice bursting on your tongue."

Yes, apricots. Jane's mouth watered. The summer seemed remote, far away across a wasteland of sleet and rain.

Miss Smith reached for her gloves. "I trust my little repair lasts for the rest of your bacchanal, Miss Austen."

The spell was broken. "Oh, yes, indeed. I thank you. I am much obliged, Miss Smith." Jane snatched up her glasses of punch, her face heating. She bobbed a curtsy, clumsy and off balance; turned; walked as fast as she could across the room, dodging the people who milled about, laughing and talking while the musicians took their break; and arrived at Mrs. Bigg's card table only slightly out of breath.

Chapter 2

"Why Jane, you are quite flushed," Mrs. Bigg exclaimed as she accepted the glass of punch. "Most kind, my dear; how very thoughtful you are. I was just telling Mr. Smith what famous dancers you and Catherine are, and how you will not be without a partner the whole evening long."

"I beg your pardon, ma'am, but Catherine is by far the better dancer." Mr. Smith? Yes, Miss Smith had mentioned a brother.

"Now, where did he go?" Mrs. Bigg looked around. "Ah, there he is. Mr. Smith, this is Miss Jane Austen, my daughter Catherine's best friend." She beamed at the gentleman as though he were an old acquaintance.

"Your servant, ma'am." The gentleman bowed.

"Sir." She dipped a curtsy. Did not Mrs. Bigg see him for what he was? Was she spellbound, by one means or another, by the gentleman's extraordinary good looks, the restrained simplicity and elegance of his superb tailoring, or simply because he was what he was? She could not think that Mrs. Bigg was deflecting the gentleman away from Catherine, sensing his innate danger; that was unworthy of this well-meaning if slightly foolish woman.

"Miss Jane, may I have the pleasure of standing up with you?"
She could hardly refuse. Mrs. Bigg beamed approval, her good-natured face slightly flushed, as Jane accepted the offer.

"You have met my sister, I believe," he said as she took his arm.

"Yes, Mr. Smith, I have. She saved my gown, and my reputation, from certain ruin."

"She remarked upon what lovely women you and the elder Miss Austen are, having encountered you both earlier. I was bold enough to ask for an introduction."

Jane smiled. "And what brings you to the wilds of Hampshire, Mr. Smith? You must find it a far cry from the elegance of town."

"We have acquaintances in the neighborhood, and you do yourself an injustice. I have rarely met more pleasant society."

Who on earth could be one of his kind in Hampshire? Before she began a mental inventory of her neighbors, he added with a slight smile, "I do not believe you know them, ma'am."

The musicians assembled again, instruments at the ready, and at a nod from the fiddle player, who acted as their leader, played the opening chords of the next country dance. Mr. Smith and Jane formed a set with Miss Smith and another of the London party, a Mr. Hughes, who bowed with great affability but showed rather too many teeth in his smile.

The dance began. "Mr. Smith" and "Mr. Hughes," indeed. Jane was fairly sure the party traveled under assumed names but could not imagine what their purpose might be, unless it satisfied the *ton*'s notorious appetite for novelty and as a solace for boredom.

"I have the impression, Miss Jane, that you do not approve of us," Mr. Smith murmured as he took her hand.

"Indeed? Why would you think that, sir?"

He smiled, his canines brushing his lower lip before turning her so that she faced Mr. Hughes.

She was shocked at such a blatant display in public, but realized that the steps of the dance, each dancer gazing into their partner's eyes, made the moment as intimate as though they were alone together in a room. Probably no one else had even noticed.

"You know why, Miss Jane. You suspect we have nefarious designs upon the good people of Hampshire," he said when they faced each other once again.

"And *do* you?"

His dark, handsome eyes narrowed slightly. "We are what we are, Miss Jane. One could argue that what we do comes as naturally to us as, say, dancing and flirtation do to you."

"Alas, my reputation as a flirt precedes me as naturally as your nature does you, sir."

"The only difference, Miss Jane, is that flirting is what you do, and my nature, as you refer to it, is the core of my being."

She laughed. "You have not talked about me sufficiently with those who know me, sir."

He laughed and took her hand to lead her down the set. "Why, Miss Jane, should I talk about you to others when I have you here, your hand in mine? I should be a fool indeed."

They separated briefly to cast off around the couple at the bottom of the set.

"I suspect you are quite a flirt, yourself, Mr. Smith," she said as they met and took hands once more.

"It passes the time."

She raised her eyebrows (arched, well-shaped—she had received compliments on her fine eyebrows). "Well, you may certainly flirt but you do not flatter."

"I meant, Miss Jane, that since I have much time at my disposal, I should spend it in the way I find most pleasant."

She flushed. That he should refer openly to his—his condition—was provocative in the extreme. They passed each other in a hey, shoulders brushing, and she caught his scent, a stronger, muskier version of Miss Smith's. So Miss Smith had not been wearing an expensive perfume; it was the essence of the woman, and now of her brother (if indeed that was who he was), that had captivated her senses. And Mr. Hughes—as she passed him, he too had a distinctive scent, overlaid with a sandalwood cologne—but his was not nearly as attractive as Mr. Smith's.

Could they smell her as the scent of sun-warmed apricots? Did everyone have their own distinctive scent? She thought of waking with Cassandra every morning, her sister's sleepy, familiar smell; she had always thought that would be one of the more pleasant aspects of marriage. Why was it, then, that married women would complain (sometimes with pride) of male demands in and out of the bedchamber, but not share experiences of the more pleasant aspects of matrimony?

Now face to face with Mr. Smith again, hands joined, they had progressed through the dance so now they formed a set with Cassandra and her partner, a Mr. Beecham who owned land nearby.

Cassandra frowned and raised her eyebrows, her expression one of alarmed curiosity, and Jane smiled back, thinking with delight that she alone of all the women at the assembly had been chosen by one of the London visitors to dance. She managed to introduce Mr. Smith as they danced, and beheld a most correct series of exchanges between him and her sister concerning the size of the room, the weather, and the beauties of the nearby countryside.

"What a charming gentleman!" Cassandra whispered in her ear as they passed each other. "With whom does their party stay? Do they dine with us?"

"I don't know. I—" Mr. Smith took her hands and swung her away.

"Your sister is a very lovely woman," he commented.

"Yes, she is generally considered the beauty of our family."

"And you, Miss Jane? How does your family consider you?"

As a failure. "I should not be so immodest as to tell you, sir. You must ask my sister." She managed a light, flirtatious laugh.

Surely she had not said aloud the shameful words that first came into her mind? But Mr. Smith's eyes gleamed with a sudden quick emotion she could not fathom—sympathy, pity?

Before he could say anything, she made a polite inquiry as to the state of the roads from London and learned they were exceedingly muddy. The dance continued with no surprising revelations, nothing more than some mild flirtation and conversation of the most conventional sort. She should have been relieved, but admitted to a slight disappointment that her brush with wickedness was so slight. It was unlikely she would meet Mr. Smith, or any more of his kind, in the future.

The dance ended, and as Mr. Smith bowed, he said, "If it will not cause scandal, Miss Jane, I should be pleased to stand up with you again."

She laughed. "I assure you my reputation will not suffer. If anything, it is you who will be talked about and speculated upon for a good many days, but as you are a visitor to the neighborhood, that would happen anyway."

"I am duly warned, ma'am." He bowed again. "Then I daresay tongues will wag if I offered to escort you to take some refreshment."

"It would give us all the greatest pleasure."

He offered his arm and led her into the side room, now busy with couples who intended to fortify themselves for the next dance. Miss Smith and Mr. Hughes were not there, and Jane saw Cassandra and Catherine briefly across the room. She knew they would grill her mercilessly later for details of her encounter and imagined their disappointment that there would be so little to tell.

As Mr. Smith returned with two glasses of punch, the music struck up again. "I fear I shall ruin your reputation," he remarked. "It seems you are not destined to dance every dance tonight. Shall we sit and talk awhile, or does your chaperone wish you to join her?"

"Mrs. Bigg is happy playing cards. I shall not disturb her."

He drew out a chair for her at a recently abandoned table— most of the occupants of the room had hastily downed their punch or lemonade and rushed out to dance again—and sat opposite her.

"Now, Miss Jane, we have satisfied the conventions with talking of the weather, the roads, and the assembly, so we may now talk of more interesting things."

"What topic would you suggest, sir?" She took a sip of punch.

"Yourself."

She placed her glass of punch carefully on the table and prepared to say something quite original and witty, a lighthearted, self-deprecating quip. Instead she was struck dumb, a lump forming in her throat.

She managed to recover herself. "I suggest we choose another subject. I . . ."

"Ma'am, I did not mean to cause you distress." He leaned forward, concern on his face, and every piece of advice she had heard concerning his kind rushed into her mind. *They seek to seduce you . . . They cannot feel as we do . . . They are not to be trusted . . . They despise those they consider beneath them and regard them as their playthings . . .*

"I suffered a grave disappointment today, sir. I shall not bore you with the details, but I thought to come here and seek solace in dancing and conversation. I find I am unsuccessful and worse, prove bad company."

She stood and he rose to his feet too.

"You, Miss Jane, could never be bad company."

"It is most kind of you to say so, sir."

"But should you wish to unburden yourself, you might find it easier to do so to a stranger, rather than one whom you will see every day."

"Most generous, sir." She spread her fan. "But why should you wish to be the recipient of my woes?"

He took the step that brought him to her side of the table. "Because you interest me, Miss Jane. I see in you . . . something unusual: not what I expected, or dared to hope to find in a young lady in the country."

"The last gentleman who flattered me so was not able to make me an offer of marriage because he had no money. You, sir, are likely only to offer me debauchery or ruin." She snapped her fan shut. "I had best join the others in my party, sir, as had you yours."

"Afraid, Jane?"

She gazed at him, desirable, sinful, damned. "No sir, but neither am I fool to take the challenge."

"Then leave me, Miss Jane." He swept a low bow that had something of mockery about it.

"Damn you!" She'd never dared speak those words aloud to anyone, however much she had wished to. "Damn you, Mr. Smith. Very well, I shall bare my soul to you, a creature with no soul. My disappointment in love, although I am recovered from it now, took place last year and created much bitterness in my heart. This year my dear sister's betrothed died far from home. And this very day, I received word that a London publisher was pleased to send back my first book, unread."

"Your first book? That is to say, a love affair gone awry is not a surprise in such a young and pretty woman. But a book—will you tell me of it?"

She shrugged. "It is a novel, a story of two sisters who live unfashionably in the country and who have little money but wish to marry well and for love. I flatter myself—or rather I flattered myself when I thought well of my work—that my work resembled that of Mr. Richardson, whom I much admire. But now, I see I must abandon my original plan and start afresh. I am not sure how, however."

"Interesting. I should mention, Miss Jane, how handsome you are when you are passionate."

"Of course I am," she murmured. "A lady is always aware of how to present herself to her best advantage."

He offered his arm. "Shall we take a turn around the Assembly Room and continue to talk?"

She glanced around the refreshment room, empty except for a manservant gathering glasses and plates from tables onto a large tray. The man glanced at Mr. Smith and made a slight gesture with one hand: forefinger and little finger extended, the other two tucked beneath—the traditional sign against evil. His tray fully laden, he hefted it and left through a side door, leaving Jane and Mr. Smith alone.

Music, the thud of dancing feet, and merry laughter drifted into the room.

"If we return to the other rooms, I shall be obliged to introduce you to everyone I know there, which will prove a grave obstacle to conversation."

"Indeed. So you suggest we stay here?"

"Yes. The dance will last a good twenty minutes more."

He tucked her hand into the crook of his arm. "We shall take a turn around this room, then, and I shall serve as your confessor."

She gasped in mock horror. "Worse and worse. Now you confess to papism? I hardly know which is more dreadful."

"I suppose, in your view, either way I am condemned to eternal damnation."

"It is no laughing matter to me, sir. I pity you."

"You *pity* me?" His lip curled. She caught the gleam of white beyond the ruddiness of his lips.

"Yes, sir. You have all of the world and all of time, yet your kind fritter away their gifts. Have you not considered the good you could do and the wisdom you could share with us? Yet you are notorious for your debauchery and wickedness, and worse, you spread corruption throughout society with your evil ways."

"Spoken like a true daughter of the Reverend Mr. Austen of Steventon," he responded. "I must admit, I am disappointed in you, Miss Jane. I did not think you should grasp at the straws of conventional morality. Would you turn down immortality if it were offered you?"

"I would. It is against my faith and I should not wish to injure my family."

"But if you were to undo the damage my kind has done; to do good in the world with your gifts? Would not that be worth losing your soul?"

"Nothing is worth that, sir. Nothing."

"You grow passionate again." He stopped and turned to clasp her hands in his. "You are a brave woman, to argue thus with me. Should you not be afraid to challenge me, so?"

"I don't know, Mr. Smith. Should I be afraid?"

He said nothing, but a wildness entered her mind, a swirl of sensation that made her gasp in shock. The wooden planks of the floor beneath her feet spoke of wind-tossed branches and the swirl of leaves; the silk against her feet and calves became a thousand patient creatures encasing themselves in cocoons, and a clattering loom spun and blurred.

"Stop!" She closed her eyes to block the images and sounds, but more came—grapes beneath a hot sun and cool casks in a deep, stone-lined cellar; the punch, and yes, the glasses, blown in a hellish space of heat and smoke, and the gritty pour of sand.

"A little taste," Mr. Smith murmured. Cool air caressed her hand and forearm as he peeled away her cotton glove. Somewhere, dark-skinned people, mournful and angry, plucked white buds from bushes beneath a burning sun while an overseer on horseback rested his whip on the pommel, a cigar clenched between his teeth. The smoke mingled acrid with the stink of sweat and misery. Looms thrummed, filling the air with snow—no, not snow, fragments of cotton, and small, exhausted children darted beneath the unforgiving, deadly machinery.

His lips were on her arm now, and then more than his lips, a sting and wetness.

"No," she said. "No."

But the heat and glory of the moment whirled her away from the savagery and sorrow she had seen, into a place where the throb of her blood became a pleasure too great to bear.

The vampire who called himself Mr. Smith lowered the unconscious woman onto a chair. The room was still empty, and the dance, with its imperfect harmonies and clumsy thudding of feet, continued. They would not find her for a good fifteen minutes, a tiny grain of dust in time.

He licked the last of the blood from her arm and breathed the wound closed.

She was pretty, intelligent, and—although certainly able to enjoy life—unhappy. Her distress and vulnerability had called him to her. Now her troubles would soon be over, and she would go to her Christian heaven. Her handsome sister would mourn; so would her friends and family. Her novel—doubtless some earnest, girlish attempt—would remain only as a treasured family memento, to be placed in a box with a lock of her hair and other possessions. She would never fall in love, marry, or have children. With cool detachment, he recognized in himself a spark of regret, something he remembered vaguely from long, long ago.

But as he replaced the glove on her arm, pulling the tight cotton over her too-pale flesh, he remembered her passion, her courage in lecturing him on how he squandered immortality.

Miss Jane, the respectable vicar's daughter, as one of the Damned. It was unthinkable. She could be little more than the descendant of country gentry with possibly some distant aristocratic relations' blood in her veins (very little of anyone's blood ran in her veins at the moment). How would she fare if granted the gift herself?

It was almost time for him to depart, to leave this company with his sister and the others. Whatever the temptations a provincial assembly such as this could offer him, he must not forget the great undertaking to which he was entrusted, with the fate of Britain in his hands.

He placed her arm on the table next to her head. She was almost gone, the seductive beat of her pulse a weak stutter as her skin cooled and took on the color of wax. Her breath was shallow and labored and her delicious scent of summery fruit was fading fast.

He leaned forward and gave her the only gift he had. He pressed his lips to her mouth and breathed eternal life into her soul.

Miss Jane Austen was a vampire.

Chapter 3

"Jane! Jane, my dear, you must wake."

A pungent smell woke her.

"Ah, burning feathers always works. Now, where can that physician be?" A heavy, clotted *thudding* reached her ears, accompanied by a rich and salty aroma. She wanted badly to fill her mouth and drink.

Someone lifted her head and she thought for one moment wine was what she really craved, but she took a mouthful of thin, sour stuff and opened her eyes to see that she was lying on a bed at Manydown Hall. Only a few hours ago she and Catherine and Cassandra had dressed in this room and arranged one another's hair. She had been different then. Something was wrong with her, very wrong.

Cassandra sat beside her, an arm beneath her head, and she turned her face to her sister's shoulder, where a complex web of dark richness throbbed and flowed. Her mouth watered.

"Am I ill?" she asked. "Why does everything pound so?"

The one whose essence she had coveted—Mrs. Bigg, it was kindly Mrs. Bigg—leaned forward. "Do you have the headache, my dear? If you are not better by morning we shall send for your mama. Why, we found you in a swoon in the supper room and could not rouse you; you seemed half dead. We have sent for the physician."

"Oh, Jane, you are so pale." Catherine seized her hands and chafed them. "And so cold."

"You are so warm." All three of them tantalized her, carrying what she could not have.

Another pulse joined the counterpoint of the other three women, a man who brought a waft of horse and tobacco and claret, grease from a recent dinner on his coat—already she was learning to prevent each scent flying into a wild cadenza of the senses—what had happened to her? A foul odor hung about him, of sickness, and mysterious powders.

"Ma'am." He bowed to Mrs. Bigg. "So this is the young lady who swooned? You have certainly frightened your friends, miss, but I think from the look of you there is not much amiss."

"Sir, she was unconscious for the best part of two hours, and I do not think that a trivial matter," Cassandra said.

He looked at her over the top of his spectacles. "So a lady might think, but I assure you, as a man of science, that I believe little ails her. Perhaps the excitement of the evening, eh?"

"Sir, this was the Assembly Room at the Angel in Basingstoke, not the court of the Tsar of the Russias," Cassandra insisted.

The physician grunted and picked up Jane's wrist. He frowned and poked at her skin. "You must keep her warm. A little gruel and some wine, and best to keep quiet. If the condition persists, I should recommend a bleeding."

Blood. She could see it, smell its metallic odor as it dripped into a basin, rich and dark. A small, involuntary moan escaped her lips.

"Oh, Jane, does it hurt? Where? She has the headache, I believe," Mrs. Bigg said. "Why, she is hardly able to speak, poor thing. Can you do nothing for her, doctor?"

The physician peered at Jane as though he was annoyed at being roused from his bed for such a triviality, a young woman beset by the vapors. "I'll send a draught over in the morning, ma'am, if you think it necessary. May I suggest some laudanum for the night."

Jane looked at him with dislike. "You're a fool," she said. "And your maidservant is with child by you, and your wife doesn't care because she's taken the miller as her lover."

She had no idea where the thought came from, but she saw it as clear as day: the maidservant stood before a mirror, smoothed apron and skirts over her belly, and wondered how long it would be before she showed; and a man dusted with flour slapped the buttocks of the physician's wife as though they were plump sacks of grain.

"What!" The physician backed away. "She rambles, ma'am. Clearly it is a case of insanity."

"Or of truth, sir," Jane said. How easy it would be to grasp his coat and sink her teeth into the folds of his neck—even though those folds were stubbled and greasy and the blood beneath ran sluggish and unhealthily thick.

Without even bowing, the physician gathered his bag and coattails around him in lieu of dignity and left the room.

"Jane, that was a shocking thing to say!" Mrs. Bigg said. "Where did you get such a wicked, unladylike idea?"

"I did hear something of the maidservant, Mama," Catherine said timidly. "I expect I may have mentioned it to Jane, for everyone is talking of it."

Jane nodded, running her tongue over her canines. They

ached, and she hoped a trip to the dentist was not in the future (but no, she knew deep down inside it was not so—besides, why both teeth, at the same time?). "I'm tired," she mumbled.

"Of course you are, my dear," Mrs. Bigg said. "How would you feel about some laudanum? No? Some wine? You are looking a little better, but still too pale, and these pretty hands of yours are so cold."

"I am feeling well enough, ma'am, although somewhat fatigued."

She turned down offers of tea, warming pans, more coals, and the contents of Mrs. Bigg's medicine chest, and was relieved when Catherine insisted her mother go to bed. After extracting from all three a promise that they would wake her if Jane became worse during the night, Mrs. Bigg picked up a candlestick and left the room, admonishing them not to stay up gossiping.

Catherine turned so Cassandra could untie the laces of her gown. "Hurry, it's freezing. Jane, did you hear what I heard: that the miller's parts are abnormally large?"

"Catherine!" Cassandra scolded. "What a shocking thing to say. Is it true?"

"Oh, indeed. Apparently he is most popular. There, your stays are unlaced. Quick, unlace me and then we can talk."

"We mustn't tire Jane," Cassandra said. She tugged at Catherine's laces. "Oh, they're knotted, you tiresome girl. My fingers are almost as cold as Jane's."

Catherine, at the dressing table, reached for rags to curl her hair while Cassandra labored at her laces. Jane searched her reflection—she was there, and surely the indistinct quality of the image was only because the flames of the candles wavered in the drafty room.

Catherine and Cassandra, in their nightgowns and caps, their stays and petticoats and shifts tossed onto a chair, ran over to the bed. Catherine jumped beneath the covers and gave a squeal of surprise. "Jane, you are so cold! I shall send for a warming pan."

"No, we'll warm up on Cassandra." She nudged her sister with one foot. "Pray faster."

On her knees at the side of the bed, Cassandra, head bowed and hands together, gave her a distinctly un-Christian look. "Hold your tongue, and should not you pray, too?"

"I'm ill," Jane said.

"I'm cold," Catherine said with an exaggerated chatter of teeth. "Oh, do come to bed, Cassandra, I'm sure God won't want you to catch your death."

". . . and restore my dear sister to health. Amen." Cassandra climbed into bed on the other side of Jane and tied the ribbons of her nightcap beneath her chin.

"I cannot believe you swooned from being kissed," Catherine said. "What did Mr. Smith do?"

"He kissed you?" Cassandra sat up.

Catherine gave an annoyed squawk. "Pray lie down again, you let cold air in so."

"No, he didn't kiss me." Had he? She remembered his mouth on hers and a sense of fading away and then fading back, if that were possible, and a deep and profound change that she could barely define. But she wouldn't think of that.

"Liar. Did he kiss as well as Tom Lefroy?"

She was silent. She rarely thought of Tom now. How foolish and innocent that seemed now; how young they had both been.

"Jane, dearest," Cassandra said. "We should not tease you, for you are not well, I know. But did anything—anything untoward happen with Mr. Smith? He did not hurt you?"

Touched by her concern, Jane put her arm outside the bedclothes and hugged her sister. "He was a perfect gentleman."

"She's being ironical," said Catherine, yawning. "We shan't

get anything more out of her. A pity. He was so very handsome, wasn't he? But really, who would have thought to see their kind here in Basingstoke?"

"I was pleasantly surprised. They were quite civilized. Why, they even danced, and Mr. Smith was quite pleasing in his manners, almost like a real gentleman."

"Or a duke."

"Not a duke. You have seen the wicked pictures of them. They are all so profligate and fat and disagreeable."

Their voices faded as they slid down into sleep, their bodies becoming heavier, pulses slowing and softening.

Would she need to sleep? What would happen to her in the light of day? She ran through all the myths and rumors she had ever heard and wondered when a terrible wickedness would infect her. Was she always aware of others' pulses in a quiet room? Or the sounds of a room that was almost quiet: the slight crackle of the fire, a rustle and pattering of a mouse (that rapid thrum—surely not the little creature's heartbeat?), the creak of centuries-old timber settling as the room cooled?

So she did need to sleep after all, and she awoke hungry. Beside her, Cassandra, bedclothes up to her nose, snuffled quietly in her sleep. Although it was not quite light, it was later than they normally slept, and a maidservant, at her knees at the grate, made up the fire.

Jane asked the girl to lace up her stays and gown, and swathed in a shawl, ventured out into the house in search of . . . breakfast. A cup of tea and some bread and butter would do very well, she assured herself. She descended the stairs with their elegant iron balustrade—it was a handsome house some hundred years old— and was hailed by a familiar voice, that of Catherine's brother, fifteen-year-old Harris Bigg-Withers.

"Miss Jane! They told me you were here last night, but I had gone to bed by the time you came home."

"Good morning, Harris. Yes, we were out shockingly late; you know how dissipated Basingstoke is. You have been out walking?"

He grinned, and slung his cloak over one arm. "Yes, and it's dreadfully cold." He looked around. "Where is Flash? Why, you silly creature, come here. It's our friend Miss Jane."

Flash the spaniel growled and bared his teeth at Jane.

"What's wrong with him?" she asked. Her heart sank. There was nothing wrong with the dog, but there was a great deal wrong with her.

"I don't know, but if he has not better manners I shall send him out to the kennels. Lie down, sir!" He smiled at Jane, all shy boyish charm. "Will you come in to breakfast with me, ma'am?"

She placed her hand on his arm and, to her horror, his thoughts intruded into her head.

She's so pretty but she thinks I'm a child . . . Maybe when I am a man I shall marry her . . . I hope I shall be taller than her soon . . . I wish I could stop stammering when I speak to her—and that other thing, that dreadfully embarrassing thing, is happening, I do hope she does not notice . . .

She snatched her hand away. "Yes—that is, I'll breakfast with you, Harris. And I'll tell you about the ball, as will Catherine, and Mrs. Bigg, and you will be heartily sick of the subject within a few hours. You should have come with us so we could not bore you about it."

"Would you have danced with me, Miss Jane?"

"Of course."

He ushered her into the morning room where breakfast was laid out on the sideboard and Jane stared at the array of cakes and breads that would otherwise normally tempt her. The seed cake, usually a favorite, looked pallid and dull. Harris, wielding the carving knife and fork, offered her a slice of ham. The meat curled onto her plate, limp, the stripe of fat topped with golden breadcrumbs unappetizing.

Noticing that Harris, plate in hand, stared at his food, obviously anxious to sit and eat, she took a small piece of bread and butter and sat. The footman on duty in the room poured her coffee and Harris a pewter mug of ale, and then left to replenish the hot water.

Jane cut the ham into small squares, forked one into her mouth, and chewed. Salty, cold, unsatisfying.

Beside her, Harris dug into his breakfast, a plateful of ham, bread, pickles, and cake, with great enthusiasm. Jane braced herself for a polite conversation with a young man who was altogether shy, in awe of her, and more than half in love with her, something she had suspected for the past couple of years and now did not doubt. She did not want to meet his gaze, frightened that someone who knew her only a little would detect something different, some otherness in her. She watched his hands, large and clumsy—like a puppy, he seemed to grow in fits and starts—his wrists revealed by his cuffs, as though this week his arms had decided to grow too. A visit to the tailor would be necessary soon; but Harris, heir to several properties, signified by his hyphenated surname, would find a lack of money no impediment.

Harris, his plate cleared, drained his mug of ale and laid his knife and fork neatly on his plate.

"Excellent!" he declared. "But, Jane, you've eaten hardly a thing!"

"I fear I overindulged last night at the punch bowl," she confessed, wondering that she could sustain light conversation while staring at Harris's hand and wrist. His fingers were curled still around the handle of his pewter mug, and his wrist, bared as the ruffles of his shirt cuff fell away, was revealed to her. She caught her breath at the sight of the blue veins against his pale skin.

"I w-wish you rode, Jane," he said, oblivious of her attention. "For we have a mare, a very gentle mare in the stables that Papa and I bought for my sisters and—"

He stopped and his face took on an expression of fright, or delight, she really couldn't tell which, as she reached across and grasped his wrist, shoving his plate out of the way. He resisted a little, but not much.

"Wh-why, what are you about?"

She didn't answer but drew his wrist toward her. As clear as day she heard his thoughts—*Good heavens, what if Papa or Mama—should I kiss her? Does she want me to? Does this mean I shall have to marry her? Oh Lord, that embarrassing thing's happening again, but the tablecloth—*

She shoved the excited babble aside and raised his wrist to her mouth and breathed in his scent. The delicate tracery of blue veins and the ropes and hollows of tendons were close to her lips; the back of his hand was rough with springy, fine hair as her fingers closed over the bones. He resisted a little more with a gasp of surprise, but she had him fast.

"Jane, s-stop, it is not proper—" He stood and tried to shake her off, but she was stronger than him now.

Her teeth ached again, smarting at the gums and sharp against her own lower lip. She ignored the waning voice of her conscience that warned her that what she was about to do was depraved and wicked. Instead she looked into his eyes and saw his frightened, bewildered expression.

"Don't be afraid, Harris."

He sighed and relaxed a little—oh heavens, it was so easy—but his heartbeat still thundered. His eyes became dreamy and still and he took a deep breath. A surrender.

She breathed onto his wrist, delaying the pleasure, and darted her tongue to his skin to feel the pulse.

The morning-room door opened. Shocked, she dropped Harris's wrist. His hand lay inert at his side.

"Good morning to you," cried Mr. Bigg-Withers. "Why, what are you two about? Are you feeling quite well, Miss Jane? I heard you were taken ill and actually had to miss a dance. I'm somewhat surprised to see you up and about so early. No, no, sit down, I beg you." He tucked his newspaper beneath his arm and proceeded to carve himself some thick slices of ham. "You should be at your lessons, soon, Harris. Your tutor is looking for you. May I help you to another slice of ham, Miss Jane? By heavens, you are in good looks today, despite your indisposition. Do you not think so, Harris?"

"Thank you, sir," she managed, severely disappointed, and her mouth watering.

Mr. Bigg-Withers placed another large slice of ham on Jane's plate. "There. From our own Berkshires—the best breed of pig, I always say."

Harris blinked as though unsure of what had just happened. "Good morning, Papa."

Jane stared at the slice of ham on her plate with loathing and listened to Harris and his father talk of his lessons and estate business, with much earnest discussion of a badger's sett that Harris had noticed on his walk. She dared a glance at the mirror on the wall—to her relief, she did indeed have a reflection—and saw that although pale, she was indeed in good looks. But then, their kind were noted for their beauty.

Or rather, *her* kind, for what had happened this morning left her in little doubt.

She pushed back her chair and stood; Harris and his father rose to their feet. "I beg your pardon, sirs. I am still not quite the thing. I must go home."

"You should not have risen so early," Cassandra said as they rode in the Bigg-Witherses' carriage. She put her hand out to feel Jane's forehead and Jane shrugged away. She did not want to be touched, did not want to find herself privy to Cassandra's thoughts, and be reminded yet again of what she had become.

"You must rest on the sofa when we get home. I shall read to you if you like. Do you have the headache still?"

Jane closed her eyes. They were almost home now, and she knew the inhabitants of Steventon who were taking the air would notice the carriage and remark that the Austen sisters had come home earlier than usual. Soon they would have plenty to discuss over tea, or dinner tables, or card games.

And she was hungry, so hungry, yet she could barely take a mouthful of food. She dreaded Cassandra and their mother forcing delicacies upon her and being obliged to swallow small bites that stuck in her throat like sawdust. She feared she might lose control and bite her sister—oh, she could imagine it only too well, the hot, sweet pulse, the release, the gratification.

The carriage stopped. Last time she remembered descending from this carriage she had been a girl, distracted by the unhappiness of a rejected manuscript—how strange, she had barely thought of it since last night when everything changed—and now she was another creature entirely.

"We're home," Cassandra said.

Jane gathered the cloth bag that held her overnight clothes

and stepped down from the carriage, slightly dizzy, to the familiar sight of the Rectory, her mother standing in the doorway.

"Why, Jane, what has happened?" her mother said. "You look most handsome, but ill . . . Come into the house."

Jane evaded her mother's embrace and saw the hurt in her eyes. "I am unwell, I regret."

She made her way into the drawing room and collapsed onto a chair, her eyes closed. Her mother called out to the servants for tea and hot bricks for Miss Jane's feet.

"Cassandra, what has happened to your sister?"

"I don't know, Mama. She swooned last night and we could not revive her for some time. She has been a little strange in her manner."

Jane opened her eyes. "Ma'am, I must talk to my father immediately." She rose to her feet, clutching a chairback for support.

Cassandra darted forward. "Oh, Jane, my dear, I beg of you— will you not sit and rest? We can talk to Papa later; surely he must be busy—"

"I beg your pardon, I must speak to him alone." Jane ignored her and headed down the passage to her father's study. She knocked and walked in, not waiting for a reply, and closed the door firmly behind her.

"My dear!" Mr. Austen rose as she entered and came around his desk to greet her. "So you are home, earlier than we expected. Is everything well? But no, I can tell it is not—"

"Sir, do not touch me!"

He hesitated and drew a chair forward for her. "Sit, Jane."

She remained standing. "Sir, I am one of the Damned. I have become a vampire."

Chapter 4

Her father sank back, propping himself against his desk. He took off his spectacles and massaged the bridge of his nose, silent.

Jane braced herself against the closed door, as though expecting the wood to give her strength, pressing her palms against it, and saw branches reaching to the sky, heard the wind, and then the thud of the axe and rasp of the saw, smelled sap and leaves and sawdust . . .

"Do your mother and sister know?" Her father's voice was harsh, cold.

"No, sir."

Her father straightened and retreated to the other side of his desk. He gestured to her to sit. "I trust this heinous act was committed against your will, that you did not give in to temptation and the pleasures of the world. Who is responsible for this—your condition?"

"I am not a serving maid caught big-bellied, sir. I am responsible, as is a gentleman who called himself Mr. Smith."

"The blackguard! I thought we were safe, here in Hampshire, from their kind." His voice became kinder, although the hand that gripped his pen on the desk was clenched hard. "My dear, forgive me if I am harsh. All know these creatures are full of wiles and temptations, and you have been in the world so little; how could you know what to expect? Had we known that any of their kind were to attend the assembly, of course we would never have permitted you to go."

Her father reached for his brandy decanter and glasses and poured them each a glass. He sat at his desk looking older and diminished, his bright hazel eyes brimming with tears. "I do not want to lose you, my dear."

"I am lost. I am damned." She warmed the glass in her hands. It might be more palatable if warmed.

"What are we to do, Jane?"

"I don't know, sir."

His eyes glittered; she sensed his fear and anger and helplessness. "Tell me, child, that Cassandra is untouched."

"She is well. At the moment I still feel some family connections, but I fear the craving for blood is strong and becoming stronger." Her mouth watered. "Sir, you must send me away."

"Jenny . . ." He had not called her that since she was very young. "Jane, there is one way we can take. We shall go to Bath and you can take the cure."

She nodded. The cure. If she did not fade away entirely from lack of sustenance, the waters at Bath might cure her; but the cure itself could kill. "It is a risky business," she said. "I may not survive."

"It is possible," her father said. "I have heard you will become exceedingly ill, for the waters are poison to their kind."

"To my kind."

He flinched. "It is my duty. I could cast you out, send you to London to fare for yourself, to sink into dissipation and vice with them, but I will not lose you." He picked up a knife to sharpen his pen and regarded his trembling hands with dismay. "Some would say it would be the correct way to proceed. Tell me, Jane, this Mr. Smith did nothing more to you? No further violation?"

"No, sir." Oh, the irony. What if he had? Everyone knew vampires could not carry diseases or bear children. As for her virtue, she might not survive long enough to congratulate herself on its preservation. "Allow me, sir." She took the pen and knife from him, not wanting to embarrass him. If his hand slipped and he cut himself—but she could not think of that.

"I shall write to your aunt and uncle and send the letter on the next post," her father continued, drawing a fresh sheet of paper toward himself. "We shall arrive tomorrow, shortly after they receive the letter. It is our only hope, but you will not be able to start the waters until Monday. What may we do to keep you alive, Jane?"

She took a deep breath to ward off unseemly laughter. "I need blood, sir."

"Would our dinner suffice? In a raw state, that is?"

She handed him the sharpened pen and laid the knife on the desk. "I shall visit the kitchen, sir. I hope it will sustain me."

He dipped the pen into his inkwell. "I know only a little of these matters, but I am sure time is of the essence. I fear by Monday it may be too late, but we must try."

She sat and listened to the scratch of his pen and, although she tried not to, the steady beat of his heart.

Mr. Austen sprinkled sand on the letter, folded it, and held a stick of sealing wax to melt over the candle on his desk. The wax dropped, heavy and liquid, scarlet, onto the creamy paper. He sealed it with his signet ring and turned it over to address it.

"I cannot thank you enough, sir, for all you do for me."

"You may repay me by becoming well and proceeding with your writing." He tapped the letter on his desk. "I shall talk to your mother and Cassandra and you must begin packing for Bath. I expect you will want to buy a few new things when you're better."

"Yes, I look forward to it." She smiled, sustaining the pretense that the cure would be successful and that the trip would become the usual sort of Bath visit—shopping and plays and concerts. Her father knew as well as she that the more her condition advanced, the more dangerous and painful the waters would prove. She knew too that the longer she went without blood, the weaker she would become. He might lose his daughter yet.

She left the study and found Cassandra and her mother in the morning room, both of them settled with tea and sewing, talking of the ball. They fell silent as she entered the room.

"Well, now, Jane!" Her mother reached for the teapot. "Some tea will set you up, I am sure."

She shook her head. "Thank you, no, ma'am. Father wishes to see you, if you please."

Her mother and sister exchanged a long, eloquent look before they busied themselves in putting sewing and teacups aside. They glanced at her with mingled concern and hurt that she had chosen to confide in Mr. Austen first, and apprehension at the undoubted severity of what had happened.

She watched them leave and tap at the door of her father's study, and then went upstairs to the small parlor between her bedchamber and Cassandra's. Her manuscript, still neatly tied with string, lay where she had left it.

She pulled at the knots, wishing her sailor brother Edward was there to help her, and the stout hemp cord snapped in her hands. Her newfound strength horrified her.

She read and turned a page. It could have been written by a stranger. Had she written those words, read them aloud to friends and family? She remembered the delight and laughter her words had caused, but she might as well have been reading, or attempting to read, something in Latin. The words were familiar, but the phrasing, the sentences, did not make sense.

With an impatient gesture she flung the pages aside. She yearned for fresh air—this was odd, surely. Did not the Damned of London sin all night and sleep the day away? But she must guard her strength. In three days she would take the cure and she must not exert herself, for if she did she would require sustenance.

She wandered downstairs, hoping to take solace in music, but as soon as she touched the keys she was assailed by visions of great gray beasts, the elephants from whom the ivory had been taken, moving in stately procession along a wide, flat landscape of high golden grass broken by an occasional graceful tree. And the notes sounded wrong; her hearing had sharpened, making her aware of infinitely subtle faults in the tuning of the pianoforte.

She would walk; she would find the solace she craved. Snatching her hat and cloak from the row of pegs near the front door, she let herself out. A cat, lurking outside to gain entrance to the house, fluffed up its tail and arched its back, hissed, and fled from her.

"Unfriendly creature. I'll have your blood for your bad manners," she muttered, and wondered whether she was serious.

She set out away from the house, onto a favorite walk where she and Cassandra gathered blackberries and hazelnuts in season, the hedgerows now frozen into a tangle of bare branches and tattered leaves. A few birds whistled in the gloom. The sun was low in the sky and the promise of darkness had to be responsible for the surge of energy in her limbs. She turned aside to climb a stile into a meadow, and instead of using the wooden steps—skirts modestly tucked around her ankles—ran and vaulted over, with a rip of fabric. She landed clumsily, exhilarated, and a series of thumps and scampers of small furred bodies toward shelter told her she had disturbed rabbits at their evening feed.

Not all of them. One crouched nearby, immobile, too panicked to run.

The little creature trembled, whiskers and ears quivering, eyes bright with fear.

"All is well," she murmured. "All will be well."

She stared into the dark eyes. The rabbit shuddered, eyes glazing over, and its rigid posture softened.

She could take it. Her teeth ached and extended, ready for the quick, efficient kill. The rabbit's pulse slowed as she crooned to it, lulling it into calm. She would be kind. Death would be fast and merciful. And its blood—oh, so warm and sweet—tasting of clover and grass and the sunshine of the creature's only summer . . .

No! She stood shuddering with disgust as the rabbit sprang to life, thumped its hind feet, and shot away into the hedgerow. A scuffle and rustle of vegetation, and the rabbit's escape was complete, the monster thwarted.

"I am a monster," she said aloud.

The next day, as the hours progressed in the carriage on the road to Bath, she yearned for what she could not have, neither blood nor the ready affection and quick, loving embraces of her sister and mother. Her mother, tired and with the lines on her face all too evident, wept quietly as they traveled, despite her father's attempts to cheer her.

And her family watched her—that was the hardest part to bear, those quick, sidelong glances when they thought she looked away (of course she knew)—as though they feared their beloved Jane might turn on them. She feared it too.

When they stopped to change horses and take refreshment, the world was loud and overwhelming. There were so many scents and loud noises. The worst was the contact with other travelers, the inadvertent brush of a stranger's elbow filling her with a jumble of thoughts and concerns. One time, a gentleman, elegantly dressed, pale—too pale—touched his hat and bowed with an ironic smile, saluting one of his own kind.

A chambermaid, brushing against her, murmured, "Oh, drink from me, miss, you'll like the taste of me. A shilling, miss, and you can do anything you wish. My neck or thigh, miss, whatever you fancy."

She was shocked, and tempted, and she longed for the young woman's surrender to her fangs (blatantly extended, her body quivering with expectation), before Cassandra drew her away, blushing, talking loudly of tea and bread and butter and the chance to have a moment of quiet away from the bumpy carriage. Poor Cassandra, trying to pretend they were going to Bath for pleasure, a visit to her aunt and uncle to enjoy the city and its entertainments; talking with great good cheer of the fashions they would encounter and new trims for gowns and bonnets that must be bought.

She did her best to add to Cassandra's chatter, for to think she would not be cured was unspeakable. One day, quite soon, she would write again, and laugh, and enjoy silly chatter about fashion and balls and partners, and this dreadful episode would be quite forgotten.

The day lengthened. The carriage, with its fresh horses every few miles (the expense was not to be thought of) rattled on down the Bath Road, and her father counted off the miles to their destination as they passed each milepost.

And then the carriage began the long descent into the city, Cassandra exclaiming over a house where a party was to be held.

Elegantly dressed guests spilled onto the pavement, their carriages stopped at all sorts of odd angles in the road, with liveried servants bearing flambeaux.

The Austen family arrived at the Leighs' elegant house at Number One Paragon Place, tired, travel worn, and with one of the passengers ready to hunt for blood but too weak to do so.

"Jane, my dear. Open your eyes."

She did so with great reluctance and found herself lying on a sofa in a well-lit room. Her father knelt at her side, a glass of brandy in one hand.

"I'm dying," she said and turned her head from the brandy he offered her. What was the point of delaying death? She was not afraid. Soon the hunger and fear would be over; she might be damned but she had harmed no one, not even a rabbit. The gates of heaven might not be closed against her.

"You cannot die now," her father said.

"I appreciate, sir, that you have gone to a great deal of trouble and expense so I may die in Bath. I'd rather have died at home and saved you the money. We are at Bath, are we not?"

"Yes, yes. We arrived but two hours ago." Her father gripped her hand. *Not my Jenny, not the delight of my eyes. Lord God, let me keep her awhile.*

"Pray let me go, sir. It is too much."

It wasn't what she meant, but he released her hand and his desperation and sorrow retreated from her mind. "I fear you will not survive until Monday. I am willing to do anything to keep you alive, Jane. I shall not see you drift into ash for lack of sustenance. Not my little Jenny. You are my blood, my flesh, my daughter."

"What do you suggest, sir?"

He did not answer but brought a small penknife from his

pocket, then stood, and unbuttoned his coat. She watched, with growing fear (and anticipation, she could not deny that) as he removed his coat, folded it, and laid it over a chair. With great deliberation, he unbuttoned one cuff and rolled the linen back.

"No!" she said. "What would the bishop say?"

"The bishop is the least of my worries. I fear your mother more. Have you considered my offer, miss?" His voice was playful as though she were a child and he offered her some delicious treat.

She turned her face aside. "When I was at Manydown I almost bit Harris."

"Poor lad. You must have scared him half to death."

"At first, but I . . . I lulled him. I do not know what would have happened, whether I could stop." She turned to see him hold the penknife over his arm, frowning.

"He'd make a good match for you in a few years; a very good match," her father said. "His health should be improved by then too. Now, where do you think I should cut?"

"I don't know," she snapped back at him. "I haven't been a vampire long enough to know! I've not drunk from anyone yet. And what if I can't stop?"

"Good heavens, I was not suggesting you drink from me. This glass of brandy should answer, I think, fortified by my blood. I read a treatise on the subject when I was young. Let us consider this a scientific experiment."

"Papa!"

He shrugged. "Possibly I could write a treatise upon it myself, and then we'd have two authors in the family, eh?"

"I shall only do it this once. Never again."

The knife moved, nicked, and blood welled on her father's wrist and dripped into the brandy.

He held the glass to her lips and she sipped, the brandy made stronger and more potent by the few drops of blood. If she tasted of apricots, her father had a particular scent: apples and leather, safety and comfort.

"All is well, child." He stroked her head. "All is well. I see you rally. I think that's enough, eh? We don't want you drunk, just strong enough to continue."

She lifted her head. "I can never thank you enough, sir."

"Ah, nonsense. You may be one of the Damned, but you're still my daughter." He blew his nose and gave her a brave smile. "Not a word to your mother."

Later that night she lay sleepless, listening to the sounds of the city—the deep tolling of church bells, the rumble of carts, the cry of the nightwatchman. So she would live a little longer, thanks to her father's blood, but meanwhile the current of others like herself tugged and wakened her. The night was her element now, the time she felt most awake and alive. Others like herself walked these streets, and the urge to seek out her own and learn from them nagged at her. How long would it be before she preferred their company to that of her family? Tomorrow night, the night before she took the cure, would the urge to find other vampires and the craving for blood be stronger than it was now? Or would she be so weak that she would lapse into a half swoon, as she had by the time they arrived in Bath? She could still barely remember the arrival, although she had a vague memory of the shock on her aunt and uncle's faces.

The room was dark but she could see quite clearly, walk with assurance over to the window and push back the curtains. Outside, a group of late revelers weaved its way down the street, and a pair of footmen carried a sedan chair. A cat strolled across the cobblestones and faded into the shadows. She might yet live.

* * *

"Come, Jane." Her mother helped her into the sedan chair, her bare fingers touching Jane's wrist above her glove. *Always our daughters; they are all he cares for, and he is not concerned about my well-being, however ill I may feel. How dare she put herself forward so, reaching above her station . . .*

Did her mother not know Jane knew everything that ran through her mind—the resentment and anger? If she hadn't felt so ill and tired, Jane might have warned her. As it was, she experienced only a very mild distress that her mother's cheerfulness and deference to Mr. Austen was nothing more than a façade. The sedan chair rose and wobbled and jolted its way along the streets to the Pump Room. The street was crowded, a mass of voices and scents—anonymous people who meant nothing to her. Her mother and Cassandra followed in another chair, with her father walking alongside.

She could hear their conversation with her newly sharpened senses.

"I have a recommendation for a Dr. Phelps," her father said. "He replied to my note and said he is able to call this afternoon, but with this unfortunate timing it was of vital importance that Jane start the waters immediately."

"The shame, that such a man will call at the house!" Her mother's voice was querulous. "It is bad enough that my sister and Mr. Leigh know of Jane's disgrace, but I daresay all the neighbors will talk of it, and the servants too."

"I believe we may count on the family's good sense not to gossip," her father replied. "And there is no point in frightening the servants by sharing the bad news with them."

"Oh, poor Jane." Cassandra sounded tearful. "I cannot think of her that way."

"You must be careful," Mrs. Austen said. "Everyone knows they have the power to sap the will of an unsuspecting girl—is not Jane herself an example of that?"

"She is my beloved sister!"

"We must pray for strength for her and for us," Mr. Austen said after a pause. "And yes, she is still our daughter and sister, even if she has sinned."

"I did not sin," Jane muttered to herself. She had flirted with a gentleman at a provincial assembly, something she had done before and would likely do again; in fact, if she had the opportunity at this moment she would flirt and enchant any available gentleman and sink her teeth . . . But she could not think in those terms, however hungry she might be. She concentrated on the breath and smell of the two footmen carrying the sedan chair, strong men whose blood would doubtless be invigorating and cheering.

How she longed for an etiquette book for the Damned. Surely there were guidelines on whom it was permissible to drink from, rather as the Church of England dictated that cousins could marry but niece and uncle could not. Would a servant expect a vail for allowing you to open a vein, and for how much? More than for calling a carriage, certainly, or handing around a tray of wineglasses. Was it indeed proper to expect a servant to perform such an intimate act?

For it was an act of great intimacy, and surely it must be a sin to think of such a thing. She peered out of the chair at the brief glimpses of passersby and cream stone buildings stained with soot and tried not to think of her hunger and the anonymous bodies of blood that passed nearby. If only she were stronger . . . But she could only become stronger by drinking . . .

A slowing pace, the glimpses of fashionable clothing, and the deep toll of the Abbey bell indicated that they were close to their destination. A slight tremor and the sedan chair came to a stop on solid ground. Jane drew the curtains back and took her father's offered hand.

"So we are to be fashionable, sir," she said—more of an effort to put Mr. Austen at ease than anything else. He gazed at her with a mixture of affection and guilt, and, yes, fear; and if their hands had been bare she would have felt his emotions. "I shall not be your partner at whist anymore," she added.

"What do you mean, Jane?"

"Your face reveals your feelings too clearly, sir. You have nothing to fear from me."

He tucked his hand into her arm and held out his other hand to Mrs. Austen, who ignored him, concerning herself with the set of Cassandra's bonnet and in guiding her eldest daughter around a puddle.

Jane caught a slight scent of something sulphurous and bitter—it must be the water—before she and her family were caught up with the swell of fashionable people who paraded into the Pump Room. The Austen family received a few glances that faded from mild interest to indifference.

"I feel quite a dowd," Cassandra remarked to Jane.

"It's quite remarkable that you feel well dressed when you leave the house, yet a mere fifteen minutes later are hopelessly aware of your failings in your gown and bonnet," Jane replied. She was rewarded with a brave smile from her sister.

The scent of the water became stronger as they made their way across the room.

"Sit, my dear. I'll fetch you a glass," Mr. Austen said.

Jane sank into the chair he offered. A few feet away, Mrs. Austen and Cassandra stopped to exchange pleasantries with a couple they knew slightly from a previous visit to Bath. Jane could not remember their names and did not want to waste precious energy on trivial conversation.

"I beg of you, ma'am, do not do it."

She turned in astonishment to see who had addressed her in a frantic whisper. A man of about thirty—or at least giving that appearance—slender and of medium height, with a fine-boned, handsome face. Dark eyes gazed at her beneath a head of tousled brown hair that sparked gold in the weak winter sunlight.

"I do not believe we have been introduced, sir." But there was no need for an introduction; she recognized him for what he was, and allowed herself for the briefest of moments to meet his gaze. For the first time since she had become one of the Damned she felt a connection, a knowledge that she was talking with someone who understood her. She could have wept with relief.

"Luke Venning, ma'am. You should know we do not stand on ceremony."

"I know nothing." She looked around for her father, who had disappeared into the throng around the fountain.

"Do not let them do it to you, ma'am. It is against your will, is it not?"

She shook her head. "I don't know."

He frowned. "You are but recently created, I believe. You need sustenance."

"Sir, my family wishes—"

"And what do you wish, Miss . . . ?"

"I am Jane Austen."

He bowed. "I beg of you, ma'am, consider carefully what you do." His gaze shifted away from her, to a beautiful, frail woman in a wheelchair.

"Who is she?" Jane asked.

"Mrs. Margaret Cole. She risks her life for the sake of mortality. Twenty years ago she left her husband for me. Recently she changed her mind, and attempts to take the cure."

"So that is why she looks so ill. I am so very sorry!" she exclaimed, and caught his hand in a burst of sympathy. He squeezed her hand briefly before returning it.

The woman looked near death, her lips bloodless, purple shadows beneath her eyes.

"That is what the cure does?" Jane asked.

He shrugged. "She has been one of us for some time, so the turning back is of necessity painful and dangerous. She may not survive. She turned down immortality—and myself—for twenty acres of grazing land and respectability. And children."

A stout, balding gentleman hurried to Mrs. Cole's side, carrying a glass. She looked at the yellowish, steamy water and took it with one thin, blue-veined hand.

"That is Mr. Cole." Luke shook his head.

"I see vanity is not absent," Jane murmured. "That she should turn down a young, handsome man for that."

"Oh, I am far older than Mr. Cole," Luke said. "But I am sure once she has the children she craves and he needs she will take a younger lover. I—oh, I do beg your pardon, sir."

Had he deliberately jogged her father's elbow? Mr. Austen looked at the empty glass and splash of water on the floor with dismay. "My dear, I am afraid I must brave the fray once more." He turned to Luke. "I regret we have not been introduced, sir."

"A thousand apologies, sir!" Luke produced a handkerchief and patted him down. "A dreadful crush in here today, as I was mentioning to Miss Austen. You know Lord Barnhill, I believe. No? Oh, a capital fellow. He has some most interesting theories on the old Romans of the city; why, everywhere you see a hole dug in the ground there's all sorts of Roman rubbish—allow me to introduce you."

"Most kind, sir, but I—"

"Do not be concerned, sir. With your permission, I shall fetch Miss Austen as much water as she can tolerate."

Jane watched with some interest as Luke made fluent introductions and Mr. Austen was whisked away by a group of gentlemen passionately debating the ancients. Her father cast a concerned glance back at her and she smiled as best she could.

"How do you do that?" she asked when Mr. Venning returned. "Why does my father not know you for what you are? When I—the gentleman and his sister who—that is, the whole company recognized them."

He smiled. "We learn to dissemble and of course we can charm. Sometimes it pleases us to reveal ourselves; it is most amusing to see the mortals stare and whisper and find excuses to seek us out. And there are also a few, a very few, who recognize us for what we are, whether we will or not; you must be careful of them. I can see you have a lot to learn, Jane. May I ask how long . . . ?"

"Last Thursday."

"Last Thursday!" He looked at her with alarm. "No wonder you are so weak. I could scarce feel your spark. What is your Bearleader about, to let this happen to you?"

She smiled a little at the term. "You mean, as though I were a young gentleman taking the Grand Tour with an unfortunate, long-suffering tutor to keep me out of trouble? Why should I have a Bearleader?"

"The one who created you, is he or she not with you?"

She shook her head. "The gentleman who—who bit me—left. I do not know what he was supposed to do. Or what I am supposed to do."

"You're slipping away. He should have stayed to see you through these first few months. Who was he?"

"A Mr. Smith. I doubt it was his real name."

"Ah. And so you have not dined since?" He gazed at her with concern and compassion.

"I'm not hungry."

"No, my dear Jane. Not food."

"My father gave me his blood."

He raised his eyebrows. "Well, Mr. Austen has hidden depths, it seems."

She glared at him with all the outrage she could muster in her weakened state. "He is the *Reverend* Mr. Austen, something you should probably know since you have greeted him as an old acquaintance, and his offer was made for love of me."

Luke bowed. "I stand corrected." He offered his arm. "Come with me, Miss Jane Austen."

Chapter 5

Jane hesitated. The last time she had been alone with a gentle-man—no, a vampire, and certainly no gentleman—had not been to her advantage.

"Do not fear," Luke said.

"But—but I owe it to my family to—"

"To die? For that is what will happen if you do not dine soon." He led her, half supporting her, through a doorway at the far end of the Pump Room into a narrow, dark passage and then into a small, dim room.

"I am come here to take the cure," she said, her resistance ebbing away.

"A cadaver cannot take any sort of cure, my dear Miss Austen, and that is what you'll be soon enough. It's a delicate matter, the cure; you must be strong enough to withstand the poison of the waters—for such it is to us—yet the stronger you are the more dif-ficult and painful the cure will become."

"What is it to you? Why will you not leave me alone?" She hated herself for the whimper in her voice.

He pushed her into a chair. He stood over her, hands moving to the buttons of his coat. "My honor, as one of my kind, demands it, Miss Austen. This Mr. Smith abandoned you, a most dishonorable act, and it is my duty, honor, and privilege to do what he should have." He shrugged the coat from his shoulders and let it fall.

"But what about me? My family fears me and rushes me to take the cure. Your honor, frankly, is no business of mine. No one asks me what I want . . . I . . ." Her voice faded away as Luke unbuttoned his shirt cuff. He raised his wrist to his mouth and breathed upon it, then showed her the blue veins against his pale skin.

"I cannot," she said faintly. "Please, sir, do not . . ."

"My name is Luke." He bent and held his wrist to her lips. "Your canines extend. We call it *en sanglant*. You cannot help yourself. You feel pain but that's only because it is a new sensation. With time you'll recognize the condition of *en sanglant* as a sign of desire, of need, of the pleasure you'll anticipate—oh, I beg your pardon, you are the daughter of a clergyman; I doubt you'll appreciate the—"

"Hold your tongue!" She grabbed his wrist and bit, hard.

"Ouch! A little more finesse, Jane, but no matter, you'll learn."

Through a mouthful of blood she growled—yes, Jane Austen, the cultured and respectable daughter of the Austen family *growled*, and then laughed messily.

And the taste—like lightning, like the way she felt once, in another life, when the words flowed and she laughed aloud at her own cleverness and the delicious interplay of her characters. This was a far cry from the tender comfort of her father's blood.

She raised her head and looked up at him, a warm trickle running down her chin.

"Dear, dear, you are a sight. No manners at all," said Luke, handkerchief in hand.

"You taste like . . . like heaven."

"Of course I do. I'm old. Now, hurry up before we're discovered."

"I don't care if we are."

He laughed. "Spoken like a true vampire."

She drew away. "I am not a vampire." Even as she spoke she flicked out her tongue to catch the last few precious drops.

"Indeed. You sit there *en sanglant*, blood on your lips, and claim you are not a vampire? By the way, it's customary to breathe on the wound, a small courtesy, if you have finished."

"I beg your pardon." She did so.

He dabbed at his wrist with the handkerchief, a pained expression on his face, and she became aware that she had breached etiquette once more in not cleaning the wound.

"I meant," she said, "that I shall not be a . . . that is . . . I shall take the cure." For the first time she looked at their surroundings, a dusty room with a pile of chairs, some with broken legs, in one corner. A dirty window let in a little light. "Now I feel a little more revived, I must return to my father."

He knelt in front of her, not attempting to hide his extended canines, and placed a hand on hers. "Say it, Jane. Say what you are."

She shook her head. "I beg your pardon, sir, I cannot."

He stood, his hand still resting on hers. "Very well. How do you feel, now?"

She considered. "Strong. As though a new world opens up. Excited." She shivered. "No, I really cannot . . . But will you tell me something, sir? Why is it that your kind do not drink only from each other? For then you would be no threat to the rest of us."

He let her hand drop and reached for his coat. "Ah, you have a lot to learn. It is considered a high honor for one of the Damned to drink from another; such occasions as the present do not count, of course, for I seek only your survival, whichever path you may choose.

"Besides, there are many mortals who wish us to drink from them. They find the sensation stimulating and delightful, the lightheadedness that follows enjoyable. In short, it is a sensual experience. And of course, we vampires have both charm and skill in the amorous arts that often accompany such an experience—we've had years to practice them. Oho, now you look shocked, Miss Jane."

"Of course I am." She hesitated. "On the journey, a maid at one of the inns offered herself to me. She wanted money."

"Indeed, that is also a possibility for us, that we buy mortals' favors. A pity you did not accept her, for you would be much stronger now. But as to why we do not dine often from each other—we are vampires, dear Jane, put upon the earth to seduce and delight mortals. However, when one of us becomes a Bearleader, it is his or her duty to teach the fledgling manners."

"Oh. You mean you have become my Bearleader?" And then, "But I don't feel wicked. And my manners are generally acknowledged to be beyond reproach. What you have just described sounds dreadful."

He squeezed her hand before releasing it. "You are quite charming. I am sure that under my tutelage you will assume what you call 'wickedness,' and we 'polish,' soon enough."

"But I don't want to." She stood. "I thank you—at least, I think I do. I am not sure, although I do feel much better. But, Mr. Venning, my family cares for me deeply and it is my duty to take the cure."

"You'd turn down immortality?" He raised an eyebrow as he adjusted the cuffs of his coat.

"Yes, sir. I would." She stood and bounced a little on the soles of her feet. How she would like to run, or at least take a vigorous walk. "I love my family, my friends. I have no wish to outlive them."

"You feel well, I see," he said. "Well, my offer stands, for the moment, Jane. And if you refuse, you'll surely have a story for your grandchildren. We must return so your reputation may be preserved."

She lingered, not wanting to leave the company of the only person who accepted her condition with calm rationality instead of fear and bewilderment. Although what he had done was shocking, he had shown her kindness, even if it was only to lay more temptations in her way. There was so much she wanted to ask him; when would she get this chance again?

"Probably never," he said. "Shall we leave, Miss Austen?"

"You knew what I was thinking?"

"Of course. You have my blood. I am part of you now."

"Oh!" She raised her hands to her mouth, horrified. "Could—could you try not to?"

"Listen." He raised a hand. "What the devil is that?"

She listened, and she could hear something now, a heavy toll of the Abbey bells, the sound of voices shouting, and a general tumult outside.

"Something's happened," Luke said. "Were we in the north I would suspect a riot—but here in Bath? We should go and investigate. It's been an odd sort of day, so far; you know the post failed to arrive this morning."

"What can that signify? You mean I should accompany you?"

"You're a vampire who's just dined. I don't believe you are in any danger. You're no shrinking spinster now."

"I am never a shrinking spinster!" She almost growled again. "So you need me for protection?"

"No, for company. We like to stick together with our own kind, dear Jane." He offered his arm.

He led her down a dimly lit passage, and she realized they took a different way out. "My father will—"

He pushed a door open with some caution onto the Pump Yard. Small knots of people stood around, talking, gesturing, some weeping; groups dispersed, gathered, surged, restless and unsettled. It reminded Jane of an anthill: so much scurrying activity and no apparent purpose. Overhead, the bell tolled and tolled and the stone angels of the Abbey, oblivious to the noise and the human passions below, continued their journey up and down the ladders that graced the frontage.

A man passed by pulling a handcart piled with a heap of possessions, a bird in a cage on top of a motley collection of furniture and clothes, a couple of children and a dog running alongside. A woman followed, a baby in her arms.

"What's happened?" Luke asked.

"The French have taken Bristol," the man replied. "My advice is to get out of the town, sir, for they'll be here soon enough."

"What!" Luke exclaimed. "You're sure?"

"Boney eats babies," one of the children gravely informed them, glancing at the bundle in his mother's arms.

The man shrugged and bent his shoulders to the cart again, threading his way through the crowd.

A gentleman approached Luke and Jane, clearly agitated. "A horse, sir, do you have a horse I could buy? Or do you know of any who might have a nag to sell?"

"I'm afraid not, sir," Luke said.

The gentleman wandered to another group.

A cry came up from the depths of the crowd. "Soldiers!"

"Don't be a fool, it's the militia," someone shouted back and sure enough, a troop of men on horseback entered the square, harness and weapons jingling.

"I don't care overmuch for our chances," Luke murmured.

Jane was inclined to agree. The pasty complexions of several of the soldiers and their awkwardness with their mounts suggested they had but recently abandoned shop counters and warehouses. Their leader was a middle-aged, handsome man, sharp-eyed and alert, a retired officer for sure, Jane thought.

The officer held up a hand and reined in his horse, and the soldiers behind came to a ragged halt. "Good people!" he called. "Pray, calm yourselves."

A silence fell for a moment before people started shouting questions. Where were the French, was it true they'd taken Portsmouth and London, what about the King, was it true they were cutting off heads already?

Again the officer called for silence. "We are here to protect you and we shall fight the French for it is almost certain they shall try to take our city. We expect them to arrive by nightfall. They have taken Bristol and many inhabitants of the city rallied to them, but it shall not happen here. Any gentlemen who wish to join us may do so, although you will be obliged to find your own weapons and mounts. Good people of Bath, pray go to your homes and stay calm. God save the King!"

There were a few ragged "Huzzahs!" and near them a man muttered to his companions, "I daresay the French might have more to offer us than poor, old, mad George. Everyone can vote there, they do say."

"Unless you're a woman," Jane said.

Luke smiled.

The gentleman of Jacobin leanings regarded her with horror and then addressed Luke. "My good sir, your wife is obviously unwell, distressed by this news. You must take her home, sir, for she will not be safe in the streets."

"Oh, she's not my wife," Luke said, with a genial smile. "And in quite good health, are you not, Jane?"

At that moment Jane's father came pushing through the crowd toward them. "Mr. Venning, my thanks for looking after my daughter. Jane, I have sent your mother and sister back to Paragon Place already. We must follow them. This is a dreadful day, indeed—the French on our shores; it is hardly to be countenanced."

Luke bowed. "I was honored to be of service, sir. Miss Austen is altogether charming."

"Do you intend to join the militia, Mr. Venning?" Jane asked.

"Oh, I don't know if my tailor could run me up anything before the French arrive, which I imagine will be a matter of hours," he replied. "A dreadful inconvenience, but I am afraid they will have to do without me."

Mr. Austen stared and then laughed. "Why, for a moment I thought you were serious, my dear sir. Good heavens, Jane, such a time we live in." His eyes filled with tears. "The shame," he said. "The shame that the men of Bristol rallied to the French; I can scarce believe it."

"Come, Papa." She took her father's arm and turned him slightly so that Luke would not see him weep. "Good day, Mr. Venning."

Luke stepped forward. "I insist, Mr. Austen, Miss Austen, that I escort you home. Doubtless there will be unrest on the streets. I am at your service."

"Most kind," her father murmured to Jane's dismay and stared aghast at the hubbub in the square. "A chair, do you think, Jane? No, I do not think it will be possible. We must walk, if you are strong enough."

She agreed and they set off through streets where shopkeepers boarded up their windows and, according to their irate and voluble customers, had hastily marked up prices. People seemed to be dashing around buying up the oddest articles in some sort of desperate panic, as though shopping would hold back the French, or that the possession of half a dozen stone crocks and a couple of brooms could be wielded against the might of the invading army.

Mr. Austen stopped outside an apothecary's, where the owner of the shop was engaged in nailing boards across his shop window. He tapped the apothecary on the shoulder and asked if he could make a purchase.

"Very well, sir, but I will take coin only. I regret I cannot extend you credit." The apothecary led them inside, although Luke announced that he would wait outside, and gave Jane a piercing look. "The young lady has come to take the cure, I see."

"I—yes—that is correct." Mr. Austen glanced at Jane and then at the apothecary. "With this unfortunate occurrence, it is possible we shall not be able to take the waters. Do you have any remedy that may ease her?"

The man laid his hammer on the counter and took several jars from the shelf behind him. "I can mix a draught that may ease the cravings. It will not effect a cure, sir. Only the waters can cure the condition."

"Yes, I am aware of that." Mr. Austen laid a sovereign on the counter.

"No, no, sir. A shilling will suffice." The apothecary measured, stirred, poured ingredients into a bottle, and topped it up with liquid. "I trust this will give the young lady some comfort." He pushed a cork into the bottle and sealed it with wax from a candle. "I would suggest some laudanum, too."

"That may help your mother," Mr. Austen murmured to Jane. Placing both bottles carefully in his coat pockets, he led Jane outside.

A crowd of drunken men surged onto the street, their arms full of bottles of wine, shouting and swearing they'd kill half a dozen Frenchies each before they saw the *tricouleur* fly over their city. "You'll drink a toast with us to the King!" one of them demanded, waving a bottle in their faces.

Luke paused to draw a blade from his cane and the man with the bottle took a step back, tripped, and fell flat on his back onto the refuse of the street to the great amusement of his companions.

"Mad, quite mad," murmured her father as two women shrieked over a length of calico cloth, eventually ripping it in half. The shopkeeper's howls of rage mingled with those of her customers, who immediately began bickering over who had the greater length.

They passed more families, struggling elderly people, and weeping small children, carrying a few hastily snatched possessions—one woman carrying an iron pot that, from its scent, held the day's dinner—trying to escape. Her father tried to remonstrate with them that they might well be safer to stay in the city, but fear of the French left them beyond reason.

"What do you think will happen?" Jane asked.

"I trust that *fraternité* will hold sway," her father responded with a flash of his usual spirit. "But I fear there will be bloodshed. We must be brave, my dear. I fear your mother will not take it well."

They passed a trap stuffed full of people. "Five guineas each, sir, to escape the French," the driver shouted to them.

"Where on earth does he think we will sit? On their laps?" Jane felt sorry for the horse, an old and bony specimen that struggled to pull its load. Several of the passengers looked exceedingly stout, stuffed like sausages into several layers of clothes.

"Outrageous!" Mr. Austen exclaimed. "Yet we shall leave the city, for I am sure we shall be safer at home, and take your aunt and uncle with us."

"We do not know the state of the surrounding countryside, sir. You may do better to shutter your windows and sit tight until more is known," Luke said.

"You may be right, sir, but Mr. and Mrs. Leigh—my sister-in-law and her husband—keep a carriage and horses. We must discuss it with them."

They continued through streets full of hurrying, anxious people, passing houses with the shutters closed tight, until they reached Paragon Place. Luke refused Jane's father's offer of refreshment.

"I must return home to shutter my windows and take stock," he said. "If I may be of service, my lodgings are on Queens Square—here is my card. I am generally home unless I am visiting patients." He shot Jane a glance as he handed the card to her father. *Find me there, Jane, you will need to dine again, whatever the French do. Or I shall find you, now I know where you are.*

Oh, do leave me alone.

"You are a physician, sir?" Mr. Austen asked.

"Indeed I am. May I be of some assistance to you and your family? I see that Miss Austen is indisposed; it shows quite clearly to me, for I have had much experience with cases such as these."

Jane opened her mouth to tell her father he was deceived, but the words failed to come. Her father instead gripped Luke's hand with his own, expressing his extreme gratitude, and begging him to call on them the next day for a consultation.

Luke smiled and bowed. Jane watched him walk away. Her

Bearleader. A slender man who walked like a dancer and twirled his blade as though it were a toy; she did not doubt he could use it. He had had years, possibly centuries, to practice swordplay.

"Quite a gentlemanly sort of man, but somewhat whimsical," her father pronounced. "My dear, the waters have made an improvement already, I can tell—you look quite remarkably well, and I am most grateful for Mr. Venning's kind offer."

Chapter 6

As the footman opened the door to the house, Mrs. Austen hurried to meet them, Cassandra following close behind.

"My dear, this is dreadful indeed, and what's worse, my sister and her husband are out goodness only knows where—"

"There was talk of a christening, some distance outside the city," Cassandra added.

"Yes, they left shortly after we did, according to the servants, the few that are left, and have not returned. And they have the carriage!" Mrs. Austen wrung her hands. "Oh, if only we could afford our own carriage we could escape the horror. What shall we do, sir?"

"Why, make the best of things, Mrs. Austen. Come, we'll close the shutters. How many servants are left?"

The news was grim indeed, with only two footmen, the housekeeper, and a maidservant currently suffering from the toothache to run the large house. All the others had fled.

"We must all keep calm," Mr. Austen declared. "Possibly you and the girls could help the housekeeper prepare dinner, for I am sure we shall all feel better for dining."

Mrs. Austen drew herself up, her whole body expressing outrage. Once again Jane heard her mother's inmost thoughts. *Why, I thought to have a rest from drudgery and this is the best he can do? How dare he look so cheerful while I suffer so?*

"Here's a small consolation, ma'am. We may be murdered by the French within hours, thus saving you years more in servitude." The words burst from Jane's lips before she could restrain herself.

Her mother glared at her, and forcing a smile, declared there was nothing she liked better than to help prepare dinner. She led her two daughters downstairs to the kitchen, where the housekeeper and the maid, her jaw swaddled in a poultice, labored at preparing dinner.

Jane, knowing her hands would be the coldest, offered to make pastry for the oyster pie. She could see the history of the ingredients in her mind, the fields of grain rippling in the wind, a pig rooting in mud, a cow standing docile in the stall for milking. Around her the air was thick with fear and apprehension as the other women exchanged speculation on what would happen to them. One time the clatter of hooves and jingle of harness on the street brought the conversation to a sudden, frightened stop, until they heard the reassurance of a shouted command in English.

"Heavens, must they make such a noise!" her mother exclaimed at a distant burst of gunfire.

"Very inconsiderate, indeed, ma'am," Jane said. She clumped the pastry into a ball and reached for a rolling pin.

The strongest emotion Jane could feel was that of Betty the maid, in agony from the toothache. She could bear it no longer. Dusting her hands clean on her apron, she went over to the girl, who peeled potatoes at the other end of the long scrubbed table.

"Your tooth pains you greatly, I believe," she said.

"Yes, ma'am, it does," the girl replied. "I tried cloves and willow and some other stuff that tasted nasty, but nothing helped."

"Let me help." She wasn't even sure what she was about to do, but she leaned forward and unwrapped the bandage around the girl's face. To her embarrassment her canines popped out and she clamped her mouth firmly shut—it had to be the proximity to another, that was it; surely she did not wish to feed again?

The maid gazed up at her with fear on her freckled face. She could not be more than twelve years of age. "I shan't have to have it pulled, shall I, ma'am?"

Jane touched the girl's swollen jaw and felt fear and pain, dreadful pain; how could this child not weep with it? And some thoughts of a sister about to give birth, a brother pressganged into the navy, a father she feared for his drunkenness and violence, terror at the thought of an apothecary ripping the tooth from her mouth. The girl started. "Beg pardon, ma'am, your hands are so cold."

Betty opened her mouth.

Jane stared at the blackened, infected tooth and the grossly swollen gum and then looked into the girl's startled eyes. "Don't be afraid," she said, as quietly as she'd said to Harris Bigg-Withers. "I'll make it better. It won't hurt anymore."

Betty's eyes drooped half closed and her face relaxed. Jane helped her into a chair. She took a quick look at the others, who clustered together over the stove, Cassandra and her mother mostly getting in the way of the housekeeper, she suspected.

She raised her hand to her mouth and bit, quickly, a small puncture on one finger deep enough to produce a drop of blood that she smeared onto Betty's gum.

Betty jerked upright in her chair, eyes wide, and screamed, shaking violently.

Jane stepped back, horrified; she had obeyed her instincts entirely without thought, not knowing what the outcome could be. Mrs. Burgess, the housekeeper, rushed forward, a wooden spoon in her hand. "What's wrong, Betty?"

Betty leaned forward, clutching at her apron, and spat out blood and pus. Something small and blackened fell from her mouth and rolled onto the flagstone floor. Jane bent to pick it up. "The source of all your ills, I believe, Betty." She held out the decayed tooth that had come out entirely from the roots, or what was left of them.

"Beg pardon, ma'am." Betty spat out another mouthful into her apron and looked up, wide-eyed. "It doesn't hurt anymore."

"Come on over to the sink, girl, you've no business making a mess in front of the ladies." Mrs. Burgess led her away from the table, and Mrs. Austen and Cassandra joined them at the sink, making suggestions about further treatment and the use of tooth powder and brushes.

"I've never seen such a thing!" Mrs. Austen declared as Betty spat into the sink. "Rinse your mouth out, now. Some vinegar, maybe, Mrs. Burgess, to clean the wound? What happened, Jane?"

Jane shook her head. She was *en sanglant* still and could barely speak. Raising her apron to her mouth as though she felt unwell, she managed, "I—I must go outside."

"But the French! Cassandra, tell her she must not—"

"No!" Jane gazed at her sister, who stopped halfway across the kitchen. "Roll out the pastry for me, if you please."

"Oh. Very well." Cassandra picked up the rolling pin with the obedience of an automaton.

"Put flour on the rolling pin, else it will stick," Jane continued, debating whether she should tell her sister to get on the table and dance. "I shall be back soon."

She took the knife Betty had used for the potatoes and plucked a woman's jacket from a peg by the kitchen door before leaving the house. The air was cold and damp in the dimness of the late afternoon. Bursts of gunfire, shouting, the clatter of hooves filled the air, but from some distance. Here it was quiet. A wheelbarrow, its wheel smashed, lay in the gutter with a scatter of broken china and glass around it. The wind blew acrid smoke into Jane's face, and, ridiculously, she was reminded of an earlier visit to Bath, with fireworks in Sydney Gardens—except here the explosions and flashes of light were of battle.

She should be afraid. Instead she felt invincible, powerful, and yes, hungry, doubtless her appetite stimulated by the scent of Betty's blood. She moved into the shadows, aware of the precision and grace of her movements. She remembered Luke's strut as she had seen him last, the set of his shoulders and his long, handsome legs.

She heard the man before she whirled around to face him, the thud of footsteps and jingle and clank of weapons, and then the stink of sweat and cheap wine. His uniform was unfamiliar, but his swagger and leer told her all she needed to know. For a moment she considered drawing herself up and declaring she was a gentlewoman and would scream for help—not that anyone would believe her, with her floury hands and apron and jacket. He strolled toward her, one hand at the fall of his breeches, the other holding a musket.

"Eh, *ma petite*, you walk alone?" His voice rasped. "You like to welcome a Frenchman to your town, yes?"

She hid the knife in the folds of her gown and waited. She could smell his blood now that he was closer, hear the excited thrum of his heart. As though afraid she backed against the railings that led down to the front area of her aunt and uncle's house.

He laughed and lunged toward her. He was against her now, almost overwhelming her with his stink and lust and the heat of his blood, grabbing at her skirts. She raised one hand and ripped at his stock and jacket, tearing the fabric—how strong she was, how powerful—and lunged for his neck beneath the greasy pomade-scented black hair.

Now she was the one who attacked. He yelled in fear and the musket clattered to the ground.

"Silence, s'il vous plait!" she hissed at him, looking into his eyes as blood pulsed from his neck—what a waste!—and to her relief his expression became dreamy and distant. He slackened in her grip as she drank, blood spilling over them both, darkening her gown and apron, his boots scrabbling on the flagstones for purchase until he collapsed beneath her.

Astride him, she raised her head to gasp for breath and he came to life beneath her, his eyes wide with fear and rage, while he cursed and heaved. She remembered the knife as he gripped her throat—he was strong, but not as strong as she—and jabbed it into him. The blade struck something hard and jarred her arm. His terror became overwhelming, and she saw a farm and apple trees blooming in the spring and . . .

"Maman. Maman." His eyes glazed over, he shuddered and the last of his blood pumped out.

"Forgive me," she said, too late. She rose and stepped away. The knife was buried in his side and after a moment's hesitation she bent and removed it. She swiped her hand over her mouth and straightened her skirts and the apron, heavy and sodden with blood. As ravenous as she had been she seemed to have wasted as much blood as she had drunk, and the taste of it was strong with garlic—well, what else would she expect from a Frenchman? But weren't they—her kind—afraid of garlic? She stared down at the dead soldier, the man who had called for his mother as he died— and hardly a man; the monstrous, threatening Frenchman had been little more than a boy.

She should close his eyes at least—but no, to do so might arouse suspicion if anyone should care about one dead soldier who was not an officer.

"Did he hurt you, miss?" She whirled to see a group of men approaching. Some of them were armed; all of them looked fierce and disheveled. If she had not drunk she would have been frightened by their appearance, but she was full of courage and strength. They stared at her with horror and curiosity.

"No, I—I'm well. I stabbed him."

"Go home, miss. This is no place for you," one of the men said. "The French are coming in on the London Road."

She opened her fist and showed them her knife. "I killed this one. I'll kill another."

The men exchanged glances and a muttered conversation arose. "We've women on the barricade now. Let her come . . . But she's a lady, you can tell by her speech . . . She's *something* . . . We can't leave her here . . . For sure, she's deranged . . . No, I tell you, she's one of *them* . . ."

The man who'd spoken first to Jane held up a hand to quiet his companions and Jane recognized him now—he was the apothecary who'd sold her father a vial of what she suspected was a panacea that very morning. "Come if you wish, ma'am, so long as I have your word you'll not turn on us. You remember me, I trust? William Thomas, apothecary."

"What the devil could she do? She's only a girl," another of the men said.

To her relief Mr. Thomas did not attempt an explanation, but pushed his spectacles more firmly onto his nose. Jane saw he had a musket in one hand and a large pestle, a formidable club of marble, tucked beneath his arm. "Come along with us, ma'am. Time is wasting. They've held the Frenchies off so far, but we've come to help."

"What is happening elsewhere in the town, sir?"

"The French marched from Bristol, and the militia fight to hold the bridge and the roads against them. We had word they were coming along the London Road too, so that's where we are bound."

They passed Walcot Church and turned right onto the London Road. Ahead of them a bonfire burned in the streets, and a crowd of people moved, dark against the red glow. Two men emerged from a house, dragging a heavy, old-fashioned table between them toward a barrier some six feet high across the street, constructed of furniture, pieces of wood, and flagstones. Jane ran forward to help them as they upended the table onto two legs and attempted to hoist it onto the barricade. She could have laughed at their expressions of astonishment as she grabbed the blackened oak and hauled it up. She clambered aloft and peered cautiously over the edge.

"Any sign of them, miss?"

"Not yet." She climbed over and dropped down to the other side. Walking farther up the road, she listened carefully, then dropped to a crouch and laid her bare hand on the ground to get a better sense of the faint tremor she had detected. Yes, men and horses, and something iron and heavy that lurched along the road—it had to be a cannon.

She ran back, and climbed over the barricade. "I can't tell how far off they are, but they bring artillery."

"I suppose they're not ours?" someone asked.

Jane shook her head. "I don't know, but they're probably not far off. We'll know soon enough."

Mr. Thomas shook his head, staring at the barricade. "They'll reduce this to splinters."

"Then take cover and attack them after they come through," Jane said, astonished by her own decisiveness—telling grown men what to do, or, for that matter, telling anyone what to do, although her mother frequently complained of her willful nature. "Fire your weapons and then run before they can fire the cannon again, for the best we can do is delay them and maybe kill a few."

"True enough," Mr. Thomas said. "We have some muskets, but not enough for everyone."

"Cobblestones!" someone shouted, and the crowd tore at the surface of the street.

"And now we wait," the apothecary said. The crowd positioned themselves in the steps leading to the servants' quarters, silent, muskets loaded, handfuls of cobblestones at the ready.

Jane listened. From far off down the road came the orderly clop of horses' hooves moving at a quick trot, the squeak and rumble of the gun carriage, the jingle of harness and weapons. She watched the faces of those around her and observed that they too heard the sounds. A command to halt rang out. She imagined what they saw—the makeshift barrier with the glow of the bonfire behind it.

"In the name of the Republic, citizens, lay down your arms!"

"Damned Frenchies, excuse me, ma'am," the apothecary muttered. His spectacles glinted red, reflecting the flames of the bonfire. He bit his lip. "Do they know we're here, do you think?"

"I don't know. They'll expect an ambush."

She listened, hearing whispered orders and the scratch of a tinderbox, precise metallic sounds and the creak of the gun carriage; the quiet sounds of a well-trained cavalry unit waiting to attack. She rose and gestured to the waiting townspeople to keep down, then sank down to her former position.

A deafening bang burst the barricade into pieces, scattering debris over the road. Paving stones and pieces of wood flew through the air and smashed to the ground, with coals from the bonfire scattered throughout. From a cloud of smoke the French cavalry emerged, negotiating rubble and flames, to encounter a hail of musket fire and cobblestones as the townspeople emerged from hiding.

"Got you!" the apothecary crowed as a soldier fell from his mount, and pulled another musket ball from the pouch at his belt.

Beside him Jane hurled cobblestones—Edward would be proud that his little sister had developed such a strong bowling arm, she thought as she caught a Frenchman square on the forehead. Around her, the townspeople scrambled from their hiding places, dodging between the horses and running around debris. What had begun as a disciplined cavalry charge had turned into hand-to-hand fighting. But not for long; already the cavalrymen formed a tight formation, and sabers swinging, charged ahead.

"Call them off!" Jane shouted to Mr. Thomas. "The French have the advantage over us!"

But the apothecary was gone—Jane saw his spectacles glinting on the ground among the blood and mud. She picked them up, hoping he lived still. Around her, townspeople fought to escape the cavalry sabers, and foot soldiers followed.

"Run!" Jane shouted above the screams and shouts. "We're outnumbered. Save yourselves!" She watched in horror as French soldiers poured into the front areas of houses, bayonets at the ready, where a few townspeople still remained. She saw a man and a woman hammer at the servants' door in a basement, screaming to be let in, and then saw them cut down.

"Run!" Jane shouted again. She picked up her skirts and ran ahead of the cavalry, guessing that they would take the most direct route into the center of the town down Cornwall Street. A crowd of people, some supporting the wounded, followed her.

"Where shall we go, mistress?"

"To your homes. The city will fall," Jane said.

"The wounded may come with me," said a voice behind her. Mr. Thomas the apothecary blinked shortsightedly at her. His face was blackened with smoke and smeared with blood. "Bravely done, ma'am. And where will you go?"

"I'm so glad you're alive, Mr. Thomas. Good night to you, sir." She handed him his spectacles and shook his hand.

She could not return home covered in blood and stinking of smoke and have to explain where she had been or what had happened. But there was one place she could go; once again she felt the bond that drew her to the Damned and distanced her from her family.

She had a Bearleader and surely he would know what she should do. Although Miss Jane Austen would not be so foolish as to walk alone through a battle, the new Jane—Jane the vampire, who had killed and fought—was fearless.

In Queens Square all of the houses but one were shuttered and silent; only the Damned could be so ostentatious as to keep candles blazing in every room and curtains open at such a time. Inside, some sort of gathering seemed to be taking place; she heard laughter and music and saw people moving around inside. She walked up the steps and tugged at the bellpull, angry that they should amuse themselves while the people of the town, barely armed, fought and died.

The door swung open to reveal a half-dressed man. His coat and waistcoat were discarded, his shirt open at the neck. He had a familiar, dreamy expression on his face.

"Another one." He swayed toward her and tipped his head to one side, revealing small wounds on his neck. "Drink from me, beauty."

Chapter 7

"Beauty? Hardly. Let me pass, sir, if you please." Jane pushed the man aside and he fell against the wall as though drunk. She stepped onto the marble slabs of the hall. A door opened and a gentleman dressed in a militia uniform emerged.

"Good God, girl, what has happened to you? Venning! There's an injured woman here, a servant, I believe, who must have fallen foul of the French." He rushed to Jane's side and gripped her arm. "Sit, if you please. Where are you injured?"

"I am not a servant. I am Miss Jane Austen."

Luke emerged from the same room. "So it is." He looked at her coolly. "Am I to take it that you have made your first kill?"

"I have been fighting the French."

Luke was silent, merely raising an eyebrow.

Jane continued, "You should have been there, not entertaining! All of you!"

"Indeed."

"Well, what did you expect me to do? Sit at home and quiver in fear? So far I have found only one useful facet of my condition— my cold hands make me excellently suited as a pastrycook."

The gentleman in militia uniform looked from Jane to Luke, burst into laughter and bowed. "Pardon me, ma'am, your appearance gave me quite a fright. A pastrycook, eh? You're a brave woman, Miss Austen."

"Come with me, Jane," Luke said. "Colonel Poulett, excuse me while I deal with this. You're welcome to join the others upstairs in dancing or cards."

"I think your excellent claret will suffice my needs," the officer said. "Your servant, ma'am." He returned to the room from which he had emerged.

"You," Luke said to the man who had let Jane into the house, "behave yourself, and take care who you admit, do you hear? Tell the others to send hot water to the bedchamber, if you please."

Luke grasped Jane's wrist none too gently and pulled her upstairs.

"Where are we going?" Jane asked, alarmed at his reference to a bedchamber.

"To make you decent." His tone was curt. "You have much to learn, and the first is that you do not allow yourself to appear in such a disgraceful condition."

"The country is being invaded and you are concerned only with appearances?" Jane fought to free her wrist. "Are you all mad?"

He ignored her and stopped at the first landing. The sound of music was louder here and through the open doorway Jane saw couples dancing. "Stay here. Do not wander off."

"What is the matter with you?" Jane asked but he ignored her and entered the room. He walked over to a sofa and whispered in the ear of a woman who sat there with a young man reclining next to her, his head on her lap. She nodded, stroked the man's hair, rose, and accompanied Luke to the doorway. The man slumped back onto the couch and his head rolled to the side, revealing a smudge of dried blood on his neck.

"This is Clarissa. I must return to the colonel downstairs." Luke bowed briefly and went downstairs.

The woman eyed Jane and sniffed. "The French, I presume? Phew, you stink. Come with me, if you please."

"Why? Where's Luke going?"

"If you prefer he helps you bathe, then you do not need my services."

"Oh!" Obediently Jane followed the female vampire up the stairs.

"Your name?" the woman threw over her shoulder.

"Jane. I am sorry if I disturbed you."

"You should be. He was such a delicious young man and I had not quite finished with him. Now probably someone else will take him." At the landing she opened a door and beckoned Jane inside. "We shall burn your clothes. I'll find something else for you."

She led Jane into a bedchamber and into the dressing room beyond it. Two maidservants poured steaming water into a tin bathtub while a third placed a large kettle into the embers of the fire.

"You may go," Clarissa said. "Yes, you too, Ann," as the maid at the fireplace lingered. "You may fetch this lady some of my clothes."

"Yes, ma'am." The girl curtsied and grinned, then followed the others out through a doorway cut in the paneling of the room.

"A cheeky little piece," Clarissa said, "but palatable enough. Off with those filthy clothes, Jane."

"Do you live here?" Jane fumbled with her apron strings.

Clarissa pushed her around, untied both apron and gown, and

then began on the laces of her stays. "Several of us do. So Luke is your Bearleader. I have never known him to create anyone before."

"He didn't." Jane was relieved as her stinking clothes fell to the floor in a sodden heap. "I suppose he adopted me."

"Allow me." Clarissa reached for her hand and uncurled her fingers from around the knife. "You do not need this. You are among friends now." Her voice was a little more gentle. "It explains why your manners are so bad."

"I do not have bad manners!"

"Among us you do. You are unschooled and uncouth, but it is not entirely your fault if your Bearleader abandoned you." She examined Jane's clothing. "We shall burn all of these, but your stays are unmarked. Ann shall clean the shoes for you."

"Is she a vampire too?" Jane stepped into the hot water.

"Ann?" Clarissa's eyebrows lifted. "Indeed not. She is a servant who likes to perform certain services outside her normal duties. We of the Damned are of impeccable lineage, many of us descended from princes. We are not peasants."

"Oh." A barrage of gunfire nearby made Jane jump. "Have you heard any news?"

"They're taking Bath," Clarissa replied as if commenting on the weather. She handed Jane a bar of lavender-scented soap. "The militia's gallantry is of little use against Bonaparte's army."

"What will happen?"

Clarissa shrugged. "We shall go on. The rest of them—oh, they'll scurry around and panic, and in a century this will seem as nothing."

"But . . ." The water turned reddish brown and cloudy as Jane turned the soap in her hands. "Then why is Luke talking to Colonel Poulett of the Somerset Fencible Cavalry downstairs?"

"Is he?" Clarissa sounded uninterested. "Possibly it amuses him. You must wash your hair, Jane."

Jane closed her eyes as Clarissa poured water from a ewer over her head and scrubbed scented lotion into her hair.

"Why is Luke so cold to me?" Jane asked.

"What do you expect? You turn up at his house covered in blood and stinking of garlic, which many will find offensive. You make your first kill without him being present, which is a grave discourtesy and you have not sought his advice on finding someone on whom to dine. Do you wonder at it?"

"I didn't know."

"You will learn." She raised her voice. "Yes, Ann, I know you are at the door. Come in, you insolent girl. Very good. Pray clean the dirt from Miss Austen's shoes." She took a gown from the maid and held it up for Jane's approval. "This should do well enough."

"Thank you. It's beautiful." So it was, a white muslin with a gauze silver overdress.

"Ann will help you dress. I have business downstairs. When you are ready, Ann will take you to join us." Clarissa stroked the maid's neck. "Maybe I shall·call for you later, my dear."

"Thank you, ma'am." When Clarissa had left, Ann said, "So you're a new one, then, miss."

"I suppose I am." She hesitated. "Do you mind being bitten, Ann?"

"Mind? Ooh, miss, it's better than anything. Better than gin or plum cake or Christmas, and you won't get a baby from it. And the Bible says you can do it and it's not a sin."

"It does? Whereabouts?" Try as she could, Jane could not think of any Bible passage condoning relations with vampires.

"Well, miss, it doesn't say you can as much as it doesn't say you can't." She wrapped a towel around Jane and giggled. "Some girls give themselves to vampire gentlemen, for they won't leave you with a baby or a disease, but I'm saving my virtue for marriage with my young man."

"And your betrothed doesn't mind that you . . ."

With brisk efficiency Ann dropped a clean shift over Jane's head and proceeded to lace her into her stays. "Oh, not at all, miss, for I make more than him in vails and the more we save, the sooner we shall marry. Shall I help you with your hair, miss?"

"No, I can do it myself." But when Ann stepped forward and took the comb from her hand she allowed her to do so.

"You still have a reflection, miss. You must be very new. I'll take you downstairs now."

Even if Jane had not entered a drawing room full of the Damned, this gathering was unlike any other she had seen. The room itself was far more opulent and fashionable than any she had ever visited, its walls decorated with painted panels and with gorgeous silk hangings at the windows. The furniture, also upholstered in silk, consisted mostly of sofas in the classical style, or heaps of satin pillows forming inviting nests. Gauzy draperies suspended from testers created fantastic tents, in which entwined bodies were visible. The air held an enticing, spicy scent.

Blood.

She walked into the room, her feet sinking into the luxurious carpet, self-conscious in her borrowed finery but aware that her elegant entrance made no impact whatsoever upon the gathered company. No gentlemen sprang to their feet; in fact, the gentlemen who lounged upon the sofa opposite were otherwise occupied. Clarissa lay between them, her slippered feet upon the thighs of one while she guided the wrist of the other, the beautiful young man whose company she was so anxious to retain, to her lips. As Jane watched, she blew on his wrist, released his hand and then pulled his head to hers for a long, passionate kiss. She withdrew her head from his, smiled, and then lifted her face to his to run her tongue over his lips.

"Don't stand there staring." Luke came to Jane's side and pushed her forward.

He was accompanied by Colonel Poulett, who looked excessively ill at ease. Jane saw the colonel gaze around the room, noting the amorous play that took place on nearly all the sofas and pillows. A woman walked forward and ran her finger along the gold frogging of his uniform coat. "Why Colonel, your heart beats so fiercely. I should fear to engage you in battle. You must be a formidable opponent." She parted her lips to reveal herself *en sanglant*.

"Behave yourself, Maria. There will be time for dalliance later." Luke walked past Jane into the center of the room. "Ladies and gentlemen, our friend Colonel John Poulett has a proposition to make to us. Mark his words well."

Colonel Poulett stepped forward, incongruous in his uniform. "Ladies and gentlemen, the bridge to the city has been taken and within hours we shall negotiate a surrender. We have fared badly in the skirmishes in the streets and we fear retaliation on the populace should the fighting continue." There were a few brief exclamations; one of the liveried servants cursed and then looked around guiltily. "We have heard that Portsmouth and Dover and London itself have fallen. We do not know the whereabouts of the Royal Family, and we expect the worst. Our only hope is that the Navy may cut off French supplies, but until then we must hinder the movement of Bonaparte's troops. Undoubtedly there will be a curfew in the city at night and it is then that the French will move weapons and supplies. I understand that the French intend to leave a garrison quartered here in the city and to store munitions and supplies, probably in the city's churches. We beg for your help, for you can do what an army cannot."

"So, you think we seek to prove ourselves?" A voice came from the shadows that made Jane start and shiver with fear and anticipation as recognition thrummed through her body. Once when she was very young and walking with her father she had lost sight of him, bursting into howls of fear and abandonment before he appeared and swept her into the blissful refuge of his arms. She remembered the piercing joy when Tom Lefroy smiled at her across a crowded ballroom, the recognition of two like minds thinking the same thoughts, the happy anticipation of talking and flirting and touching hands. And kissing. She'd never told anyone of that, not even Cassandra.

It was he, she was sure, the one who had created her. Mr. Smith.

She came to her senses in the midst of an argument that occupied all the vampires in the room, the women as articulate as the men.

"Of course we should fight!" Clarissa said. She sat upright on the couch between her two companions. "What else is there to do?"

"This is not a game, ma'am," the colonel said. "Neither is it a fit pursuit for ladies . . ." He paused as she parted her lips and displayed herself *en sanglant*.

"You think not, sir?" She rose in one fluid, graceful movement, pushing the beautiful young man aside. He slumped against the arm of the sofa, eyes closed, a smile on his lips.

"Clarissa!"

She ignored Luke's warning and approached the colonel with a sinuous, predatory stride. "Try me, Colonel."

He looked alarmed. "Ma'am, I . . ."

In a moment Clarissa had felled him, her slender hands holding his wrists, pinioning him to the floor. "Not a fit pursuit for ladies, sir? Can you escape?" Her gaze was on his neck.

"Enough, Clarissa!" Luke strode forward and grasped her arm. She raised her head and snarled at him.

"Let him go, Clarissa." Again, that familiar voice from the far shadows of the room.

Clarissa rose to her feet, looking distinctly sulky, and returned to the couch.

Colonel Poulett stood and brushed off his uniform. "I understand you perfectly, ma'am. Yet even your immortality will not withstand the effects of a cannon shot. War is not a polite business, ma'am, and neither is it an entertainment."

Clarissa's lip curled. "My words, sir, indicated there was no alternative for us. We are obliged to drive out the French, for we have our own quarrel with them for what they have done to our kind. You are correct, Colonel. We can survive neither cannon shot nor Madame la Guillotine."

"So we are decided, then? Does any of us wish to speak further?" Luke waited for a response.

"What do we gain from this?" A handsome fair-haired man strolled forward. A woman, her loosened gown revealing most of her bosom, hung on his arm, a dazed smile on her face. "And surely you do not expect us to fight alongside the rabble of the town?"

"Your reward will be the satisfaction of knowing you have done your duty and the thanks of a grateful nation," Poulett replied. "As for the rabble of the town, as you call them, I assure you there are plenty of them who are equally ill at ease in fighting alongside the Damned. You will have to make the best of it, sir." Jane could see he was doing his best not to stare at the woman's exposed breasts.

"So we will receive no reward of a more material nature?"

"Pray do not be so vulgar, James. This is a matter of honor." Luke glared at the speaker, and then stepped forward and pulled the woman's gown into place. She giggled and tipped her head to one side, presenting her neck to him.

"His Majesty may well be prepared to consider something of the sort," Poulett said. "That is entirely out of my control, sir."

James shrugged and hoisted the woman into a more upright position as she began a slow slide toward the floor. "This one proves tedious. I tire of her."

"Revive her, else she'll be dead by morning," Luke said. "Are we in agreement, brothers and sisters?"

A chorus of "ayes" resounded through the room, followed by a silence when Luke asked if any dissented.

"Excellent. England thanks you," Colonel Poulett said, and then addressed Luke. "I must leave you now, sir. I have to negotiate the terms of our surrender." He bowed and turned away. His face showed despair and exhaustion, and Jane, feeling as though she had intruded on his most intimate thoughts, looked away.

But she could wait no longer. She pushed through the room—a dance set was forming, the musicians having picked up their instruments—and to the double doors that stood open revealing a card room. Mr. Smith, in shirtsleeves and silk breeches, sat at a table with some others, frowning at the cards in his hand. James, with his female companion clinging to his arm, passed by Jane and took his place at the same table.

As Jane approached Mr. Smith placed a handful of gaming pieces on the table.

"Sir!"

He looked at her and there was a moment of recognition before his face became a polite mask. He gave his companions a knowing smile and turned his attention to his cards.

"Mr. Smith, what is this? Why do you not speak to me?"

He laid his cards on the table. "Madam, I regret I do not have the honor of your acquaintance."

"But—but you do. Do you not remember? You—"

"Pretty enough, if somewhat green," one of the others at the table commented. "Your play, I believe, William. James, why do you not give that girl to her to deal with?"

"An excellent idea." James shoved the half-conscious girl off his lap and toward Jane. The girl giggled and wrapped her arms around Jane's waist. "Here, make yourself useful. Revive her."

Jane disentangled the girl from her, pulled the descending gown into place, and shoved her onto a nearby chair. "Mr. Smith—"

"What is this, Jane?" Luke joined them. "William, your charge is safe? Excellent. Come, Jane, do not bother the gentlemen."

"Stop treating me as though I am a child!" She shook off his hand. "This is he. This is Mr. Smith."

"On the contrary, ma'am, my name is William and I do not believe we have ever met, although I am delighted you wish to spend some time with me. After the game, of course." He turned his attention to the table.

Luke looked from Jane to William and his face hardened. "To my study, sir, if you please. You too, Jane."

William stood and his chair tipped backward with a thud onto the fine carpet. "You do not have the authority to speak to me so, Luke."

Luke's canines lengthened. "I care not for age and rank. What you have done may well undermine us all in these perilous times. Have you forgotten France already? Your memory will be refreshed, I am sure, when a guillotine is erected and the *tricouleur* flies above every town in England." He turned to Jane with an irritable air. "You should not be *en sanglant* in polite company, if you please. It is most improper. Correct yourself."

"This is polite society? I do beg your pardon. As for my teeth, I regret they seem to have a mind of their own."

"Good God, you know nothing yet and I am to blame. Come with me."

She dodged away from him before he could take her arm, and walked with him through the tables of card players and the dancers, into the hall, and into a room at the back of the house. Recent signs of male activity were in evidence—Luke's coat flung over a chair, the scent of tobacco, a half-full bottle of claret and two empty glasses. A map of the city lay on the desk.

"Sit, if you please." Luke bent to light a spillikin at the fire and touched it to an oil lamp that sat on the desk. William, who had followed them, stalked to the fireplace and kicked at the coals.

The room filled with light, allowing Jane to see once again the features that had so enchanted her at the Basingstoke assembly, the handsome aquiline nose and sensual mouth, the piercing dark eyes and straight brows. She remembered his mouth on hers, and yearned for him to touch her or even acknowledge her, but he stared resolutely into the glowing heart of the coals.

Luke propped himself on the edge of the desk and sat, one foot swinging. "This is a fine predicament, William. She's fed from me. If we had time it would be a different matter, but the French are underfoot and I have other business on my mind."

"I regret I too am otherwise occupied." William shrugged. "I cannot be Bearleader to both, and the other is of the greatest importance."

"Why did you do it?" Jane asked.

Both men turned and stared at Jane as though she had spoken out of turn, and it struck her that she probably had, by their standards.

"Was it for sport?" she continued. "You thought so little of me that you used me and abandoned me? Knowing you had another—another engagement? I know, that is the wrong word; you know my meaning, I think. You have damned me and made me a stranger to my family—oh, good God, they do not know where I am. I must return immediately."

"Do not agitate yourself," Luke said with slightly more kindness than he had shown so far. "I have sent them a note explaining that my sister and I passed by in our carriage and persuaded you to dine with us."

"In the middle of a battle?" Jane said, incredulous.

"Yes, with you wandering out to take the air wearing your servant's clothing. Most strange, is it not? But to return to our problem, William, I have taken her on and you know there will be difficulties. Regard how she yearns for you."

"I beg your pardon, sir, I am able to speak for myself, and I assure you I do not yearn for anyone!"

Luke ignored her. "The bond between me and her barely exists. She has drunk from me once and now you reappear. Her metamorphosis will be difficult at best. She may never reach her full strength."

William shrugged. "It was the whim of a moment. I needed to dine, I found her charming and pretty, and I created her. May I remind you, my dear sir, of the most urgent business which I undertook for the sake of Britain?"

Luke shook his head. "We'll talk later, William. I am afraid you are stuck with me, Jane."

"No, I am not. I am here to take the cure and that is what I shall do. I hope the French will allow the sick to take the waters. If not, then I shall die." She stood. "Thank you for your hospitality, sir. I must return home. I want to be with my family. I want my sister."

"Oh, good God, tears." Luke shoved a handkerchief into her hand. "Well, it might be for the best. I am afraid you might not be cut out to be one of us after all. I shall see you home."

In silence they left the house.

"We seem always to be saying farewell, Jane," Luke said as they approached the house. The body of the soldier still lay on the street. "I shall remove the corpse for you lest it cause your family any embarrassment. I regret I failed you."

"You did not." She hesitated. "Thank Clarissa for the loan of her gown. I shall return it soon. Thank you, and I wish you well, Luke."

Chapter 8

Jane prowled the bedchamber, pausing to stroke the delicate fabric of Clarissa's gown, which now lay crumpled on the bed. She half imagined a faint odor of blood, even a scent of Luke himself, rose from the garment. She glanced down in distaste at the gown she had changed into, a modest striped cotton day dress that was once a favorite but now seemed dull and unbecoming. But it was not only a desire for finery that caused her restlessness. She needed to feed again, and yet in a matter of hours she would go to the Pump Room and take the waters for her cure. Cassandra had taken one look at her this morning and fled, muttering that she would see about some beef tea, if there were any beef in the house, and how would they buy food with all these Frenchmen in the city.

Downstairs there was a commotion, a loud banging at the door and shouting, male voices raised in anger, and the clump of booted feet in the hall. Something fell over with a crash.

Her father's voice and her mother's sobs joined the hubbub. Jane could make out some French words. So they were in the house! How dared they!

She ran downstairs to find her parents with a French officer and a couple of soldiers in the hall, a side table lying smashed on the floor, and much shouting. The footman leaned against the wall, bleeding from the mouth.

She looked away quickly, but it was too late. Already she hungered, becoming *en sanglant*. She raised a hand to her mouth and touched the exquisitely tender, aching canines, which retracted beneath her fingertip. *See, Luke, I don't need you after all.*

"What is it, sir?" she asked, touching her father's sleeve.

"Some problem, I believe—this officer is asking for your aunt and uncle. I don't know what to do, Jane." He shook his head.

The officer addressed her in rapid French, too fast for her to understand, and he seemed to have some sort of regional accent that made his words even more unintelligible. He thrust a handful of papers at her that carried the pungent scent of printers' ink. She leafed through them. "They are our identity papers. We must carry them at all times, but he needs to write in our names. I believe he is confused because we do not own or lease this house. And this . . . this says the officer is to be quartered with us. He is Captain Jean-Auguste Garonne."

She explained in French that the owners of the house were not in residence. The captain frowned at her and she was struck by his youth—he could not be much older than she—and the exhaustion and the nervous energy that drove him like a man might ride a foundering horse. He must have been awake all night, if not for several nights.

"Some ink and paper, then," Garonne said. To Jane's surprise, his English, despite his uncouth, unshaven appearance and his uniform soiled with smoke and blood, was quite good, if hesitant.

His mouth tight, Mr. Austen led the way into the study, where Garonne sat at the desk, carelessly pushing papers aside. Jane spelled out their names.

"Here, ma'amselle. It is spelled correctly, no? You take these. You are safe. Do not forget them."

"But we have only one paper, in my name, for the whole family," Mr. Austen said.

"So? You will manage, monsieur." Garonne yawned. "Later I shall make more. Now I sleep. My men, they sleep too. Your house will have food now I am here."

He pushed past them and they heard him and the soldiers clumping up the stairs and then the outraged shriek of Betty, who was at work cleaning fireplaces.

Betty came dashing downstairs. "There's Frenchies in the master and mistress's bedchamber. They'll murder us in our beds."

"Don't be silly," Jane said, then addressed her father. "Sir, is it true the city has surrendered?"

"I regret it is so." Her father adjusted his glasses and looked up from his perusal of the papers. "I see here there is a nine o'clock curfew at night unless accompanied by a French officer and we need a pass to leave the city. I shall see about applying for one directly, for as soon as you are well, my dear, we must return home. When you are ready we must venture out to the Pump Room. I hope only that we may be allowed there."

With the identification papers tucked firmly into Mr. Austen's pocket, he and Jane set out for the Pump Room. At first Mrs. Austen complained loud and long that she and Cassandra were to be left alone in a house full of Frenchmen, but an exploration upstairs showed all three of the soldiers asleep, still in their uniforms. Garonne had got as far as removing one boot, revealing a dirty stocking with a large hole in the heel, before falling asleep on the bed. The other two lay sprawled on the floor, and Jane was reminded with a shudder of the corpse of the French soldier the night before.

Outside, the chilly air held the scent of gunpowder and masonry and, to Jane at least, blood. The city was in disarray and chaos. She and her father walked in silence past an old woman picking over a barrow of goods and mumbling to herself, past corpses of horses and of men in what had previously been elegant and well-kept streets, although soldiers were engaged in clearing these away. A shopkeeper wept over his looted goods and nailed pieces of wood over his shutters as further protection. A woman, bright-eyed, went from one person to another, asking after her little Bill, only ten, and she was sure he would come home soon, but if you see him, sir, ma'am, he is small for his age with fair hair and the prettiest blue eyes—pray tell him to come home.

Many walls and windows bore the distinct marks of bullets and cannon shot, leaving shards of stone underfoot.

And everywhere the French, so many of them. Jane thought it might have been better if they had been hotheaded, swaggering conquerors; but they patrolled the streets, wary and thorough and coolly threatening. At every turn, it seemed, a soldier demanded to see the Austens' papers, which were scrutinized at length, and they were questioned each time about their destination.

"Ha. Your mayor is to speak," a soldier stationed at one of the checkpoints said. "Outside the big church with the angels." He grinned. "We will keep horses in the church, maybe. You will see, *citoyen, citoyenne.*"

The deranged woman seeking her little Billy approached the soldier, who told her with a rough kindness to go home and wait. "It is war," he said to Jane with a shrug. "And she is mad." He handed the papers back to them. "You go."

Sure enough, in the Abbey courtyard a crowd gathered, silent and shocked. Only yesterday a crowd had heard the Abbey bell toll its warning of the unthinkable—the first invasion of England in nearly eight centuries. Now many of the people looked stunned, beyond tears or rage.

A rough stage had been erected outside the west door of the Abbey, and the crowd showed a little animation as three men—Colonel Poulett, a French officer, and a stout gentleman (who must have been the mayor) wearing an old-fashioned full-bottomed wig—made their way up the steps.

The French officer stepped forward. "I am General Philippe Renard. This town is under the rule of the Republic of France."

A few soldiers called out "*Vive la France. Vive la république d'Ingleterre.*"

The crowd remained silent and sullen.

Renard gestured to the mayor, who stepped forward. "Good people, I am to tell you that the French are our friends, bearing liberty, equality, and brotherhood. Colonel Poulett of the Somerset Fencible Cavalry and I have negotiated terms of surrender that will avoid further bloodshed in our city. There is a nine o'clock curfew. No man may carry a weapon. None shall be allowed to leave the city unless they carry the proper papers. We shall be allowed to worship in the Abbey and the Octagon Chapel. Life in our city shall continue much as usual, and we are asked to show hospitality toward our French guests."

"What about bread?" someone called from the crowd. "How do we feed these extra mouths?"

"Shame on you, that you give the churches of the poor to the French!"

Jane couldn't help agreeing with the last speaker, who had drawn the obvious, and probably correct, conclusion, that only the fashionable places of worship were to be preserved. Remembering the conversation last night, she concluded that other churches might well be used to stable horses or store supplies.

"Supplies to the city will resume once the countryside is pacified and brought under French rule," the mayor replied to the first speaker. "Commerce will take place as usual."

Jane couldn't tell whether the mayor's matter-of-fact acceptance of the city's defeat derived from shock or reflected the desperate hope of preventing further loss of life. Poulett stepped forward, drew his sword, and presented it to Renard, who smiled and extended his hand. His smile faded as Poulett made no effort to offer his own hand.

"*Vive la France,*" Renard called out, although again it was only a few French soldiers who responded.

The three men trooped down from the stand, and a few angry mutters were exchanged in the crowd. The French soldiers straightened, muskets at the ready, and the crowd dispersed, heads hanging.

"So, like that, it is all over," Mr. Austen said. "If I were a younger man . . . but what does age have to do with honor?"

Jane gripped his hand, glad they were both gloved and she could not feel the full impact of his pain and shock. "Let us go into the Pump Room, sir."

They made their way through the crowd and showed their identification to a soldier outside the Pump Room, who regarded Jane with much interest but finally allowed them inside.

"I shall fetch you a glass of water," her father said.

"No, sir, do not."

"What is this, Jane? I have heard the cure may be painful—I was pleasantly surprised that you had so little ill effect yesterday—but you must bear it, my dear."

"So I shall, when the time is right."

"What do you mean?"

"I mean, sir, that the Damned of the city intend to fight the French, and I shall be one of them."

"What!" Mr. Austen looked around, but there were no French nearby, only a few invalids. "No, Jane, you cannot. I forbid it."

"If I were your son, what would you say?"

"Well, I . . . but you are not! It is unseemly. And Edward or any of the others would not risk their soul in the process."

She smiled at him and slipped her hand into his arm, leading him on a slow circuit of the room. "I am in less danger than you think, although I cannot speak for my soul. But as a vampire I am more or less than a woman. I am very strong and I will be stronger. Also, I did not take the waters yesterday. I met another of the Damned, who allowed me to feed from him, an act of supreme kindness, for in their eyes I am an orphaned and shameful creature. I regret I had to deceive you."

Mr. Austen shook his head. "What! Surely you do not talk of that Mr. Venning?"

"Yes, sir. He offered to be my Bearleader—that is, a patron of sorts. I do not understand it fully myself."

He stopped and gazed at her. "What else do you hide from me, Jane?"

She tightened her lips and shook her head. "It is of necessity that I must confide in you, sir, for the respect I bear you. I believe I can learn to hide my condition from my mother and Cassandra, and I shall do so to protect them. But you, sir, do not need my protection."

They stood in silence for a moment while her father removed his spectacles and polished them on his handkerchief.

"Promise me, Jane, that if—or rather, when—your business is concluded you will take the cure. I fear the lure of the company of the Damned may prove stronger than the ties that bind you to your family and your God."

"I promise."

He nodded and they resumed their walk.

"I beg your pardon, ma'am, sir." A voice came from behind them.

Jane turned to see the fragile, sick woman in the wheelchair who Luke had pointed out to her the day before. She looked even more ill today.

"I regret we have not been introduced," the woman said. She waved away the maid who pushed her chair. "I could not help hearing the name of Luke Venning in your conversation—I assure you I did not mean to overhear, for it was obvious that your talk was of a private nature. I am Mrs. Margaret Cole."

Jane's father introduced himself and Jane. "I cannot help noticing, ma'am, that you look most unwell. May I fetch you some water?"

"No thank you, sir. I know you mean well, but it poisons me, as it will poison your daughter if she takes the cure. I beg of you, tell me, how is Mr. Venning?"

"He is well," Jane said. "If we are to speak frankly, I should tell you that I know of your former association with the gentleman."

She straightened a little in her wheelchair. "And I heard of your decision, Miss Austen, to fight against the French. I am full of admiration for you. I may speak freely since my husband is not here. You noticed the difference in our age, yesterday? Almost twenty years have passed since our wedding day and he has aged and I have not. I truly thought I wanted children and the life of an ordinary woman, but these are by no means ordinary times. You have helped me decide what I must do. Will you take me to Luke?"

"Gladly, but . . ." Jane could not think of a polite way to say she thought Margaret looked on the brink of death.

"The others in the house will revive me and bring me to my strength. As for Luke, I have injured him, and I no longer know his mind."

"I do not know if I am the right person to take you to the house," Jane said. "I have refused Luke as my Bearleader."

Margaret frowned. "That was unfortunate. You do not realize how great a privilege it would be to have Luke as Bearleader. I have never known him offer to do so. But I would see him and the others, for the last time, if that is what it will be. For I shall not survive the cure, I am convinced of it. I have been one of the Damned for too long. Will you call my maid, Miss Austen? I shall need my shawl. And may I presume further on your kindness, for I must ask you to help wheel my chair to their lodgings."

"I shall accompany you," Mr. Austen said. "I cannot condone an adulterous relationship, but neither would I see you suffer, ma'am. Besides, as a matter of practicality, I imagine Mr. Cole has your identity papers. And," with a glint of his usual humor, "whatever you two ladies may indeed be, you look like ladies and it is only proper that a gentleman should accompany you."

"Thank you, sir. Mr. Cole has gone to look at the houses destroyed last night by cannon fire on the Bristol Road—I regret many regard this as entertainment—and he will be some little time. I thank you for your kindness."

In silence they left the Pump Room and set off through the streets of the scarred and battered city.

"Let us look upon this favorably," Jane said in an effort to cheer her father. "If food becomes scarce, as I think is all too likely, you will not have to worry about providing for me."

"Oh, dear. I suppose you are right. That is, you will, ah . . ." Her father suddenly started talking loudly of the weather and concentrated very hard on steering Margaret's chair around a heap of rubble. The scent of blood was strong here, causing Jane's canines to ache, yet the mortal side of her was repulsed and dreaded seeing a corpse among the fallen masonry.

When they arrived at the house on Queens Square, her father made no move to embrace her as he might once have done.

"I shall return home when I can, Papa," Jane said. "I will send word. If you tell my mother and sister I visit friends, I think that should suffice."

"Very well. I shall pray for you."

Jane watched her father walk away as she tugged on the bell-pull. He did not look back.

"They may not yet be awake," Margaret murmured, to Jane's relief. She had not said a word on the way over and Jane feared she was unconscious, or worse. "Try again."

Jane did so and after a while heard a scuffling as though someone approached while trying to force their feet into their shoes.

The door swung open to reveal a footman, bleary-eyed, his wig on crooked, coat half buttoned. "They're not at home," he announced, closing the door.

Jane grasped the door and held it open. Even as hungry as she was, she was stronger than the man, who stepped back, apologizing. "Pray announce that Mrs. Cole and Miss Austen are here."

"I don't like to wake them, ma'am."

"Well I am certainly not going to! Go!"

"Help me," Margaret whispered. She pushed herself up from her chair, swaying, and clutched at Jane's arm. Tears ran down her face. "I don't want him to see me like this. Once I was beautiful."

Jane half carried her into the house. "He knows what you look like."

"I can't. You must revive me."

Jane pushed open the door to the dining room and settled Margaret onto a chair. "What may I do?"

"Fetch me a glass of wine, if you please."

Jane found Madeira and glasses on the sideboard and poured them both a glass.

"Now," Margaret said, "add a drop of your blood to my glass."

"Is my blood strong enough? I'm hardly much of a vampire."

"Not strong enough to kill me," Margaret whispered. "Hurry."

Jane bit her finger and watched the drop dissipate like smoke in the wine. "Last night I cured our housemaid's toothache with a drop of my blood."

"Ah. Luke has taught you well."

"He didn't. I—" She paused as, with a sudden burst of energy, Margaret snatched the glass from her and swallowed it in one gulp, then lay back shuddering.

"Fetch me another. Two drops. No, four."

"Two," came a voice from the doorway. "You seek to destroy yourself one way or the other, Margaret."

"No, I seek to become foxed," Margaret said. "Good morning to you, Luke."

Luke came into the room, yawning and rubbing his head, his hair rumpled. He wore a shirt open at the neck and breeches, his legs and feet bare as though he had risen hastily from his bed. "You're up devilish early."

Jane handed Margaret her second glass of wine.

"Your blood isn't too bad," Margaret said. "A little too much garlic, though."

Luke dropped into a chair and called out to the footman. "Fetch Miss Austen some parsley, if you please, and bring us some tea."

"Could I not bite someone who had eaten parsley?" Jane asked, attempting to lighten the situation.

They both frowned at her.

"Don't be vulgar," Luke said. He turned to Margaret. "So Mr. Cole proved incapable of providing you with babies?"

Margaret wrinkled her nose at him. "I have scarcely been able to sit up, let alone resume my marital duties."

They sat in silence as Margaret sipped her wine, eyes closed, as though that moment of animation had cost her dearly.

Luke yawned but Jane noticed his gaze never left Margaret. Once he reached out to steady the glass, touching the back of her hand with his fingertips. She stirred and opened her eyes and Jane thought she smiled a little at him. Luke looked away as though unsettled by the brief exchange.

The footman entered with a limp bunch of parsley on a plate and tea things on a tray. "Yesterday's parsley, sir, and yesterday's milk, too, but I think it's still good. The housekeeper is out looking for supplies."

Luke directed Jane to a tea caddy on the sideboard and she made tea; after which, seeing that Luke was quite serious about the consumption of parsley, she took a handful of the sorry-looking herb.

"Do we eat in the normal course of things?" Jane asked.

"Of course. We do not need to, but it is—or should be—a pleasurable pursuit. You may have noticed how things taste and how you can sense their origin. But if you need sustenance, food or drink will be of little use." Margaret sat up a little straighter on her chair. She was still pale, but her skin had lost its translucent fragility and Jane could see now the traces of the extraordinary beauty that the Damned possessed.

Upstairs, someone started to play scales on a pianoforte, an ordinary, familiar sound.

Luke stood abruptly and moved away, teacup in hand. "And what are we to do with you, Jane?"

She looked at his unyielding back and then at Margaret for support. "I told my father I wished to join you in the fight against the French."

"Indeed. And then you intend to leave us, I suppose."

"You forget a precedent has been set," Margaret interposed.

Luke shrugged. Upstairs, the musician launched into a sonata by Clementi that Jane recognized.

"You are horrid when you are cross," Margaret commented.

"My apologies, ma'am." Luke turned and bowed. "Allow me." He raised one hand to his mouth and dripped a little blood into her teacup. Jane heard him release his breath as Margaret drank and smiled at him.

The intimacy of the moment sent a pang of loneliness through her. She wished to leave but scarcely knew what etiquette demanded. What was worse, Luke probably sensed her unease but did little to reassure her, with his attention on Margaret.

"Jane," he said, without looking at her, "if you have finished your parsley, you may go upstairs to the drawing room and meet our newcomer. Then I suggest you go home to your family and return here at six o'clock, when we dine."

Dine? She hoped he meant she could feed again.

She stood and dropped a curtsy. Luke now sat next to Margaret, her hand in his. He raised the other to her cheek and swiped away a tear.

Jane closed the door, glad to escape the intensity of the moment, although she also found it excessively interesting. She must remember it for a book, if it did not smack too much of indecency. An adulterous relationship might be frowned upon, but possibly the reunion of two former lovers overcoming their injuries to each other could prove an interesting topic; and certainly the gentleman would never appear unshod and in his shirtsleeves.

Upstairs, the drawing room was empty, apart from a man who sat, his back to her, at the pianoforte. His musical skills were superb, and to her great pleasure, the instrument was perfectly tuned. He nodded his mane of chestnut-colored hair to indicate that he had heard her enter and she bent over his shoulder to take the page and turn it for him.

As she did so she studied him. There was something familiar about him, the curved nose and arrogant set of the head, the bright blue eyes.

She gasped and he stopped playing as she dropped into a curtsy. "I beg your pardon, Your Highness, I did not expect . . ."

She could not finish the sentence. No one expected the heir to the throne to be one of the Damned.

Chapter 9

"Bless my soul," the Prince of Wales said. "Or rather—since I have no soul at the moment, I beg your pardon, ma'am. Pray do not stand on formality with me. I did not mean to take you by surprise."

He stood, offering her a hand, and raised her from her deep curtsy.

"But you!" she said. "You have become—I am all astonishment. How long since? By design?" She stopped, remembering her frequent breaches of etiquette.

"It seemed the best course of action," he replied. "Certain among us knew the French were to invade at any time, so only a few days ago I was created. Capital fellow, William—I beg your pardon, ma'am, did I speak out of turn?"

"He is your Bearleader?"

"Indeed, yes. Who is yours?"

I have none. "Luke, but he did not create me. He adopted me, so to speak."

"My commiserations. They will treat you like a poor cousin, you know, as though it were your fault."

"I know, and to make it worse I fear I have offended him."

"Oh, he's a Bearleader with a sore head." The Prince of Wales laughed uproariously at his own joke. "There's some trouble with a lady, I believe. It's why they all came to Bath, for normally they wouldn't be here—the waters are poison to our kind, as you know. I can't countenance having all of eternity to bicker with one's beloved. I was adamant the Princess of Wales should not be created, nor the rest of the family."

"Are they safe?"

"I believe so. I don't know where they are, and they don't know where I am or what I have become. It's safest that way, you see, although the French are welcome to Her Highness."

Jane was silent. Everyone knew of the Prince of Wales's animosity toward his wife.

"So, you must call me George, and you are . . . ?"

"I am Jane."

"Capital. Would you care to play a duet?"

"I'm most honored that you asked, but you play far better than I." She tried to smile. Jilted by William for the Prince of Wales and the security of the succession—it was an honor of sorts, she supposed.

"Odd, ain't it," George continued, "you and I both know we're young for the Damned, but I'm damned if I can tell the age of the ladies. But then I've always favored ladies somewhat older than myself, although I never thought I'd meet ladies who were several hundred years my senior. So how do you get on, Jane? Can you retract your canines yet?"

"I certainly can." She showed him.

"Very good. I tend to lisp if I do not watch out."

She laughed, and realized then that he could sense her distress and had attempted to put her at her ease. "You know, I always thought you were fat and stupid."

He burst into easy laughter and slapped his flat abdomen. "I'll never have to hear a doctor or my tailor complain about my girth while I'm one of the Damned. And to be honest, Jane, I'm not the cleverest of fellows, and those devilish caricaturists have no mercy for my expanding waist or my mishaps. But I think I could be a pretty good vampire and prove myself against the French. Poor old Papa would never let me go for a soldier. Now, about that duet—do have pity and play with me, Jane. I fear I shall lose the knack and I need someone to keep me up to scratch. I am sure you are a clever woman and can play and sing and embroider and do all those things young ladies have drummed into their head."

"Mostly indifferently, I fear. My greatest, or rather my only true accomplishment, is as a writer." She paused. "Or as a former writer. I have a novel written and ideas for several others. But since this—since I was created—I had almost forgotten about it."

"Well, there's no denying it's a shock to the system. Turns you upside down and inside out. D'you feel hungry all the time? But to return to your writing—I'd be most honored if you'd let me read your novel. My friends have told me I have an eye for a well-written page."

She shook her head. "I regret I cannot let anyone read my imperfect work at the moment."

"I apologize. I did not mean to press you." He handed her a book of music. "Please, choose a duet you know or one you can read at sight."

He was kind to her and she was grateful, even if he had what she could not, William's care and regard. She found a duet by Haydn that she and Cassandra had played. They argued politely over who should take the top part, and she insisted she should take the bass part, suspecting he would enjoy the flourish and melody of the upper. Her extreme sensitivity to the ivory and ebony of the keys had faded and she was able to enjoy the experience, even when the pianoforte began to lose its pitch.

They finished the piece with a resounding, triumphant chord, and both winced.

"A mixed blessing where music is concerned, is it not?" Jane said.

"I don't think I could bear to hear anyone sing," George commented, fishing the tuning key from its hidden compartment. "You play exceedingly well, Jane."

"Thank you.. You too."

"I'm interested in this sort of thing. Music, books, art. Architecture. Or I was. Now I tend to think only of the next feed."

"Some would say little has changed."

He laughed. "*Touché*, Jane. Do you stay at the house with us?"

She shook her head. "My family is nearby. They brought me here for the cure and my father knows of my condition and that I intend to fight the French, but the rest of the family think I take the waters. And so I will, when the French have gone. You too, I suppose?"

He nodded. "An unpleasant experience, from what I have heard, but you and I shall suffer together. Misery loves company, as they say."

"Indeed. I don't enjoy deceiving my mother and sister; I'm not even sure I can."

"William taught me a little of that. It takes some concentration. You have to look into their minds frequently and tell them what they want to hear. They don't want you to be a vampire, you know, unless they want you to drink from them, and you'd know that soon enough." His eyes gleamed. "Some very pretty girls are in and out of this house. Gentlemen too, for the ladies of the Damned, and I daresay they'll find a way even with the curfew. We shan't be hungry for long. It's rather like gambling or laudanum, you know. Why, in London, some of the most respectable matrons of the *ton* bare their necks and raise their skirts for handsome vampires. Has not Luke introduced you to a suitable partner yet?"

"I believe he will tonight." She tried to keep her voice calm. She wanted to dine but the circumstances appalled her; she could not imagine such intimacy and gratification with a stranger, but the more she tried not to think about it, her excitement and extending canines shamed her. She touched a discreet finger to her lips.

He burst into one of his sudden laughs. "All this formality— it's almost as bad as being at court, but here most of them—or rather us—are half undressed and mad for blood. Well, Jane, at least you don't have to look like a hot-air balloon in one of those damned silly court gowns to meet me."

"I've enjoyed meeting you very much, George." She slipped from the piano bench and offered him her hand. "I shall return tonight."

He took her hand and raised it to his lips, then backed away, looking exceedingly embarrassed. "Dreadfully thorry," he said, and brought a finger to his mouth.

Back at the house at Paragon Place, Jane found her sister once again in the kitchen.

"I am so glad you are home," Cassandra said. "Where have you been?"

Jane concentrated hard and drove the question from Cassandra's mind.

Cassandra blinked. "What did I just say? This is dreadful, Jane. Papa has shut himself into our uncle's study, and Mama will not be comforted. She has taken to her bed. The only good thing is that the French soldiers left the house and then they brought back this, so we shall have something for dinner tonight." She indicated a large cut of meat that lay on the kitchen table. "I think it is mutton. At least, I hope it is so."

Jane laid her hand on the cold, clammy stuff. Woolly bodies shoved against each other in a windy field, seeking warmth. "Yes, it is mutton. Would you like me to make pastry again?"

"Yes, indeed. Your pastry is excellent, and we have some lard and flour still. Our chickens—or rather, our aunt and uncle's chickens—still lay, but I wonder how soon it will be before we must eat them. Papa told us commerce will return to the city, but Mrs. Burgess says everything is so expensive and there are French soldiers everywhere." Cassandra picked up a cleaver and regarded the meat with trepidation. "How shall I cut this up?"

Mrs. Burgess took the cleaver from her. "I'll do that, Miss Austen. They're not letting anyone into the city and they say the countryside swarms with French troops, Miss Jane, so heaven only knows when we can buy fresh stuff again."

"I have been invited to dine by Mr. Venning and his sister," Jane said, "so you do not have to worry about my share."

"Oh, was that the young man who escorted you and Papa home?" Cassandra said. "Papa said he was very droll and a physician by profession. Is he handsome?"

"Quite handsome and his sister is most amiable." Jane measured flour into the bowl of the scales, tipped it into the mixing bowl, and then weighed a block of lard. Calculating the amount she needed, she cut it off and chopped the fat into small pieces in the flour. How easy it was to lie, or tell a half truth. She wasn't quite sure what Clarissa's relationship with Luke Venning was, for she was fairly sure the Damned did not marry—on the contrary, they were notorious for their lax morals and disdain for the married state. She was also fairly sure that Luke and Clarissa were not related. But "brother and sister," however unlikely that might be, was a relationship that could be accepted with ease by the Austen family and thus define Clarissa and Luke as fit company for a gentlewoman.

Close by, the cleaver fell with a splinter of bone and spatter of blood.

"You should go and write after we've helped Mrs. Burgess," Cassandra said. "You've scarce talked of your writing. Is it because you don't feel well?"

"Partly, although today I feel better." Upstairs, her manuscript lay in its brown paper wrapping. She dreaded having to look at those pages, remembering how unintelligible they seemed the last time she had looked at them at home in Hampshire. "It is difficult to think of our usual occupations at such a time, but I suppose we must do so."

"I wish we could persuade our mother of that," Cassandra said. "I shall do my best to make her dress and come down to dinner. I think it will help Papa."

Household duties completed—Jane thought it was more that Mrs. Burgess found them only of limited use in the kitchen, and Betty had returned from the garden with an armful of cabbage and a basket of eggs, ready to be put to work—she and Cassandra went upstairs to the morning room. Cassandra picked up her sewing and Jane stared at her manuscript, turning the pages over. Now and again Cassandra glanced at her.

"You are not yourself," Cassandra said. "Normally you talk and smile to yourself or scribble notes. Maybe you should put it aside."

Jane rested her forehead on her hands, elbows on the table. "It is as though someone else wrote it, and not well. It does not make sense. I don't know what to do."

"Perhaps you could start something else? Maybe you need a change." Cassandra rose and lit a candle from the fireplace.

Jane nodded and drew a sheet of fresh paper toward her. She sharpened a pen, dipped it into the ink, and sat staring at the blank page.

"Remember, you told me several weeks ago, when we were reading that letter from our aunt and uncle, of the idea of a novel set in Bath," Cassandra continued. "Maybe something gothic. I remember how we laughed about the silliness of some of Mrs. Radcliffe's books, yet we agreed that we always felt compelled to read to the end. And you said—"

Jane stood. "I—I don't think I feel well. I shall go upstairs. No, I shall do perfectly well on my own. Please do not concern yourself." She ran out of the room and up the two flights of stairs to her bedchamber, noting that she was not at all out of breath, and sank onto her bed.

She couldn't write. She couldn't talk freely to her sister, and, what was worse, yearned to be a few streets away with her own kind. She longed for nightfall. She stiffened as she heard footsteps on the stairs—not Cassandra; she would know her tread. Almost certainly a woman's, for she could hear the rustle of skirts.

It was Betty. She could recognize her scent. The maid paused outside the room and tapped at the door.

"Enter," Jane called.

Betty entered with a cup of tea. "Miss Austen said I should bring you this and see if you needed help in changing your gown."

"Thank you. Put the tea on the table."

"My mouth hardly pains me at all, Miss Jane."

"Good." Her voice sounded harsh and unfriendly. "You may unlace my gown." She did not dare face Betty. It would be so easy to trap the girl here, drink from her—she could hear the pounding of Betty's heart and smell her warmth.

"That's a very pretty gown, miss."

"Yes." She held her breath as Betty dropped the gown over her head and tied the two laces, one at her neck and one at the waist. She could turn and grasp her, slake her hunger. Other than a little weakness after, Betty would never need to know.

"You look most elegant, miss."

"Thank you. Go." Jane turned her head to the window, willing darkness to fall.

"Yes, Miss Jane." A rustle of fabric, a breath, and Betty turned and left the room.

An hour later Jane, her pass tucked securely into her stays, left the house again. Her father had come downstairs, complimented her on her looks and offered to escort her. She forced a smile, looked into his eyes, and told him with great firmness she had no need of an escort. Her father meekly called for a chair and allowed his daughter to leave the house in the dark of the early evening in a city full of an occupying army. Little did he know that any stray soldier would be in more danger from this elegantly dressed lady than she from him. Her canines extended. She was hungry, so hungry.

She reversed her *en sanglant* as she stepped up to the front door of Luke's house, once again its every room glowing with candlelight and full of the sound of music and laughter. The footman asked her to wait in the hall.

After a little while Luke came down the stairs, wearing a coat and breeches but with his shirt open at the neck. He looked at her and nodded as though finding her appearance satisfactory.

"Yes, indeed, the headdress is a new style," Jane said with an elaborate curtsy. "Most kind of you to admire it so, sir. My sister thought I should add more feathers but instead I used the silk flowers, and I think it most elegant—"

"Come with me." His stern look cut off her facetious chatter.

He opened the door to the dining room and ushered her inside, shrugging his coat off. He unbuttoned his cuff. "Drink."

With a whimper of relief she grabbed his wrist and bit, rewarded by a surge of blood that thrilled through her body. Just one gulp, and Luke lifted her chin away. "Enough."

She only just remembered to breathe on the incisions and lick the wound clean. He nodded and wiped her chin with his thumb. "Thank you," she said, confused. Was that all she would be allowed?

"Good."

"Luke, is this some sort of game we play, that I speak, and you answer with one word? I assure you I am able to talk at great length, but such an unequal conversation may bore me. I—"

"Let me explain, Jane. You are to dine upstairs tonight in company, and I need the edge to be taken from your hunger so that you do not shame me or yourself."

"You mean, I have to drink from someone I do not know in the drawing room? In front of everyone?"

"Oh, you'll know the person quite well by the time you have finished, I should think." He smiled. "Or as much as you care to. I assure you no one will take much notice; the others will be busy too."

"But—that's shocking." She had a fairly good idea what sorts of activities would keep them busy.

"So shocking you are *en sanglant* again." He pulled two chairs out from the wall and placed them together. "Sit."

He took the chair next to her and undid another button on the ruffled placket of his shirt, tilting his head away from her. "Do be careful not to get blood on my shirt, Jane."

"You want me to bite your neck?" She was appalled, ravenous, afraid.

"Oh, yes—yes, if you please," he breathed, in a parody of genteel surrender, and winked at her. "Now, gently, Jane, do not chomp at me, if you please. Put your lips on my neck first. Ah." He gave a long sigh.

"You are laughing at me."

"No, I assure you I am not." He had achieved full *en sanglant*; his eyes were bright and his scent filled her nostrils.

"Where do I put my hand?"

"What a question to ask a gentleman. First, allow me to place your fan aside, so. On my other shoulder will do quite nicely, although if you wish to—"

"I believe you are not entirely indifferent to my intentions." She blew gently on his neck and saw him shiver.

"And why should I not enjoy it, my dear Jane? I find bearleading to be a tedious occupation. I deserve some reward."

She gazed at his neck, at the pale skin with a hint of stubble where his razor had missed a spot. She had never been so close to a gentleman before—but of course she had, when William had created her, although she remembered it only as a swirl of confusing, startling pleasure.

"Don't be afraid," Luke said. "You decide when you are to bite. Slowly. Allow your canines to sink in; it's easier than a wrist, the skin is softer. Ah, very good."

She whimpered as his blood flowed onto her tongue, a sweet flood of power, before pulling away. She breathed on his neck, licking the last drops. "I can't drink any more from you."

"What's wrong?"

"You're so sad."

He grinned and wrapped an arm around her waist. "On the contrary, my dear, I am quite cheered at the moment."

"Consider the gravitas of your position as my Bearleader, sir."

"You are quite right. I am behaving disgracefully." He released her, and pulled his shirt front straight.

"Not a drop spilled," she said, cheered by her success.

"Excellent. Now remember that if the person is excited, which invariably he will be, the blood will pulse. Take care not to choke, and pray he has not eaten onions recently." He handed her her fan.

"How will I know when to stop?"

"You'll know. If you seem a little too, ah, enthusiastic, I shall let you know. I shall be nearby." He rose and, pulling his coat on, walked to the sideboard, where a decanter of wine and wineglass stood. "Some Madeira? Now, others will be dining when you enter the drawing room. Pray do not express too much interest; it will be considered excessively vulgar. In particular you must avoid meeting the eye of one who dines, for he or she will consider it a request to join. Since you are a fledgling it would be monstrously improper of you to solicit an invitation thus, and you should await for one senior to you to make a proper introduction—"

"Good heavens!" cried Jane, nearly choking on her wine. "It reminds me of a Basingstoke assembly!"

"As I was saying: if, on the other hand, another of us invites you to join, it is considered proper to accept, for it is a high honor. If you wish to decline, you may do so by bowing your head and dropping a curtsy."

"And at what point should I remove my gloves?" Jane asked, struggling to keep a straight face.

Luke shot her a stern glance. "If one of the mortals requests you dine from him or her, you must be careful they do not ask to stir up trouble between us. Some of our group are jealous of mortals they consider their own." He added, "Unless it is Ann, for she is with the household, although Clarissa tends to regard her as her property. Apparently Ann has a certain way of darning stockings that is most rare."

"I see," Jane said, again suppressing a smile. "But she does not darn stockings while one dines upon her, I think."

"Indeed not." Luke took her empty wineglass and held the dining-room door open. "Let us proceed to your debut among the Damned. By the by, George told me he very much enjoyed meeting you. It is good for him to have the company of another fledgling."

"I must admit, I liked him better than I should have expected."

"Oh, he's a good enough fellow."

They started up the stairs.

"How is Margaret? Is she recovered?"

"She is well enough, I believe." Luke's voice was cold and formal once more, his playfulness gone. He walked ahead of her into the drawing room, and a woman ran forward and grasped her hands, leaning to whisper in his ear. He put her aside and gestured with his head for Jane to follow him.

The woman gazed at Jane with curiosity, but most of the other occupants of the room, intimately twined together in groups of two or three, gave her only the most cursory of glances. She was careful to keep her gaze modestly lowered. To her relief she could not see William although she knew that almost certainly he was nearby.

"Luke bearleads her," she heard someone say. "It is most good of him to take her on."

"Ah, she is the one who fancies William is the one who created her. She aims high." An insinuating laugh.

She raised her head and followed Luke across the room. He stood with someone who looked familiar, although it took her a moment to recognize him in evening clothes and not in regimentals. He was one of the few men in the drawing room who wore a neckcloth. He bowed low over her hand. "Miss Austen, the pastrycook. Your servant, ma'am."

"Colonel Poulett! How delightful to meet you again. Do you come to talk tactics with Luke?"

"Heavens, no, ma'am. I abide by the terms of the truce." He winked at her. "But Venning suggested I offer my services to you."

"Your services?" she repeated.

"Indeed, ma'am." He cleared his throat. "That is, my blood."

Her canines shot out and Luke glared at her.

"I beg your pardon," she muttered, restoring her canines to their normal state.

"If you'll have me, that is, ma'am. When I was younger I frequently indulged myself, but of late . . . Well, Luke thought you might be more comfortable with me rather than one of the others." He smiled, but she could see he was ill at ease. "Do have me, ma'am."

"That is most considerate," Jane said. "Shall we sit? You realize, I hope, that I am somewhat inexperienced, but Luke will be nearby to make sure no harm comes to you."

Poulett threw up his hands. "Good heavens, ma'am, I trust you implicitly. You are a gentlewoman!"

"And a vampire." She sat on a nearby sofa and after a moment's hesitation Poulett sat next to her and untied his neckcloth. He unbuttoned his coat, waistcoat, and the placket of his shirt with a determined, if not enthusiastic air. Jane sighed. Was she destined to drink from reluctant military men? She wished she had not thought of the French soldier at that moment.

She leaned forward and placed a hand on his wrist. His pulse hurtled and she sensed the pain and humiliation that lay beneath his stoic façade—the burden of his defeat and the men for whose deaths he had been responsible.

"I trust I may provide you with some solace, sir. Will you not call me Jane?"

"My pleasure, ma'am—Jane, that is. My name is John."

She laid her fan on the sofa and slipped her hand inside the collar of his shirt, overwarm skin and rough hair. She'd never touched a man so, never even thought of daring to slide her hand below the cambric of a shirt. His heart thudded in time with the pulse in his neck. His hair was touched with gray and curled into the back of his neck and over his ears.

She leaned into him, placing her other hand on his shoulder, and he took a deep, sudden breath. *I have power over him.* She touched her tongue to his neck and to the taste of sweat and bay rum, wine, and tobacco. Her canines sank into his neck and the blood pulsed onto her tongue, a rich tide of pleasure and strength.

He groaned and placed his hand on hers, large and rough, the hand of a soldier, as she drank his sadness and defeat away.

Chapter 10

Jane woke on the sofa where she had settled after dancing for several hours and reflected on how she had spent the previous night. In fact she had enjoyed herself thoroughly. She wished she could tell Cassandra about it, but that was impossible. What would Cassandra say if she knew her sister had languished in the arms of a gentleman she barely knew, and if that wasn't bad enough, had drunk his blood to their great mutual enjoyment? She didn't know which would shock her sister more.

On the other hand, there had been some very interesting gowns and headdresses, and she had danced and flirted with several partners, including Poulett, who was shy and grateful and apt to tread on her toes. To her relief there was no sign of him, for meeting in cold daylight after the intimacy of the previous night could only be awkward.

"Devil take it, daylight," someone else grumbled; so at least one of the household was awake.

"I'm hungry," said a familiar, plaintive voice.

"Stow it, George."

"But I am. I'm a big fellow, you know." The Prince of Wales loomed over her. "Good morning, Jane."

"Good morning." She sat and looked around the room and wished she hadn't. Opposite her on a sofa, Luke lay asleep between two women whose gowns were more off than on and wearing little else besides. Clarissa sprawled close by on a pile of pillows with three men clad only in cotton drawers.

"Messy, ain't it?" said the heir to the throne with great cheerfulness. He walked over to the fireplace and tugged the bellpull to summon a servant. "They—we, that is—tend to favor sleeping in heaps. You'll learn to fight today, you know. I want a cup of tea."

Jane struggled to connect these seemingly unrelated sentences. Someone on the floor beside the sofa sighed and she looked down to see a young man who wore only a cushion on his lap. Really, she should be a little more shocked, should she not?

"I'm Jack, miss," he said.

"Good morning, Jack."

He blinked long beautiful eyelashes at her. "I need to be revived, if you please, miss, for I have to get to work."

"To work?"

"Yes, miss, I'm a stonemason. I repaired an angel on the Abbey. It's the one on the bottom on the right-hand side."

"Stop chattering and get your bottom down to the kitchen, where it belongs," a masculine voice growled. "And for God's sake put some clothes on."

"Yes, sir. Thank you, sir."

After some scuffling around, Jack emerged more or less dressed. He bowed in a vague sort of way to the room at large, and left.

George gave a cry of triumph and pounced on a half-naked

woman, rolling her aside to pluck a gaudily embroidered waist-coat from the floor. "I knew I'd left it somewhere. I'm going downstairs for some tea."

Jane rose and followed him, stepping carefully between sleeping bodies sprawled on pillows.

"One thing puzzles me," she said to George as they went down the stairs. "Everyone seems to tolerate daylight quite well."

"If you stay up all night you sleep most of the day. I never go to bed before four, generally. It's thought to be vulgar to be seen in daylight, that's all. I daresay they—we—might have fried in sunlight once upon a time, but that's long past. Of course, some of them don't sleep at all, but they're old." He opened the door to the dining room. "Good morning, sir."

William, impeccably dressed, sat at the dining-room table, drinking tea with a slender young man. He nodded at George and ignored Jane. She had not expected him to be other than indifferent to her. Could he feel her misery at his coldness? She suspected that he could and attempted to block off her feelings from him.

The other man, dressed in an elegant dark blue coat and tan buckskins, rose. Glossy dark brown curls tumbled over his brow, and his face was just saved from prettiness by a bumpy nose. "Why, Your Highness—George—it's true—you're one of us!"

"George!"

"You cannot both be called George, it's damned confusing," William said. "Try numbers."

"I may anticipate myself by taking on the number four," the Prince of Wales proclaimed.

"But damn it, we can't find two more Georges for your sake; your head will be even more swelled than usual," said the other with easy familiarity. "And which number would I take? But won't you introduce me?"

"Oh, I beg your pardon," the future King said. "This is Jane. She's a lady novelist, you know."

"Indeed? Your servant, ma'am. George Brummell." He looked at Jane with interest. "What do you write?"

"Very little, at present."

"Of course, these times are not conducive to literature. George, go and find Luke, there's a good fellow."

Jane had been trying to adapt herself to the laxness of life among the Damned, but seeing the Prince of Wales ordered to fetch someone as though he were a lackey was astonishing, far more shocking than the casual nudity and debauchery she had witnessed upstairs. Even more surprising was the enthusiasm with which George left the room on his errand. She stole another look at George Brummell, admiring his pale, handsome face, and thought he might well be much older and more important than she had at first thought.

"Well?" William said.

She stared back at him and poured herself a cup of tea she didn't want, pleased that her hands did not shake. "Good morning to you, sir."

As she left the room she met Luke and George coming down the stairs, Luke rubbing his hair and yawning. "Ridiculously early, but I hope there's some good news from London. What are you doing down here, Jane?"

"I invited her," George said, and muttering again of cups of tea, returned to the dining room.

"You did quite well last night," Luke said.

"I'm gratified I did not cause you any embarrassment."

"I too." He paused. "You may return to your family. Oh, heavens, don't look at me like that. You will return, of course. Clarissa will call on you later this morning to invite you to take the waters and you'll return here. We must teach you to fight with the others, after all."

"Very well. Luke, I don't understand. What can we do that the militia cannot?"

He smiled. "We are not just a handful of the Damned in Bath. There are thousands of us all over the country, fighting the French, and we do not need the Royal Mail to keep us informed. We are superior at night, curfews mean nothing to us, and by nature we are stronger and faster than any well-trained soldiers—even a fledgling such as you. What's wrong?"

"When . . . when first I met William I accused him—us, the Damned—of being merely irresponsible and interested only in self-gratification."

"And so we are," Luke said. "We do this for our own amusement and because the royalty of England, sorry clods though the present lot may be, have been kinder to us than the revolutionaries of France."

"I see." She lingered while Luke tapped one impatient foot. "I don't want to go home. Well, it is not my home, but I hate being there. I hate deceiving my family."

"The choice was yours," Luke said.

"I see I am to get little sympathy from you." Greatly daring, she extended her canines at him.

He laughed. "I'll send a footman with you. *Au revoir*, my dear Jane."

"Every morning I wake and for a few seconds all is well." Cassandra stabbed her needle into her embroidery. "And then I remember that England is invaded and you are unwell and there is a French officer here in our house—well, not our house, but our aunt and uncle's house, and we don't even know if they live or not—and we cannot send letters. And I must keep my spirits up because maybe that will help Mama. At least you have some friends."

"Fellow invalids," Jane said. "We have the most tedious conversations about our illnesses. Where is the Frenchman?"

"Out. He's out most of the time. He did not dine with us last night but came home late, and we were glad for there was more food for us. Oh, Jane, you look so thin and pale."

"I am well enough." What Cassandra interpreted as a sign of illness Jane recognized as the pallor and lean beauty of a vampire. She stole a look at her reflection in the mirror that hung over the morning-room fireplace; sure enough, her cheeks, formerly round and pink, inspiring her brothers to compare her to a well-fed dormouse, were now hollow, her cheekbones sharp. Was there a slight fuzziness in her reflection?

She reached for the teapot. "I'll take Mama some tea. Where is Papa?"

"Out trying to get us a pass to go home, for when you are well, that is."

Jane laid a hand on her sister's, bracing herself against the wash of emotions. "I am sorry. I feel you deal with everyone's distress."

"I do. And the worst of it is, Jane, that I am so bored!" Cassandra gave a little gulping sob. "It is a dreadful thing to say, for this is a terrible time, and I daresay we shall tell our grandchildren of how we lived through this historic event; in fact, we shall bore them to death, I am sure. But everything is so wretched, and the servants complain to me interminably of how difficult it is to buy food, and I hate cooking, but I must do something."

"You do quite enough, acting as the only sensible person in this house."

"But I don't want to be sensible. I want to go shopping! I want to go to card parties and assemblies! I want to dance and flirt!"

Cassandra gave a horrified laugh. "Oh, heavens, Jane, you know what I mean. I want none of this to have happened." She tossed aside her embroidery and laid her face on her folded arms. "To think that a visit to Bath was once synonymous with pleasure."

Jane patted her shoulder, helpless. "I am so sorry," she mumbled. "Believe me, there is nothing I should like better than for everything to be as it was before."

"It wasn't your fault." Cassandra's voice was muffled. "None of it was anyone's fault."

"I beg your pardon, ma'amselle Austen and ma'amselle Jane." Captain Garonne stood at the doorway. He held a newspaper in his hand. "I came to bring you this . . . it is the newspaper. I do not wish to disturb you."

Cassandra straightened and grabbed her embroidery, her head turned aside so the captain would not see her reddened eyes.

"Thank you, sir. Do you dine with us tonight?" Jane tried to make the question as unfriendly as possible.

"I believe so." He crossed the room to lay the newspaper on the table. "Here it says there is to be a concert and fireworks at Sydney Gardens tomorrow night to celebrate the friendship between the French and English in this town. I should like to offer to escort you ladies, if it is agreeable with all. I know my uncle, our commander, General Renard, would find your company delightful."

"I regret my health does not permit me to attend such events," Jane said. "Neither do I feel, Captain, that there is much friendship to celebrate."

He bowed. "I shall wish you good day, then."

Cassandra waited until the front door closed as the captain left the house. "Jane, what has come over you?"

"What do you mean?"

"It is not like you to be so rude. Would it harm us to go out and have a little pleasure?" Cassandra picked up the newspaper and leafed through it. "Why, here is the announcement. There are to be refreshments and a concert and fireworks, as the captain said. You know, he is quite a handsome man now he has rested and shaved. He looked like a brigand when first he came into the house. I shall ask Mama—"

"I beg of you that you shall do no such thing!" Jane cried. "We are at war, Cassandra! He is an unwelcome guest in this house, this city, this country—*our* country. How can you even think of such a thing?"

Cassandra looked taken aback at Jane's show of passion. "Don't you see, Jane—he has high connections. Maybe he can help Papa obtain a pass."

"Oh. I suppose he could. I beg your pardon; I never thought of that." Jane took the now cooling cup of tea she had poured for Mrs. Austen. She looked over Cassandra's shoulder at the newspaper. "What a sad rag—all advertisements and no news. But Cassandra, we should not fraternize with our enemies. It is not right. I am sure Papa would agree."

"I shall ask him," Cassandra said. She had a familiar, obstinate set to her mouth.

Jane sighed and went upstairs with the tea. She tapped on the bedchamber door and entered.

Mrs. Austen, in her dressing gown and cap, lay in the bed. "I am very ill," she said in a voice that dared Jane to disagree.

"I am sorry to hear it, ma'am." Jane hoped her mother would not take it into her head to visit the Pump Room, which would be exceedingly awkward.

Mrs. Austen sipped the tea. "It is stone cold."

"I'll fetch you more, ma'am."

"No, I do not wish to be a burden." Mrs. Austen closed her eyes. "It is too bad your father leaves me alone in this house full of French monsters all day."

"The captain is out, ma'am, as are the other two soldiers."

"I do not even wish to think of it!" Mrs. Austen groped among the bedclothes. "Where is my vinaigrette?"

Jane handed her the small silver box. "Miss Venning has invited me to attend the Pump Room and Baths with her today, ma'am."

"What is our connection with the Vennings?" Mrs. Austen asked. "Your father was quite vague on the subject, other than saying Mr. Venning is a physician. I am not sure he would be well-bred enough to dine with us at home."

"I believe he and Mr. Venning have some mutual acquaintances who have an interest in antiquities."

"Oh, old things. It is all very well for you, Jane, but I do not know a soul here and the town is full of marauding Frenchmen. It is too bad and Cassandra is in a most provoking mood."

"Indeed, ma'am. Maybe it is better you rest abed until you are stronger."

Her mother insisted, however, that she should rise, and spent a good quarter hour complaining about Jane's help with her hair and gown before descending the stairs.

"We cannot receive Miss Venning in our morning room. Jane, Cassandra, we must have the fire lit in the drawing room."

"But that room is freezing, ma'am," Cassandra said. "It takes a good half hour for the fire to warm it. Furthermore, the chimney smokes if the wind is from the west. Consider that both you and Jane are unwell and—"

"Just because the town is overrun with dreadful French does not mean we should let our standards decline." Mrs. Austen led the way into the drawing room and tugged on the bellpull, and then proceeded to make the life of their two remaining footmen wretched.

Jane, glad she no longer felt the cold, poked the sullen fire into life, and was rewarded by a gust of smoke. Cassandra meanwhile talked of the entertainment at Sydney Gardens the next evening and Captain Garonne's offer to escort the ladies.

"How very thoughtful of him!" cried Mrs. Austen. "And nephew to the general—why, he is better connected than I thought!"

"Is he not one of those marauding and dreadful Frenchmen of whom you were complaining, ma'am?" Jane could not resist. "Besides, I am sure Papa will forbid it, and quite rightly. They are our enemies."

The jangle of the front doorbell announced the arrival of a visitor, who turned out to be Clarissa, much to Jane's relief.

To her mortification, Mrs. Austen invited Clarissa and her "brother" to join the party going to Sydney Gardens the next evening, despite, Jane was sure, her father's anticipated refusal to allow the family to attend.

"I beg your pardon, ma'am, I must refuse. We are otherwise engaged," Clarissa replied, and turned the conversation to the weather. Jane was relieved when they managed to escape the house after some more trivialities. A troop of French soldiers passed them as they walked the short distance to Luke's house.

Clarissa growled softly, *en sanglant.*

"I do so agree," said Jane as they entered the house.

"Yes, a young man in uniform is exceedingly tempting."

"That wasn't quite what I meant." If it were not physically impossible, a blush would have overtaken her.

Clarissa led the way upstairs. "I really don't understand why you stay with them," she said over her shoulder.

"They are my family."

"No, my dear Jane. *We* are your family. There is no need to dissemble or deceive here. You are with your own kind." Clarissa pushed open the door of the bedchamber where Jane had bathed and dressed two nights ago. Before Jane could formulate an appropriate response, Clarissa added, "You had best mention to Luke they have a Frenchman in that house. He will not be best pleased that you conceal such a thing from us."

"But . . ."

To Jane's surprise a young man lounged on the bed in his shirtsleeves, directing Ann the maid as she unpacked garments from a large trunk. "That will need ironing, and see if you can remove the spot on the cuff. No, those will not do—I can see the moth holes from here. Why, Jane, you have come at exactly the right moment."

Jane blinked. The "young man" was none other than Margaret. Ironed shirts, neckcloths, and stockings lay over the bed and on the backs of chairs, and a pile of boots lay on the floor.

"You look much improved," Clarissa said.

"Thank you. I am a little weak, but getting stronger by the hour."

"Does Luke sulk still?" Clarissa pinched Ann's cheek. "You look very plump and biteable today."

"Thank you, miss." Ann giggled.

"I have not seen Luke since yesterday," Margaret replied. "Clarissa, if you distract Ann we shall appear as male slatterns, for she has a great deal of ironing to do. Jane, you must find a pair of breeches to fit you."

"Breeches?" She knew she would fight, and had thought vaguely that skirts were perhaps unsuitable—but men's clothing? On the other hand, Margaret looked quite well in hers, and Jane had always secretly been rather proud of her long legs, strong from walking and dancing.

"Now, don't be a ninny," Clarissa said, noticing Jane's hesitation. She turned so Ann could unlace her gown and then her stays. "I think you'll make an excellent young gentleman."

Jane accepted Margaret's offer to unlace her and, still wearing her shift, picked out one of the shirts that lay on the bed. It had the familiar, homely smell of recently ironed cotton.

"Wait. You'll need this." Margaret held out a long length of cloth.

"I shall?"

"You can't be a gentleman with a bosom."

"Oh. Oh no, of course not."

"And these." Margaret held out a garment that Jane had only seen previously in the family laundry, a pair of gentleman's drawers.

"How very odd these are," Jane commented as she tied the drawstring at the waist. She tied the strip of cloth around her chest, and giggled a little at the wickedness of it all, trying to ignore Clarissa, who flounced around the room stark naked, obviously enjoying herself.

Jane slipped the shirt over her head and her arms into the sleeves. After several tries she found a pair of fawn breeches that fit her quite well and she struggled with the brass buttons of the fall. Without stays she felt undressed, her posture entirely changed. Stockings and boots went on next. The waistcoat, a colorful striped one George might admire, helped matters a little, but it was not until the coat was on, her shoulders drawn back by the cut, that she was able to swagger around the room. She loosened her hair and tied it back in a queue—old-fashioned, but possibly she could conceal it beneath a hat—and admired herself in the mirror.

"Not bad." Luke stood in the doorway. "Enjoy the reflection while you can, for you won't have one for long. Put some clothes on, Clarissa, you'll be late. You've forgotten one small detail, Jane."

He handed her a rolled-up stocking.

"What's this for?"

"In the front of your drawers, at the top of the thigh; possibly you'll need to pin it into position. Pick one side and stay with it." He placed his hands on his hips, feet slightly apart, providing her with an eloquent demonstration of what the rolled-up stocking would provide.

Margaret raised a hand to her lips in a gesture Jane recognized. Either her fangs had extended or she was simply amused and hid a smile—or her anger. Yes, anger, that was it, at Luke's attention to Jane.

"Possibly I may be of some assistance." Luke took a step toward Jane.

Margaret growled, quite definitely *en sanglant*.

"I think I can manage. I'd hate to prick you."

As Jane hoped, for an instant Luke looked startled at her mild innuendo. She snatched the stocking from his hand and a pin from the dresser and turned her back to him. So she was about to learn how to fight. She was more than ready.

Chapter 11

They gathered in the drawing room, Jane, William, Luke, and George. George Brummell, it appeared, had departed again for London. Others drifted in, and introductions were made, until a dozen or so had assembled. Two footmen brought in a large, heavy trunk with contents that rattled and clattered.

Luke flung the lid of the trunk open, revealing a collection of large, dangerous-looking knives, many with misshapen, notched blades that suggested former, lethal uses.

"Choose a weapon and practice," he said. "But not you, Jane and George. You need to be taught."

"Beg your pardon, Luke, I know how to fight," George said. "I've had a fencing tutor since I was five years of age."

"Not that sort of fighting," Luke said. "You know only how to fight like a gentleman, and that's not adequate for what we are to do."

"Very well." George shrugged.

"I'll teach George; William, teach Jane, if you please."

In the silence that fell, William looked Jane up and down. "I beg you will excuse me. She is not vampire enough to tempt me."

Luke stepped forward to lay a restraining hand on Jane's arm as she stiffened, her fist closing around the knife hilt, canines extending. "Come, William, we cannot have this sort of division in our midst, not at this time."

"Look, I don't mind, damn it," George said. "I'd be honored, whoever cares to teach me, and if William doesn't wish to teach Jane, that's his loss. Look how devilish fierce she is—she scares me half to death."

Luke nodded. "Thank you." He laid his arm on Jane's shoulder, led her away to the far end of the drawing room, and spoke softly. "I beg your pardon. Generally it's best not to have a Bearleader teach his own—without realizing it he'll be too protective of his or her ward."

"But he is my Creator!" She sniffed and lifted a cuff to wipe her eyes.

"That's true. But consider that as your adopted Bearleader, I lack a vital protective instinct toward you, and I'll train you better. I shall be far less gentle, far less solicitous."

"And that was why you wanted William to train me, because you would do a better job of training George." She glanced over her shoulder.

"I do not mean to offend you, but he is of far more importance in the larger scheme than you." He gave her a friendly smile that took the sting from his words. "Good. Now, let us commence. You may remove your coat and waistcoat and neckcloth—you did a dreadful job of tying it, by the way. I shall have to teach you the finer points of male fashion."

She removed her outer clothes as he suggested.

William and George joined them and closed the connecting doors that made two smaller rooms into one large drawing room.

Grunts and thumps from behind her indicated that George's lesson had already begun.

She straightened, feeling awkward and self-conscious and took a firmer grip of the knife.

"No, no." Luke adjusted her grip. "Forget the way actors hold daggers. You are not playing Brutus, you know. So. Try to kill me."

"But I can't kill you."

He rolled his eyes. "Imagination, dear Jane. You have some I believe, as a writer—" He laughed and swayed aside. Something tickled and scraped along her side. "Now, if I'd put a little weight behind that, I'd have hurt you. Speaking of which, if you make me bleed I'll reward you with a little of my blood." He turned his back on her. "I'll make it easy for you."

"Are you sure I cannot kill you?"

"Absolutely."

She ran at him, dagger poised upward, and the room whirled as she was deposited neatly on her back, the breath knocked from her.

"Oh, that's not fair!" she gasped. "You knew I was attacking."

"Certainly I did. You came at me like an elephant."

"You are exceedingly rude." She scrambled to her feet, or rather, began to, but he was too fast for her, disarming her and pinning her to the ground.

"Now what?"

She fluttered her eyelashes at him. "That *hurt*."

He frowned.

Triumphant, she reared up and aimed a swing at his jaw with one hand.

Luke cursed as he fell back and his head bounced on the carpeted floor.

She threw herself onto him, grabbed the knife, and held it to his throat, grasping his wrist with her other hand. Her knee on his other arm and her weight on his belly immobilized him.

"Good God, you females need no encouragement whatsoever

not to fight like gentlemen." Luke twisted a leg around hers in an attempt to dislodge her. "Fangs, Jane."

"I beg your pardon—" She raised a hand to retract her errant canines and found herself flat on her back, disarmed once more, flattened by Luke's weight.

" 'Pon my word," said George, peering down at them. "May not one of the ladies teach me?"

"Concentrate!" William grabbed him by the collar and threw him down.

"Let us assume you have stabbed me or bitten me by this time," Luke said. "We'll start again. Most of the killing you do must be quick and clean, and above all, silent."

"May I dine when I kill?" Jane found herself anticipating dining this evening; her fangs had extended again. She got to her feet.

"If you have time, certainly," Luke said, "but surely you noticed with your Frenchman that it was not particularly quiet?"

She remembered the guttural bubbling wheeze of the dying man and nodded.

"So." He stepped close to her. "Give me your hand. Here, at my back. Aim upward, and you will reach the heart through the ribs. Now try again. Walk quietly. You don't want to arouse my suspicions. And Jane, if you please, save my shirt and do not use your knife. I promise you'll have opportunity enough to make me bleed, and besides, it will hurt like the devil."

He turned away from her and lounged against the mantelpiece, whistling softly to himself, and she stalked up on him, planting the knife precisely, or so she hoped, in the right spot on his ribs.

"You're dead," she said.

He spun around, grasped her wrist, and tossed her onto the floor, his own knife point pressing against the binding on her chest. "No, *you* are." He paused. "What will you do? Consider, I cannot kill you—or at least, not like this—but I can certainly injure you and weaken you enough to take you into captivity. Or I can call to my companions to help overpower you."

She struggled to throw him from her, but the point of his knife pricked through the fabric of her shirt; she heard the small sound as the threads severed. He was stronger than she was, and this time he would not allow her to overpower him.

"If you're fast, you may throw a man off yourself, and my advice is to either kill him then or run as fast as you can." He eased himself from her and stood. "But let us suppose you are in a tight corner and there is nowhere you can run and evade him, no shadows in which to conceal yourself. You must fight hand to hand and I shall teach you a little. You have the advantage of speed and strength, but doubtless your opponent will be more skilled and also have a greater reach."

She stood and faced him.

He took her coat and draped it over his left arm. "Use your coat or hat to distract him and also to protect yourself. Try it." He tossed the coat to her.

She caught it and used her protected arm to block his attack.

"Good, good, now stab beneath—aim for my belly, Jane, you seek to injure me—" He twisted away from her with the grace and speed of a dancer, circled. "Attack me, don't wait. Keep coming at me—"

Once more she found herself rudely deposited on the floor, this time landing on her bottom. "You kicked me!"

"I told you, I shall not fight like a gentleman, and neither shall you."

She rolled away as his blade whipped down. She stabbed upward, punching into something solid with a sound that reminded her again of the French soldier and of Mrs. Burgess chopping at the joint of mutton. She pulled the knife back and blood spattered over her hand.

"Well done." Luke dropped to the floor beside her. "Claim your victor's spoils."

"Oh, Luke, I'm sorry." She gazed at the cut on Luke's knee, blood darkening his breeches and flowing down his boot. Her fangs lengthened. "Did I hurt you?"

"Not much." He pushed the top of his boot down and fumbled at the buckle on his breeches leg. "You're fast, better than I thought you would be."

She bent her head to his leg, canines extending. There was a small white scar on his knee, only just visible beneath the brown hairs, and she wondered if that was a scar from childhood. Had his mother kissed it better for him, decades or centuries ago?

He drew in a sudden breath.

I shall not remember that, not even for you, Jane.

Forgive me.

George and William fell silent, watching as she lapped Luke's blood. As she breathed the wound into wholeness again she glanced up and saw them both *en sanglant*.

"And before you suggest it, sir, the victor shall not patch your breeches," she said.

Jane returned to Paragon Place that afternoon, already hungry despite the delicious but all too brief taste of Luke's blood. She went upstairs with the bundle of men's clothes and hid it in a chest of drawers beneath a shift. Downstairs, to her surprise she found her mother and sister in the drawing room—their hands at their needlework looked pinched with cold—entertaining Captain Garonne.

He stood and bowed. Sleet rattled against the windowpanes and damp, cold smoke gusted into the room from the fireplace.

"I was just telling the captain how well you play, Jane," her mother said. "Was the water of benefit to you, my dear?"

"I believe, so, thank you, ma'am." She sat and picked her work from the sewing box.

"I should be honored if you play for me, Miss Jane," the captain said.

"Pray excuse me. My hands are too cold."

"She has not been at all well," Mrs. Austen said in a loud whisper to Garonne. "She is like me—very delicate."

Jane delicately bent her needle into a hoop and straightened it out again, pleased by the strength in her hands.

Cassandra yawned.

The clock on the mantelpiece, a florid affair of ivory and bronze, ticked loudly in the silence.

The front door opened and closed, and they heard Mr. Austen talking to the footman. He came into the room, his nose reddened with cold.

"Oh, my dear Mr. Austen," cried Jane's mother. "Sit down, my dear. I shall ring for more tea and you may tell me of your day. Is the populace still discontented? Mrs. Burgess stood over three hours in the market for a sorry piece of bacon and some beefsteak that must come from a cow of venerable years, but at least we have bread now and a little cheese. And Cassandra was sharp enough to spot a milkmaid in the street, and went out directly for milk."

Mr. Austen glanced at his daughters. "You look well, Jane, but thin in the face; I do not think it suits you. I must congratulate you, Cassandra, on the purchase of milk. I wish my day had been as successful. I have nothing to show for my pains."

Mrs. Austen, in the midst of giving orders to the footman who had just entered the room, looked up sharply. "It is too bad they will not let us go home."

"Believe me, madame, you may be better off here, in the city, than traveling dangerous roads," Garonne said. "There is much unrest in the country. It is not safe."

Mr. Austen sighed. "I stood in a line for hours, and then when only half a dozen were ahead of me, the soldiers said the office was closed for the day."

"They expect money," Garonne said.

"A bribe? That does not fit in with your republican ideals, surely?"

"It is war, sir, and men are what they are."

"It is not the way we do things in England, sir." Mrs. Austen opened the tea caddy that stood on the mantelpiece. "My poor sister is almost out of tea."

"That is terrible indeed," Garonne said. "The blockade prevents more tea being brought into the country, so prices are very high."

"The Navy runs a blockade?" Jane asked.

He shrugged. "It is no matter. We shall defeat you there too, ma'amselle."

"I have a brother serving in the Navy, sir. It is no small matter to us."

"Oh, my poor boy!" Mrs. Austen cried. She turned to the footman. "We shall use the tea leaves twice. You may have the leaves downstairs after that."

"Yes, ma'am." The footman bowed and left the room, looking distinctly gloomy at the prospect of even weaker tea for the servants in the future.

"So you do not dine with your new friends tonight?" Mrs. Austen turned on Jane. "I regret we cannot ask them to dine. This is not our house. It is very good of them to have you to dinner so often."

"Oh, I don't have much appetite, ma'am, and they seem to enjoy my company." There, the truth, more or less, although her appetite felt like a raging, growling animal inside her. She glanced out of the window at the darkening sky. Soon the Austen family and their uninvited guest would dine and she would retire, claiming poor health. And after that . . .

Jane became aware that her mother was talking again of the Sydney Garden entertainment the next evening.

". . . and my dear, Captain Garonne was kind enough to offer to escort us. There! What do you think of that?"

Before her father could make a reply, the footman entered with hot water and china and Mrs. Austen busied herself with making tea, chattering on about what Cassandra should wear and whether it would be a fine night.

"And you, Jane, do you wish to go?" her father asked her as Mrs. Austen paused for breath.

"No, sir, I do not. I do not believe we have anything to celebrate."

"At least one of the family has a sense of decorum. I regret, sir, we must decline your most kind invitation."

"Oh, Mr. Austen! After I have been so unwell, I think I deserve a little pleasure. And poor Cassandra, stuck here at home while Jane gallivants around taking the waters. I think you will change your mind soon, for you will see it is the best possible thing for us."

With a sinking heart, Jane saw that a familiar pattern began to emerge. Her mother would chip away at her father's defenses like a garrulous, lace-bedecked siege engine, until, irritated and exhausted by her persistence, he would allow her to do as she wished. Jane did not want to witness the scene, particularly in front of a man she could regard only as their enemy. Muttering an excuse, she stood to leave the room.

Garonne opened the door. In a low voice, he said, "I regret

you will not come with us, ma'amselle. The party will not be the same without you."

"There will be no party, sir." She stepped past him and made her way up the stairs and into the sanctuary of her own room.

Only a few hours to go. She would pick at a small amount of food over dinner, drink tea again, and retire to bed. And after that, her real life would take up again, when, dressed as a man, she would climb down the vine that grew over the back of the house, and go to meet her own.

"Tonight we hunt."

"Hunt what?"

"Our dinner," Luke said. "And we frighten the French—it is all to the good. But first I shall teach you how to use the shadows."

He led her down the steep, narrow staircase that led to the kitchen of the Queens Square house. A few servants worked there, preparing elaborate dishes of spun sugar and fancifully stuffed and decorated fowl; rich and luxurious, but nothing like the quantity of food a normal, wealthy household would serve for dinner.

"Who will eat this?" Jane asked.

"We might, should any of the food appeal to our senses; after all, food is something that should be savored and enjoyed." He pinched a sugar flower from a dish made of spun sugar in the form of a Greek temple, an intricate work of art that seemed too beautiful to eat. "Try this."

Jane parted her lips, chewed and swallowed. "Delicious. A sugar rose flavored with rosewater."

"Or this." He offered her a small pastry tart filled with cream and custard, delicately flavored with nutmeg and lemon. "We must leave, for I cannot afford to upset our cooks, particularly our pastrycook. But you must try this wine sauce flavored with saffron." He dipped a spoon into a small copper saucepan. "This is for the pheasant, is it not, Jacques?"

A man wearing an apron with a large, lethal-looking knife tucked into the waistband nodded. "Yes, milord, it is. Don't you go spoiling your appetite on Frenchies out there."

Jane was intrigued by the man's accent, French overlaid with Cockney, and the admiration he obviously held for Luke, who started a well-informed discussion with him about the uses of saffron and nutmeg, and the different sorts of mushrooms available.

"He thinks he is English," Luke said to Jane as Jacques turned away to scream, with violent Gallic gestures, at one of his underlings. "He is extraordinarily embarrassed by the presence of his fellow countrymen here. I think he fears someone may recognize him."

"What would they do to him if they did?"

Luke dipped a spoon into another saucepan. "Take him away and have him cook for their officers, I expect, and his pride in his profession would not allow him to poison anyone. Or only in a very delicious way. But we should leave."

He took her hand and led her outside. Stone steps led up to the street level, glistening wet in what little light there was.

"Watch." He stepped into a shadow and faded from view.

She looked around for him but apparently he had disappeared. "How do you do that?"

"Quite easily." His voice came from behind her, quiet and amused.

"Oh! You startled me!"

"Now you try."

Obediently she stepped into the dark area by the steps. "Now what do I do?"

"Think of the dark."

She tried to but the urge to giggle was strong. "Am I still here?"

"Very much so. Now concentrate."

"Concentrate on what, precisely?"

"Darkness. Stillness."

She closed her eyes and attempted to contemplate the nature of darkness.

"Jane, my dear, it does not follow that if you cannot see me I cannot see you."

She opened her eyes. "It's about as logical as thinking about darkness."

"Dear, dear, and you a creature of the imagination, an authoress. Very well, think about something, a favorite object, that is dark."

The night sky? A shovelful of coal? Instead, she thought of a certain beautiful black feather she had bought to trim a hat, its dusky softness and the way it sprang against her hand. Darkness curled and lapped around her like silk. "Oh!" she said in delight. "Oh, it's like bathing in warm ink."

"What an extraordinary life you writers lead, to be sure." Luke put one booted foot on the stone steps, and flicked a drop of water from the iron rail with one hand. "Not bad, not bad at all. Now George, he thought of a black cat, and it made him sneeze, so he might have become invisible, but you could hear him all over the town. Follow me and pray do not try to trim that hat with anything bright and shiny."

She took his hand and followed him up the steps to street level. He stood, scenting the air like a hound, and nodded.

So, we go this way. Follow me.

"How do you know?"

"Ssh!" He removed his glove and touched her bare wrist. *Try to put a thought into my mind.*

At the same time as I think about my feather?

Precisely. He put his lips close to her ear and whispered, "You're a butterfly of a woman, Jane, alighting on one subject and flying off to the next."

"Nonsense. I merely think faster than most people."

He smiled and led her down the street. They passed the Assembly Rooms, where sedan-chair carriers lounged against the walls, waiting for customers. Faint strains of music floated out from the building, and as they approached, a sedan chair arrived and a woman stepped out, wearing a mask and long cloak. A French officer, who had been waiting for her in the building's portico, strode forward and bent low over her hand.

Too crowded. Luke's fingers touched her wrist.

I wish we could dance. She cast a reluctant glance at the Assembly Rooms but let Luke lead her down into streets that rapidly became unfamiliar.

What we aim to do, Luke said, *is to unnerve the French. They believe the city has surrendered, but they know their patrols are not safe. They are aware that the shadows hold dangers and that an attack may come at any moment, yet they cannot find the source. Ah, listen.*

A group of soldiers approached at a march. Jane counted. *Six? But there are only two of us!*

Keep trimming that hat, Jane. Half a dozen Frenchmen are no match for you and me with our superior powers and all the darkness of the night. Here they come. Watch.

The patrol approached and passed them, taking the next turn. Luke darted forward, a swift shadow, and in a few seconds, a soldier had fallen limp on the cobblestones, blood flowing dark from the wound in his neck. The man marching next to him whirled, musket waving randomly, and shouted in alarm. The rest of the patrol, most of whom had already turned the corner, hesitated, and at a command from their officer, turned and closed ranks, muskets at their shoulders.

Luke took Jane's hand and pulled her further into the shadows. She could smell blood on his mouth, hot and enticing.

The officer shouted another order and the patrol dispersed and ran down the street, searching for their attacker.

Take that one. Luke pointed to a soldier running directly toward them. *Use your fangs and then throw him across the street.*

Jane sprang forward and overpowered the soldier, one hand over his mouth, dragging him into the darkness she carried with her like a cloak. He barely had a chance to struggle as she bit down and gulped his blood and would have wanted more, but Luke's blade flashed once, finishing him. She was glad she felt only the soldier's surprise and shock, no panicked thoughts of his mother or his home, like that first French soldier she'd taken.

The soldier's corpse flew across the street, landing with an ungainly thud in front of the officer, who swore violently, sword in hand, and yelled at his men to keep together.

Can we not take another?

No, we cannot stay. They'll start thrusting bayonets into the shadows and we'll regret it. Come. He took her hand and pulled her away.

She ran with him. *But I'm hungry.*

You sound like George. We'll dine at home. This is to whet your appetite and teach you how to fight.

They slowed to a walk. "Will you teach me more?" she asked.

"I shall. Listen." He stilled and pulled her deeper into the shadows.

Two men walked toward them, their footfalls uneven. Even at this distance Jane could smell wine and brandy and hear their slurred speech and laughter.

Two drunken officers. We'll take them.

Luke, does it not seem that we hunt like a fox in a chicken coop?

You mean we have no mercy? No scruples? He smiled at her. *This is war, Jane. Do not be a sentimental fool. But if you insist . . .*

Jane gasped as he left the shadows, revealing himself to the two officers who approached, meandering along the street. One of them held an open bottle.

"*Bon soir, mes amis,*" Luke called in badly accented French. "You have some drink? I'll trade a girl for it." He jerked his head toward Jane.

Feigning nervousness, she stepped from the shadows and curtsied before remembering she wore men's clothes, and turned it into a clumsy bow.

The officers looked confused, and then lustful as they focused on her legs.

"It is late. I arrest you, *citoyen,*" one of the officers said with an attempt at dignity. He drew his sword with ponderous, drunken clumsiness.

The other headed for Jane, a lascivious gleam in his eye. She leaped at him, fangs out, and saw horror and deadly fear drive him into sudden sobriety. He took a step back, pulling his sword from its sheath, but she felled him and took the first, hot mouthful of blood.

Someone tugged at her arm. She looked up, growling, fangs extended, and saw Luke pulling her away. *Into the shadows. Now.*

The hat, she couldn't remember. What was it about the hat? Soldiers ran into the street, shouting, the remnants of the patrol they had attacked earlier joined by reinforcements, another half dozen or so men. The corpses of the two officers lay sprawled in the street.

The feather, you silly girl. The black feather. The beautiful black feather.

Oh yes. She melted into the darkness and licked the blood from her lips.

In the street, the officer snapped out a command, and soldiers ran to the nearby houses, pulling doorbells and hammering door knockers.

Are they likely to blame the people who live there? Jane asked.

I think not. There are some very influential townspeople on this street and many of the French officers are quartered here.

Sure enough, half-dressed people erupted into the street, complaining vehemently of the rude awakening. "I am personally acquainted with General Renard!" one gentleman shouted, his nightshirt flapping around his legs. "This is a respectable area, sir! Call off your men."

Windows were flung open and inhabitants in nightcaps leaned out to complain bitterly and loudly about the disturbance in the street, in French and in English.

Luke took Jane's hand and led her away. *We'll go home to dine. You have blood on your lips still; you did better than I, for mine had his sword out and I barely had time to subdue him.*

I shall share with you. Emboldened by the taste of hunted blood she pressed her lips to his. The kiss began as an experiment— would she learn more of him, this way?—but she learned only the greater mystery of desire as she discovered the sweetness of his mouth and fangs, and found herself trembling and clinging to him as though she would drown.

"You need not fear." Luke smiled with great kindness and toyed with a stray lock of her hair.

"What shall we do now?" Her voice was breathless. Despite the blood she had taken she was weak and mortified that the kiss had affected her so much and him so little.

"We shall go home. I think our hunting is over for the night."

"No, you and I. What do we do now? What about Margaret?"

He took her face between his hands. "My dear Jane, we have eternity, you and I, and there is no hurry. Delayed gratification is a pleasure in itself."

She knew he sensed her disappointment and hurt, for as inexperienced as she might be, she recognized a subtle rejection. She gave an exaggerated sigh. "Yes, Luke, I suppose you are right. Besides, I think I would rather like another of those lemon tarts and a glass of wine."

He gave a shout of laughter and linked her hand in his arm. "Come, then. You're a brave girl, Jane Austen."

"Where have you been?" William met them as they entered the house on Queens Square.

"Hunting," Luke replied.

"You closed your thoughts to me; you know that is unwise. She"—he nodded at Jane—"withholds something from us. Let us talk in the study."

As they walked through the dining room, Jane said, "*She* is able to speak for herself, sir. I do not know to what you refer."

"A French officer resides in your house; Clarissa tells me he is the nephew of Renard." He gestured that she sit in a chair but she remained standing. She did not want him towering over her.

"You know this is of vital importance. A child could make the connection." He turned to Luke. "Did you know this?"

"Jane," Luke said, "you know what William says is true. Why did you not tell me?"

His gentle remonstrance hurt her more than William's harshness. "I will not have my family hurt by what I—what we do."

"You're a fool," William said. "They have no claim on you now. You belong here, with us. It does not benefit you to cling to those mortals—"

"My family, who love me."

"You are one of us now. But since you insist on maintaining your façade, you must serve us, your true family, well."

"We must do what is important." Luke reached for a bottle of claret and plucked three glasses from a shelf. "Jane, you shall befriend this officer. Find out from him what the plans of the French are in the city, and anything else useful he may have to tell us. It sounds as though your family are well on the way to welcoming him into their confidence. Has he invited your family to Sydney Gardens tomorrow night?"

"Yes, but—"

William stepped forward, his eyes fixed on her. Her head swam with his presence, his closeness, his attention. "There is no argument, Jane. I created you, and I can destroy you too. Do this or leave. What sort of future do you think you have, alone as a vampire? Rejected by your Creator, and of middling blood, and with no letters of introduction? Exile from your brothers and sisters is the greatest disgrace you as one of the Damned may suffer. You shall do as I say. Use what I have given you. You are a vampire, not a silly provincial miss."

How dare he speak to her so! She retreated from his influence, tearing herself from his stern attention. Her fangs lengthened. "Careful, William, lest I write you into one of my books. You have given me much material so far—the supercilious London visitor at the provincial assembly, the faithless seducer, the gentleman too proud to acknowledge in public the woman he has wronged—"

Luke laughed and handed them both a glass of wine. "You'll be sorry, William."

"And *letters of introduction*? I have never heard anything so absurd in my life: *Madam, I wish to introduce Miss Jane Austen, who is possessed of the most elegant* en sanglant *and whose man-*

ners and deportment in matters relating to blood and dining are unparalleled—"

William raised an eyebrow. "You may laugh, Jane, but you have much to learn."

"Now *that* is something I long to learn. Can you raise one eyebrow while *en sanglant?*"

"You had best teach your fledgling better manners," William said.

Luke smiled. "Oh, you know, I rather like her the way she is. I'd hate to see her turn into another Clarissa, or, devil take it, another Margaret."

"Indeed. Another mess you have created and which you must clean up."

The two men glared at each other, *en sanglant.* Jane tried to gauge the feelings that swept between them—jealousy, resentment, love—that had to represent a complex, centuries-old relationship.

"And, by the by, I have never been a silly provincial miss," she added as a parting shot.

William spoke to Luke. "And I say again, teach her some manners. Jane, you'll go to Sydney Gardens with your family tomorrow night." He slapped his empty wineglass onto the desk and left, banging the door behind him.

Luke sank into a chair. "Please do sit. You roam around like a fierce animal."

"Isn't that what I am now?" She sat. "What is he to you? Have you been friends long?"

"A very long time, and, no, we are not exactly friends. He created me."

"Oh! So you and I are brother and sister."

"Brother and sister! I should think not." He hesitated as if about to say something else, but continued, "He and I will be civil again soon enough. As for you and me, I'll call in the morning as your physician and pronounce you cured."

"Very well."

"Come, we'll dine now. But what's the matter?"

She sighed. "Those were empty threats I made, Luke. I can observe episodes I should like to include in my books; I hear the odd turn of phrase or absurdity, but I cannot write. I tell myself I must remember what I see and hear, but maybe it is to no effect."

He took her hand. "I must tell you the truth. I have never heard of any one of the Damned who distinguished himself in the arts or letters. It is not in our nature. I have heard of those gifted in one way or another whose skills disappeared as they matured as vampires. Were you to return to your mortal state I cannot say if your gift would return; no one knows."

She regarded him with curiosity. "Then why did you not say so to William and take his part?"

He gave her hand a gentle shake. "Ah. I admire courage, Miss Jane Austen, even if you were in the wrong. You stood up to William with great bravery tempered with a generous dose of impertinence, and although he would never admit it, he admires you for it too. He would rather you fight back, even if it is with teasing and ridicule, than to accept meekly his strictures."

"Well, I suppose you know the gentleman better than I ever shall." She hesitated and took her first sip of wine, her booted feet stretched toward the fire; although she did not require the warmth, she enjoyed the homely familiarity of a burning hearth. "Shall you and I become like that? As I become stronger, shall you and I fight?"

"Possibly. William and I, we have centuries of grievances and real and imagined ills upon which to draw. We are too alike, too close in years. I was his first fledgling, and he was but a century

old when he created me, a mere stripling in our years." He gazed
into the fire. "You and I, we have all of eternity stretching before
us and who knows where we shall go. I regret that you cannot
make a clean break with your mortal family; it is infinitely preferable, for it is kinder to you, but these are unusual times."

She kicked a glowing ember from the hearth into the fireplace.
"I am to lose all I hold most dear. My family and my writing."

"But think what you gain. Eternity, knowledge, power, beauty,
love—yes, those small things. Jane, you are one of us. Come."
He stood and led her upstairs, his arm flung lightly around her
shoulders.

She shook his arm off as they entered the drawing room and
her feet sank into the carpet. Around her the Damned took their
pleasures, the air golden with lamplight and thick with the scent
of blood and desire.

"You make a handsome young man, miss."

Jane turned to meet the admiring gaze of the young man she
had met this morning. "So do you, Jack. That is, you *are* a handsome young man."

"So I've been told, miss. It would be a great honor, miss, if
you—"

A bolt of hunger shot through her and her canines extended
with a familiar, pleasurable pain as he loosened his neckcloth.
She looked to Luke for guidance; he gave a nod of approval.

You are one of us. We are your family.

She growled and pushed Jack onto a nearby sofa.

He obligingly presented his bared throat. "Would you care for
me to undress, miss?"

She didn't bother to reply as her fangs sank into his neck and
his blood leaped to her tongue.

Chapter 12

"I am happy to announce a complete cure, Mrs. Austen. Your daughter is well again."

Jane watched in fascination as Luke, sitting next to her mother on the sofa, gazed into her eyes. Cassandra, seated in a chair nearby, let her sewing fall onto her lap and seemed equally enthralled by his presence.

"Oh, my dear child!" Mrs. Austen said to no one in particular. "Yet she looks so thin, still. Her bloom has yet to return."

"My sister is most anxious to have Miss Jane's company at the Pump Room. I think those visits, and a judicious use of the waters, should put matters to rights soon enough." He paused. "I shall continue to accompany the ladies. It is safest, you know. And Miss Jane may resume her usual social activities."

"There, you see, Jane!" Her mother turned to her. "You are well enough to join us this evening. I do so wish you could come with us, Mr. Venning. Sydney Gardens are quite delightful and they say there will be braziers and hot punch to keep us warm."

"I regret my sister and I are otherwise engaged, ma'am."

Jane was silent. As she suspected, her father had given in to her mother's demands.

"You and your charming sister must dine with us," her mother said, and then looked thoughtful. An invitation to dine these days, with an uncertain food supply, was not to be issued lightly.

"When we have enough food," Jane said.

"Now, Jane, there is no need to embarrass Mr. Venning! He understands perfectly, I am sure."

"I am sure he does," Jane murmured. "We should want to give the gentleman what he is accustomed to for dinner, after all." She sent Luke a sidelong look, exposing the merest hint of canine.

"Oh, do not talk nonsense," her mother replied.

Luke cleared his throat. Jane was sure he was *en sanglant*. "My sister has mentioned that she would like Jane to stay with us as her companion. No, you need not make any answer just now, but Clarissa would be glad of some female company. Please give the idea some consideration."

"That is most kind," Mrs. Austen exclaimed, "but I do not think we can spare Jane just yet."

After a few more minutes of conversation, about the severe weather and the lack of news combined with the proliferation of fantastic rumors, Luke bowed and took his leave.

"What a charming gentleman! It is a thousand pities he cannot accompany us to Sydney Gardens. I think he is quite taken with you, Jane. But what shall you girls wear tonight?" Mrs. Austen asked. Cassandra responded with great enthusiasm while Jane picked through a pile of papers on the table that her sister had collected, ready to paste them into her commonplace book, which lay, along with a container of flour paste and a brush, nearby. The collection was of the usual sorts of odds and ends Cassandra liked—illustrations cut from a fashion paper annotated with

Cassandra's notes, a few scraps of fabric and trims, recipes and poems Cassandra had written out or copied, and drawings.

She paused at a sketch she had made of Cassandra and remembered vividly that day a month before the fateful Basingstoke assembly, one of the last fine days of autumn. They had gone on a long walk, finding a few late blackberries in the more sheltered spots, while Jane had talked of Marianne and Elinor and joked that the two sisters had almost as good a relationship as she and Cassandra did.

But maybe that's the problem with the book. Is not discord and the return to intimacy more interesting?

Maybe that's what she would do if, indeed, she ever wrote again.

"Leave that alone!" Cassandra smacked at her hand in a friendly sort of way and gathered her treasured collection of papers into a pile again. "Those are in order."

"Oh, nonsense. Your commonplace book is chaotic." She smiled at her sister. "Do you remember when I made this sketch?"

"Yes, indeed. Such a lovely day. On our walk you jumped into piles of leaves as though you were a child."

"And you had blackberry stains around your mouth that I was kind enough to omit from this sketch."

When they returned home, Jane had caught Cassandra in a few pen strokes as her sister tossed her bonnet aside and sat to remove her muddy boots, her cheeks pink with cold, her hair disordered, eyes bright. She looked particularly handsome and happy, and Jane believed then that Cassandra's pain at the death of her betrothed, Tom Fowle, had lessened, allowing her to enjoy life once more.

"Most well done, *ma'amselle* Jane."

She turned the drawing over, annoyed both at the interruption and that she had been so deep in recollection that she did not notice his entry into the room. "I did not know you were here, Captain."

"I have only just arrived. But your drawing—may I not see it again?"

She handed the paper to him, conscious that she should approach him with a little more friendliness.

He looked at her drawing, then at her sister, and smiled. "This is indeed well done. It is as though she speaks on the paper."

"Captain Garonne," cried Mrs. Austen. "Such news! The physician says Jane is recovered from her illness and can accompany us tonight. What do you think of that?"

He looked up from her drawing. "But I thought you were not willing, *ma'amselle* Jane. It was a matter of principle, you said."

"I have taken guidance from my father, sir." She did not want to appear too enthusiastic and rouse his suspicions. "He has persuaded me."

"Ah. Very good." He gazed at Cassandra. "A remarkable likeness. May I keep this drawing?"

Jane hesitated. No good could come of the captain's evident admiration of her sister—for she was certain his interest in the drawing and the subject could mean only one thing. Cassandra, meanwhile, on the other side of the room, was deep in discussion about gloves and muffs and whether her cloak would look dowdy.

"Very well." Jane watched as he rolled the drawing and placed it inside his coat.

"Your family must be very happy that you are returned to health. The waters are extremely beneficial, I believe. Many of our officers take advantage of them."

Not wishing to prolong the conversation, Jane excused herself and went upstairs to dress. Cassandra joined her, much excited, chattering of how many woolen petticoats they should wear, and how fortunate they were that it was a fine, if cold, night.

"I believe the captain admires you," Jane said.

"Indeed? I find him quite agreeable. I hope my ears will not turn red in the cold, although he told us there will be braziers and the temperature will be quite adequate. I intend to dance all night to keep warm. I hope you are strong enough to dance. I believe we shall not lack for partners."

Jane made a noncommittal answer and dropped her gown over her head. "Cassandra, do you think my book would be better if Marianne and Elinor did not agree with each other so much?"

"But I love that about the book. They are so like you and me." Cassandra turned so Jane could tie her gown closed.

"But it does not make for a good story. They are too much alike. What if they did not confide so freely in each other?" *As I am compelled to do now.*

"I don't think I'd like that." Cassandra sat on the bed to pull on a fresh pair of stockings. "But I understand what you mean. Harmony is for real life, not for literature. But how can you convey the keeping of secrets if we read only letters between them?"

"Maybe there should be narrative, too."

Cassandra paused in fastening a necklace. "I am so happy you feel well enough to write again."

Jane tried not to watch the pulse beat in her sister's neck. The only positive thing she could find about the night's outing was that she would not need any woolen petticoats.

Garonne escorted the Austen family into the inn that served as entry to Sydney Gardens, Cassandra and Mrs. Austen on his arms, while Jane and her father followed behind. Jane could tell her father was dispirited and gloomy, both at his failure to procure passes for them and at his surrender to Mrs. Austen's demands.

Garonne helped the ladies to punch, from one of many large silver bowls that stood on tables heaped high with fruits and other delicacies.

"Why, Captain, how does this food arrive in the city?" Jane asked innocently. "We haven't seen anything as delicious as this since you were kind enough to invade."

"After curfew, ma'am, but I am not allowed to tell you more."

"Your secret would be safe with me, sir!" She managed a delighted giggle while determining she could easily find out more from Garonne. "No, really, I cannot—well, half a glass more. Oh, Captain, that is another full glass. I shall scarcely be able to dance." She let the captain give orders to a waiter and then the group went outside into the grounds, where braziers and flambeaux provided light and scattered pockets of warmth. An orchestra, the musicians wearing woolen gloves with the fingers removed, played at a little distance. Under other circumstances she would have enjoyed the scene, the gaily colored paper lanterns hung from trees, and the well-dressed and elegant crowd. Doubtless if she had any appetite for food, she would have been roundly scolded by her sister for being greedy. Waiters flocked around their table, bearing china and cutlery and bottles of wine.

Cassandra looked particularly handsome in her fur tippet and matching muff, a small feathered hat perched on her head, and she and Jane entertained themselves with comparing their dress to that of other ladies present.

"It has happened again," Jane murmured to her sister. "We have failed in sartorial matters by an unnatural desire not to catch our deaths of cold. Observe that lady on the French officer's arm—she might as well be wearing her shift, and does she not realize the fabric is almost entirely transparent?"

"How dreadfully immodest! I don't know that I approve of headdresses based on Phrygian caps—and oh, even more shocking, some actually sport *tricouleur* cockades!"

"But they are the colors also of *your* flag, ma'amselle Austen." Garonne raised his glass. "I propose a toast to a greater friendship with the Austens."

The stem of the wineglass snapped in Jane's fingers and blood dripped onto the white tablecloth. She caught a strong sense of others of the Damned nearby and then the sensation was lost as her family exclaimed, and Garonne offered her a napkin. A waiter arrived to clear up the broken glass and provide her with a new wineglass.

"I am so dreadfully clumsy," she said. "No, sir, it bleeds very little now. I have wrapped it in my handkerchief, and I shall hide the offending digit in my muff so I do not cause offense. I believe enough blood has been spilled already in this city."

"True, *ma'amselle*. Your shopkeepers and militia put up a most gallant defense."

That Garonne did not attempt to deny the bloodshed in the city raised a grudging admiration in Jane's perception. The waiters approached again, with platters of food and small lamps on which to keep them warm, and the party's attention was turned to the food, which was of high quality and excellently prepared. Garonne turned out to be an attentive host, making sure everyone's glass was filled and that every dish was shared. He questioned Cassandra and Mrs. Austen about parties and assemblies in Hampshire and with great politeness asked if he could partner the Miss Austens when the dancing began. Even Mr. Austen began to unbend a little.

"But Mr. and Mrs. Austen, here is my uncle, General Renard. I have told him so much of you and your hospitality." Garonne introduced them. Jane noticed the similarities between the two men, and suspected that their relationship was in fact father and son; they had a similar scent.

Renard bowed over the ladies' hands and begged that they might each dance with him. He was an observant and clever man, that much was clear, and Jane was surprised that her family welcomed him into their midst, her father offering him a glass of wine. "No, no, I shall not intrude. But we shall see each other later, eh?"

"You are not eating, Miss Jane," Garonne commented after the general had left.

"No, I fear my appetite is somewhat diminished." *And what I should really like is to bite into someone's neck.* In a few hours she would feed unless she could find someone here—she stopped herself in horror. It was bad enough that the previous night she had gorged herself upon a compliant stranger before creeping home in her men's clothes shortly before dawn. The idea of a pursuit and flirtation followed by an exquisite surrender in the shadows of the maze tempted her with a great surge of hunger, and she raised a napkin to her lips to hide her fangs. She wished Luke were here so that she could ask his advice.

But I am here, my dear Jane.

Where? But there was no reply. She searched and received hints of conversations, desires, jealousies, worries, inebriated joyfulness—nothing useful. But she knew William was close by also and felt once again that painful, unreciprocated longing.

"The captain is really quite a pleasant young fellow," her father said, when Garonne left the table to greet some fellow officers. "If only we did not know him under these unfortunate circumstances."

Unfortunate circumstances! "Indeed, sir. I think he harbors a tendresse for Cassandra. Do you think he would make an acceptable son-in-law?"

"I beg of you, do not jest of such a thing." Her father touched Jane's hand quickly; he must find her cold skin repellent and for a moment his shame and desperation overwhelmed her.

"Papa, I—"

At that moment the band struck up the familiar opening chords of a country dance and Garonne led Cassandra onto the open space that served as a dance floor in front of the musicians.

"It is too bad he has not introduced us to some of the other officers," Mrs. Austen said. "And then you could dance too, Jane. Why, General Renard, do you seek a partner?" For the general stood bowing before them.

"I should be honored if the younger Miss Austen would stand up with me, madame."

"I regret I am not well enough to dance," Jane said.

"Oh, nonsense, I have rarely seen you in such handsome looks!" her mother cried. "She is notorious for her love of dancing, sir. She does not mean it."

"Her modesty does you credit, madame." He gave a charming, if somewhat predatory smile. "I need to learn these English dances. It would be a great favor."

Heart sinking, Jane stood, and discarded her muff. "If you insist, sir," she said in her coldest tone.

"Ah, *les anglaises*. I know beneath your stern exterior a warm heart beats."

"So you may think, sir." She wasn't quite sure of vampire physiology; she knew she had little pulse and was impervious to extreme temperatures. Yet another thing to ask Luke about, unless that was considered an indelicate subject.

"I am your enemy, that is the problem, you think, eh? But I

find you a worthy foe." He frowned. "Why, your hands, so cold. I feel it through your glove."

She eyed the flirtatious Frenchman and wondered if she could lure him away for a quick taste of his blood. On the platform while accepting the surrender of the city, he had appeared a tall man, but he was barely her height, stocky, with snapping dark eyes. She was fairly sure she could subdue him easily enough.

She subdued an inappropriate giggle. Once she had thought of gentlemen in terms of their looks, their income—for was not a large income conducive to happiness?—and their conversation. Now she dreamed, not of witty yet sensible conversation at a ball and the clasp of hands during a dance, but of how the gentleman's blood would taste.

The dance started.

"So, Miss Jane, you like my nephew, eh?"

"He seems a perfectly agreeable young man. You must set now, as the gentleman opposite does. It is a step in triplet time."

"Perfectly agreeable!" Renard repeated, bouncing with great energy in an approximation of the step. "So you are halfway in love with him, then."

"Not even a quarter or an eighth of the way, General, for as you say, he too is my enemy."

"Oh, that is a little nothing." He waved his hands, interrupting the progress of the dance. "You suit each other well. He seeks to make you jealous with your sister."

She laughed aloud. "Do you always seek to find wives for your officers?"

"Wives?" He shrugged. "I wish them to be comfortable. To be content. They fight hard. They are away from home."

"Here, General, women do not give away their virtue so easily."

"Which way do I go? This dance is confusing."

"Here." She shoved him into position and noticed his look of alarm and respect. It was easy to forget how strong she was. They both cast off around the other dancers in their set and met and joined hands.

"A woman may find her virtue is worth only a little when she seeks—oh, let us see—a pass to leave the city." His insinuating murmur was a mere breath in her ear.

She broke free. "You insult me and my family, General."

"Keep dancing, Miss Jane, for your family will not approve if you show such bad manners."

With a great deal of effort she forced her fangs back and made a great show of exchanging flirtatious glances with other, English, gentlemen in the set, barely giving the General any attention. The dance ended; she curtsied, murmured an excuse that she must find her sister, and escaped into the welcoming shadows. The sound of the music faded away as she slipped into the maze that formerly she had thought to be a playful, innocent conceit of the gardens. Now its hedged walls held secrets and pleasures.

She stepped forward with barely a sound on the gravel and snuffed the air. So, others had come this way, seeking privacy and solitude, not realizing that they might be sought in turn; pursued, desired, taken. The heady tang of blood drifted across the privet hedges as she moved forward with the quiet, deliberate tread of a hunter.

Nearby, a woman sighed in pleasure or surrender and a man laughed.

She knew that voice. She followed the twists and turns and came across them, the woman's head flung back as William feasted at her throat.

He spun around at her approach, fangs extended and bloody, eyes bright, and growled.

Jane stepped back. She should not interrupt, she knew. While it was accepted that one of the Damned might show interest as another took his or her pleasure, she must observe the etiquette of the situation. She bowed her head in a deferential greeting as courtesy demanded.

The woman moaned and reached for him but William held her away. Her blood trickled, pooled in the hollow at her collarbone, and spilled into the depths of her bodice.

"Why are you not with your family?" He glanced at the woman's throat. "Find them."

"But I—"

"Go." He licked the blood from between the woman's breasts up to its source, the small wound in her neck, as she sighed with pleasure.

Jane backed away, her hunger increased by watching William dine. She wished Luke were with her to counsel and console her. She had sensed him earlier, but now he was silent. The dark, mysterious paths of the maze and its inhabitants called to her, soft murmurs and rustles invited her to find a willing source of blood.

With great reluctance she turned back and threaded her way through the maze and out into the gardens again.

She should find her family—after all, had not Luke and William both told her to attend with them, as though she were once again ordinary Jane Austen, the obedient, youngest daughter of that bright and witty family? Perhaps they merely intended that she should have some time with the people who had once been dearest to her of all; for once her family knew her true nature, they would regard her as a monster, inhuman, unwomanly. Lingering remains of her mortal condition made the alienation from them, particularly her father and sister, painful; but how long would she feel that way? How long before she no longer cared, before she succumbed to her nature as one of the Damned?

"I beg your pardon, ma'am." The waiter swung his tray of glasses and dishes aloft to avoid collision, brought them neatly back under control and sidestepped to allow her to pass. He stopped and stared at her. "You—you're one of them, aren't you, ma'am?"

She nodded.

"I've never seen one of you so close. I've been scared. You're all too pretty."

"Oh, please do not say I am pretty; that is so commonplace. Witty or fascinating, possibly, but mere prettiness eludes me."

He balanced the tray on one hip, considering. "No, you're not pretty, ma'am. You're . . . well, I don't have the words."

"I'm hungry," she said. Her admission reminded her too much of George's usual complaint and she burst into laughter.

He stared at her mouth, at her extended canines, admiration on his face. "Would you like . . . I mean, I'd be willing, miss, but I've never seen one of you laugh before. You're all haughty and fashionable."

"I'm not very fashionable, then." It was a relief to have almost a normal conversation with this boy, whose voice held a soft Somerset burr and who gazed at her wide-eyed, his fascination winning out over fear. And she wasn't even trying to entice him, that was the odd part of it, yet he'd offered himself; and she found she enjoyed the conversation almost as much as she antici-pated sating her hunger.

"What's it like then?" he asked. "Being Damned, I mean. How old are you?"

"I'm about your age. I haven't been one for long, and there's a lot I don't understand. I'm not highborn, you see, and so I'm at a disadvantage. My name is Jane. What is yours?"

"I'm Ben." He smiled, a sweet, shy smile, and laid his tray on the ground. He took her hand and peeled off her glove.

"Aren't you being rather forward, Ben?"

But he put her cold hand on the warm smooth skin of his neck, where his pulse thudded, strong and enticing.

"I would rather have you as a friend than my dinner, Ben." Oh, how she wanted him.

"I can be both, Jane. No reason why not." He shivered. "May I touch them? Your teeth?"

She guided his hand to her mouth and it was her turn to shiver as his fingers trailed exquisitely over her fangs.

He gazed at her with heavy-lidded eyes. "Do you think I'd taste nice?"

"Very, I expect. You smell most tempting—of beer and wine and spices, and roast meat. But I shall not drink from you."

"I would like to warm you, Jane."

"I don't think you can." She pressed her fingers against his. "I must return to my family. They will worry about me."

"I'll take you to them. It's not safe, wandering around on your own."

She smiled at his gallantry. She was stronger than he, probably stronger and faster and more deadly than most of the visitors to Sydney Gardens tonight. But she let him tuck her hand into the crook of his arm and lead her through the crowd.

"Ask for me here at the Inn, if you need me," he said. "They'll take a message. Ask for Ben."

"I shall." She reached up to kiss his cheek.

The skies lit up with bright flashes and cascades of color.

His hand tightened on hers. "Don't be afraid," she said. "It's fireworks."

"Those bangs," he said. "It was like this when they took the town. I fought, Jane. I killed a man."

"So did I. I wish I had not done it, but I had to." Another series of gorgeous flowerings against the sky was accompanied by stuttering explosions and drifting clouds of smoke.

In the flashes of light, Jane caught sight of her family, accompanied by Garonne and Renard. They had left their table and sought a place to see the fireworks.

At that moment, Mrs. Austen turned and evidently recognized someone in the crowd. In the pause between fireworks, her voice rang out loud and clear. "Why, Mr. Venning, you rogue, you told us you were engaged. Fie on you! But what—"

Jane broke away from Ben; something was wrong, very wrong. The fireworks became deafening as a huge representation of a *tricouleur*, red, white, and blue, exploded into the sky, illuminating the crowd's astonished and wondering faces. By its light she saw Luke, pointing a pistol, and Mrs. Austen directly in the line of fire.

The shot rang out as Jane darted forward. "Mama!"

The scent of gunpowder gave way to that of freshly spilled blood, and exclamations of delight at the fireworks became shouts of rage and curses and demands for more lights. The music died away in a series of ragged notes.

"Renard is dead!" someone shouted. "He's been shot!"

But Renard was giving orders, while French officers converged on Luke and disarmed him. Others, swords drawn, kept the crowd at bay.

Jane dropped to her knees beside Ben, who knelt, bent over, arms at his belly. Luke's shot had gone wide to avoid Mrs. Austen, or even herself, and he had not stood a chance of hitting Renard. Instead, the ball from his pistol had found its target in Ben.

Blood soaked through Ben's long white apron. "Help me," he gasped.

"I'll make you better. My blood—" She bit into her finger and tried to feed it into his mouth, but he choked and sagged into her arms.

"No. It's no good. Finish me."

She knew now what he meant: that the ball had ripped into his entrails and there was no hope, only a lingering and agonizing death. His breath, painful gasps, rasped against her neck. She could give him the only thing she could, a clean end.

"Now. Please."

She bent her head to his neck again and took the last of his blood and his life, and was with him as his pain and terror turned to pleasure and sweet oblivion.

"It is a disaster," Clarissa said. She paced the drawing room of the house on Queens Square, fangs exposed. Jane had accompanied her and William back to the house, telling her family that Miss Venning would need comfort after the shock of her brother's arrest.

"If I had known, I could have prevented this," Jane said. "There was no reason to exclude me from the plans. I was told only to be with my family. I knew Luke was there, and I could have prevented my mother from getting in the way."

"Silence." William glared at her. "He'll hang tomorrow. You and Clarissa shall attend and bring the corpse back here."

"But—" No gentlewoman would attend a hanging.

"You'll dress as a man."

"Very well."

"It wasn't Jane's fault." George cast a nervous glance at William. "Damn it, why not just bite Renard and have done with it?"

"I did not expect such vulgarity from one of your breeding," William replied. "It is obvious, surely. If Renard was found drained of blood, suspicion would fall on us; besides, he is too well guarded for anything other than a bullet. And you, Jane, your task was to stay with your family. You disobeyed, seeking to hunt and dine instead." With a final black-browed glare, William left the room.

* * *

Jane spent what was left of the rest of the night in the drawing room, with George lounging nearby on a sofa. He offered sympathy and the occasional clumsy comment that it wasn't her fault, by God, and if William and Luke were not so high in the instep, then things might have turned out differently.

"Do you think the hanging will kill Luke?" Jane asked.

He shrugged. "I don't know. He's old, you see, even by their standards, which means he's running out of luck—like a cat with nine lives, you know. Still, if his neck isn't broken, he might come out of it. But things will not go well for you if Luke does not survive."

"Indeed. To lose one Bearleader is misfortune; twice is assuredly carelessness."

George fiddled with the golden tassel on the corner of a pillow. "I meant Margaret. She will be honor bound to destroy you. She's jealous enough already."

"She has nothing to fear from me. Luke is merely my Bearleader from a sense of duty."

"Ah, but there's the problem, you see. If he were your Creator, by tradition he could not become your lover. But as it is . . . William created you, didn't he?"

"It is so obvious? And, Luke, my lover? Pray do not be so absurd."

"Oh, yes. The way you look at him—William, that is. And the way he won't look at you. He was on his way to fetch me, you see, so he couldn't stay. He succumbed to your, ah, charms—he's only human, you see. Well, no, he's Damned, and sometimes their—our—nature gets the better of them, I mean, us, and what's a fellow to do? You know what I mean. I'm not saying it was your fault. If anything, I'm partly to blame."

"No, you are not to blame, George!" She rose and unlatched

the shutter of one of the room's tall windows. A slight lightening in the sky indicated that dawn was not far off.

She tried to reach out to Luke. She was sure he too watched the sky; he who had seen so many sunrises must know this could be the last, and according to Christian belief he was bound for hell. She wanted to pray for him, but would a prayer from another of the Damned count as anything other than blasphemy?

A world without Luke, her adoptive Bearleader, was unthinkable. No more of his blood, his sardonic wit. She remembered the circle of his arm as he taught her how to feed; his jaunty stride, swordstick in hand, as he strolled the streets of Bath; the lithe weight of his body as they fought; the tenderness of his lips. *Speak to me, Luke.*

George came up behind her and laid his hand on her shoulder in silent sympathy.

"I killed a man tonight," she said. "I beg your pardon, I burden you with my concerns."

"Not at all. You drained a man?"

"No, he was the man who Luke shot. He was there because of me. I liked him and he was too young to die."

"William told me it is not advisable to form attachments with those from whom we dine. It can get damned awkward, rather like falling in love with your cook."

The analogy made Jane smile despite her sorrow. She went upstairs to seek out some men's clothes. Clarissa and Margaret lay on the bed, Ann between them, slumped and smiling, eyes closed.

"Revive her, if you please," Margaret said to Jane, and then, as she hesitated: "Good God, did that fool Luke teach you nothing? Pour a glass of wine and add a drop or two of your blood and give it to her to drink. Otherwise she'll be good for nothing all day, dropping trays of crockery and ruining our gowns."

Jane made no reply, chilled by the venom in Margaret's voice, and did as she was ordered. Glass in hand, she knelt on the bed and shook Ann awake. The girl smiled when she saw the dark coil of blood dissolving in the wine, and drank it down, smacking her lips. "Why, you do taste nice, miss. Would you like—"

"Enough," Clarissa said. "Help Miss Jane dress."

Grumbling, Ann slid from the bed and smoothed her skirts. In a very short time Jane was changed into men's clothes, hat on head and hair smoothed back in a queue.

"It's high time you lost your reflection," Clarissa commented. She opened a chest of drawers. "Here's a pass for you. You're an apprentice to a hatmaker, so please try to assume a vulgar swagger. Ann, brush our coats, if you please. Excellent. Come, we need to get there early to get a good place." She paused and adjusted Jane's neckcloth. "I will show you how to tie an elegant knot another time, for you do not have to look like a gentleman today."

They left the house. The air was chill with frost, a light layer of rime on the railings in front of the houses. A boy with a barrow stood in front of the house, blowing on his hands to warm them, the tips of his ears red with cold.

Clarissa nodded and strode ahead, tugging on Jane's arm. "You do not need to acknowledge him, unless of course you wish to dine. He is far below us."

"Is that how you see people? As servants or sustenance?"

"How else would I see them?" She stared at Jane in amazement. "You have much to learn, but I suppose your birth is not your fault. But consider, if you had not been created, but you had married well, would you not learn to behave fittingly to your station?"

"I suppose so. I hope I should not divide the world so rigidly."

"But we must. We are what we are. It is only by keeping ourselves apart, by staying with our own, that we have survived for so long—even in England, which has long been a refuge for us."

A group of soldiers stopped them, demanding their papers, which they read, or pretended to, with great thoroughness, while making vulgar comments about the two young men's lack of beard. Jane and Clarissa maintained a bland politeness, for apprentices would not know French.

There were more soldiers in the streets than she had seen before, bayonets fixed, warily regarding the crowd that streamed toward the Pump Yard.

"They fear an insurrection," Clarissa murmured. "As though we should be fools enough to attempt an heroic rescue. I wonder how the crowd will react; whether it is the French's idea of bread and circuses, or whether there will be an outcry." She took Jane's arm. "You know it is not your fault, whatever William has said. We could not anticipate that your mother would get in the way, but we will not share everything with fledglings, for you probably could not withstand torture."

A cold shiver went down Jane's spine. She swallowed as they turned into the Pump Yard, the crowd moving slowly now as people jostled for good places. The scaffold was set up in front of the Abbey, where only a few days ago Poulett had surrendered the city. The *tricouleur* flew from the flagpole atop the Abbey.

The boy with the barrow, whom Jane learned was named John, turned it over and offered places on it to bystanders, who would pay a penny for the advantage of extra height.

"Certainly not!" Clarissa cuffed him. "If you break it you won't get your shilling. You may stand on it if you wish."

He did so, despite complaints from behind that they could not see through him, although he was small enough that even on his perch he was still shorter than Jane. Men and women moved through the crowd selling pies and gin, and a ballad singer did a roaring trade in a new song, "The Last Confession of the French Murderer Luke Venning."

A man next to them who had bought a pie spat it out, cursing. "What did you use in this? Cat or rat?"

"And crust made of sawdust!" another disgruntled customer shouted. "I want my penny back!"

The pie seller made an obscene gesture and threaded his way through the crowd where more customers, undeterred by his critics, bought his wares.

A woman, her face painted garish red and white, brushed up against Clarissa. "Sixpence against the wall, young sir. 'Twill pass the time while you wait."

Clarissa shook her head. "Not now, my pretty."

"While he swings, then? For a shilling?"

Clarissa shoved her away with the hint of a snarl. "I should not have used two stockings in my breeches," she muttered to Jane.

"Why does she want a shilling when . . . ?" She could not bring herself to repeat the whore's words.

"It arouses some, to see a man die."

Jane noticed spectators stuffed into the top windows of the surrounding buildings, craning their necks for a better view of the gallows, many armed with telescopes.

The tightly packed crowd thinned out to make space for a fiddler and his dancing dog, a terrier wearing a frilled collar. But the fiddler had scarcely played more than a few measures before the dog scented Jane and Clarissa, dropped to all fours and ran away, tail between its legs. The fiddler snatched his hat from the ground, where he had placed it to collect coins, and, fiddle under his arm, set off in pursuit of his dog.

The Abbey bells pealed the quarters and struck the hour of eight.

A great shout arose as a troop of French soldiers, bayonets

lowered, marched in formation, the crowd parting before them. Luke stood on a cart, hands tied behind his back, and was greeted with a hail of stones and a few rotten potatoes.

"Traitor!" a few called out. Jane wondered whether the French had planted them in the crowd.

"Fool for missing him!" someone else shouted, creating a flurry of boos.

Renard and a group of officers, Garonne among them, had appeared from the opposite direction, taking advantage of the crowd's attention elsewhere. More French soldiers marched into the Pump Yard and threaded their way into the crowd.

"They take no chances," Jane commented to Clarissa. "They do not know which way the crowd will turn."

The cart jolted to a stop, and Luke stepped out. He looked at the cloudy sky and briefly at the crowd. If he saw or even recognized Jane and Clarissa he gave no sign.

A couple of officers followed him onto the gallows. One read a statement in French that was almost drowned out by boos and catcalls, followed by a translation read haltingly in English that was obliterated by the crowd's roar.

Luke leaned toward him and spoke.

The two officers conferred. One of them spoke to Renard, who, astride his horse, shrugged and waved his hand in irritated submission.

"The prisoner will speak!" one of the officers shouted.

The crowd erupted again. A few called for the hanging to take place immediately, but the consensus seemed to be that the condemned man's speech was a necessary and enjoyable part of the procedure.

Luke stepped forward and a hush fell over the crowd.

"Friends, I have but one regret—that I have failed. Yet I promise that my end shall be one small setback in a greater journey.

I shall fall but others shall rise in my place, and others in theirs, until the French tyrants shall be driven into the seas. Rule Britannia!"

A few shouts of "*Vive la France!*" were overwhelmed by a massive outcry of "Rule Britannia!" and "God save the King!" with various comments on the paternity and maternal activities of the French in general.

Renard raised and then lowered his sword, and the two officers nodded to the hangman. Luke's head was shoved into the noose and the hangman pushed him off the edge of the platform. The crowd howled and yelled as his body writhed and danced at the end of the rope. Jane watched in horror and clutched at Clarissa's sleeve. How long could it take him to die?

"Courage," Clarissa said in one of her rare moments of kindness. "You can't swoon here. Breathe deeply."

Finally Luke hung limp and still, his body twisting slightly as the rope straightened. It was over.

Despite the soldiers stationed at the foot of the gallows, the crowd surged forward to be first in line for souvenirs—fragments of the rope or his clothes and locks of hair—yelling for the corpse to be cut down.

"Now!" Clarissa, with her vampire's strength, pushed through the crowd, pulling the boy and his cart and Jane with her. She waved a document at the officers on the scaffold. "I have a warrant to take my brother's body."

One of the officers took the paper and frowned at it, squinting, yet Jane recognized the relaxed, soft-eyed look of one under the spell of the Damned. "Ah. Very well. It is all in order, *citoyen*. Take the body."

Around them the crowd groaned and muttered, disappointed that the body was to be taken so soon and that there would be no reason to continue the merrymaking. Sure enough, soldiers urged the crowd to disperse.

Clarissa scrambled onto the cart and began to saw through the rope with a small pen knife. Only Jane was able to see the lightning quick flash and snap of her fangs, before Luke's body, apparently lifeless, slumped into her arms, the noose still around his neck. Jane's quick, discreet bite took care of the noose, revealing an ugly purpled welt around Luke's throat. Jane flung the rope into the midst of the departing crowd, who roiled and fought over it, with the French soldiers attempting to keep order.

She and Clarissa eased Luke's inert body into the cart.

"Is he gone?" Clarissa trailed her fingers over Luke's cheek. She stilled and Jane sensed her urgent entreaty. *Come back, Luke. Speak to us.*

"We must return home." Clarissa grasped the handle of the cart, motioning to Jane to do the same. "Come." Clarissa set a fast pace, running through the streets, dodging the remnants of the crowd, some of whom tried to follow, begging for a lock of hair. The boy who owned the cart ran behind, asking them to slow down, sirs, slow down, and when would he be paid?

As they arrived at the house, William and James emerged and carried Luke's body inside. Clarissa flung a handful of coins at John, who, red-faced and breathless, fell to his knees and scrabbled for his money among the dirt of the cobbles.

Jane followed them inside. They had laid Luke on the dining table, the nearest flat surface, and removed the rope from his wrists. But his hands lay at his sides, still clenched in the agony of death.

William shook him. "Wake, damn you!" He bent and breathed into Luke's mouth, then straightened, shaking his head. They all watched, waiting for Luke to move.

"Drip some blood into his mouth," James said. "Yours, William?"

"Certainly, if you wish to kill him. William's blood is too potent." Margaret stood in the doorway, misery and rage flowing from her. "One weaker but close to him may be able to do it."

William stepped aside and gestured to her.

She stepped forward and slid an arm beneath Luke's head, murmuring to him in a language Jane did not recognize, as intimately as though they were two lovers alone. She caressed his face and pressed her lips to his.

When she raised her head, his rolled aside, his body still. Tears ran down her face. "I cannot."

"Then who else?" William's voice cracked. "If neither Creator nor Consort can rouse him, what then?"

"So I am no longer his Consort, and you created him too long ago. There is but one hope. His fledgling." She bit the words out as though they were poison to her.

"Jane?" William took her hand and drew her forward, the first time he had touched her since he created her.

She laid her hand on Luke's, cold, inert. Dead. "What must I do?"

"Try to reach him with your mind," William said. "Breathe into his mouth."

Jane stood at Luke's side, and touched the fine bones of his face and the silky spring of his hair. *Luke, come back to me.*

She bent and lowered her face to his. His scent, the taste of his blood, lingered like a faint memory around him. *You created me, Luke, as sure as if you breathed me into being. Now I create you. Come back, friend, teacher, lover.*

Chapter 13

Luke's lips did not move beneath hers. His skin was icy cold, far removed from the normal chill of the Damned.

She straightened. "I have failed."

The others were silent, their attention shifted away from her. Something slight nudged in her mind, like a small ripple in still water.

William moved, grabbing a candle from the mantelpiece and plunging it into the fire. He brought the candle to the table and raised it high, spilling golden light over Luke's inert body.

Jane saw now the livid circle on Luke's neck pale and disappear into his normal ivory skin tone.

Speak to us, Luke. Come back.

The cotton of his shirt shifted as he took a breath, and his fingers uncurled and slid on the dark polished mahogany of the table. His eyelashes fluttered and a small sound emerged from his throat, a sigh.

She saw now other bruises and scratches change, dissolve, heal. He raised one hand and scratched his chest, a small, everyday gesture.

Hurts.

What hurts? She was fairly sure Luke spoke to her alone, aware of a babble of voices from the others that bounced around as if in a room full of echoes.

Everything. Every time I do this.

Every time you're hanged?

When I'm close to dying. This is the last time.

"Luke—" William stepped forward.

Jane snarled at William, her fangs extended, and with a small, amused smile, he retreated.

Luke's eyes were still closed, but she could see movement beneath the eyelids as though he dreamed. She raised her wrist to her mouth and bit.

As soon as her blood touched Luke's lips he came to life, snarling, fangs extended, and ripped at her neckcloth with one hand, the other digging into her hair, securing her. His fangs broke the skin of her neck, searing her with shock and relief, pain and pleasure mixed. She screamed as he bit into her.

"Don't let him harm her!" George cried, and the others held him back as he struggled to reach her.

Luke's head fell back and he sagged onto the table, but now he appeared to be sleeping.

"Allow me." William stepped forward and breathed onto Jane's neck, swiping one thumb over the spill of blood at her collarbone. "He lacks manners when he is brought back from the brink of hell."

He smiled and bowed his head to Jane, a small gesture of acknowledgment that warmed and thrilled her, the fledgling receiving praise from her Creator. Yet he picked up a napkin from the sideboard and wiped his thumb clean, a refusal of her blood, and she felt like weeping.

The others gathered around the table as though keeping watch over Luke, and Jane found herself standing next to George, disconsolate and unwanted.

"I suppose I should return home." Jane took another glance at Luke on the table and the Damned watching over him. They had cut their thoughts off from her and when she sent a tentative appeal to Luke he gave a sleepy, unintelligible reply.

"Don't take any notice of it," George said with awkward sympathy. "It's their way. Reminds me of the cliques at court. Made me damned hungry, though. I think I'll pay that pretty little ladies' maid a visit, after you've changed back into your women's clothes."

He held open the dining-room door for her.

"What did Margaret mean, that she was no longer Luke's Consort?" Jane asked as they walked into the hall.

"Ah, yes." George looked uncomfortable. "She could not revive him, and a true Consort should be able to. They've fought like cats and dogs ever since she came back. She's angry, for even though twenty years is nothing to the Damned, she was pledged to Luke as his Consort for most of them—it's like a sort of engagement, you see—and she feels she made a great sacrifice in returning to him. And for all his protestations of love when she left him and his urging her to return, now he says it's too late. And her failure to revive him proved it."

"So he is inconstant." Jane felt a pang of disappointment.

George looked uncomfortable. "I regret it's not altogether proper, but what do you do when love dies? Love may not be immortal. Lord, Jane, listen to me wax poetic; sometimes I'm quite a deep sort of fellow. William is very put out about it all, for it brings discord to the household. But you were the one who brought Luke back and they won't forget it."

* * *

Usually when Jane returned home she was able to create an illusion that she had not been out at night. If she chose to enter the house by the front door, she could meet the gaze of the footman who answered, sometimes with his wig dragged on crooked in his haste or wearing an apron, and subdue him with a glance. This time her feet dragged and she stumbled once as she walked down the street toward her aunt and uncle's house. As usual, one of the footmen from Luke's house accompanied her, and he caught her arm to prevent her falling. The events of the night and the morning, plus Luke's voracious feeding, had weakened her.

She mounted the steps and pulled the doorbell.

"Miss Jane!" The footman who answered the door looked at her with horror—no wonder, she had changed back into her finery from the night before, her gown stained with Ben's blood. "I'll fetch Mrs. Austen."

"No, please do not." She sank onto a chair in the hall.

Her mother, in nightcap and wrapper, ran down the stairs. "My dear child—what is this? We heard Mr. Venning was hanged, a dreadful business, and terrible for Miss Venning to be alone at such a time. How does she bear up, poor thing? But your gown! To think of that poor young man bleeding to death—how very sad."

"Yes, I have been with Miss Venning. I told you I would accompany her home last night." Jane stood. "I must go to bed."

Although by now she had adopted the sparse sleep of the Damned she longed for her bed and for solitude—and she was equally eager to escape the cynical gaze of Garonne, who had emerged from the doorway to the servants' quarters and stood watching, a coffee cup in his hand. *He thinks I have been with a lover.*

"Extraordinary, ma'amselle. The two men who cut Venning

down this morning, one could have been your brother," he murmured. "A remarkable resemblance."

"Good morning to you, sir." Jane acknowledged him with a dismissive bow of her head. What could he possibly suspect?

She trudged up the stairs, bone weary, feeling less like an immortal being than a tired woman who held herself responsible for the death of an innocent young man.

Later that day she and Mr. Austen sat in the kitchen of a small house on New King Street, in a less fashionable section of the town where artisans mostly lived. She had refused tea, knowing how short supplies were, and also declined to view Ben's body, which lay in the parlor of the house awaiting burial. She had found out where he lived from the inn at Sydney Gardens and, with her father accompanying, now paid a call on his grieving family.

"They told me and I said it must be a mistake," Ben's father, Mr. Weaver, said. He had said it several times before, as his hands moved mechanically, assembling and gluing fans. This was the family business, it seemed. Three children also sat at the table working, eyes shocked and blank above skilled, busy hands.

"He did not suffer long," Jane said.

"He fought when they invaded, until the militia told everyone to stop and go home," Mr. Weaver said. "I did not think he would be killed by an Englishman."

"Would you care to say a prayer?" Mr. Austen asked.

"Won't do him any good now, will it? Thanking you kindly, sir," Mr. Weaver replied.

"It might bring you comfort," Jane's father said.

Mr. Weaver's hands stilled. "Nothing shall bring me comfort, sir. Nothing. My son is dead. I thank you for coming." He reached for a handful of fan sticks, sorting, stacking.

Jane caught her father's eye and they both rose.

"I am so very sorry," she said again to Mr. Weaver.

"It was kind of you to come, miss." He didn't look at her. Maybe she should have accepted his offer to see Ben's body, but she remembered the boy's warmth and his hand on hers, the roughness of his cheek against her lips. She wanted to think of him like that, an ardent young man. She did not want to remember him in agony begging her to finish him.

She and her father left the house. They passed a group of people gathered around a brazier, who looked at them with open hostility as though guessing the prices of their clothes. This was not a poor area of the city, but these people looked wearied and worn down, despair and anger in their eyes. A pot of food steamed atop the coals, but with very little odor.

"They boil flour and greens in water," Jane said to her father. "Things must be dire indeed, that they must share their coals and food."

"We should help," her father said. "We complain at the house, but so far we have coals and enough food. Maybe I should ask Garonne—"

"I beg of you, do not ask Garonne for any favors."

They continued through the town, walking in silence along Westgate Street and Cheap Street and turning north through Bear Inn Yard to go onto Milsom Street, the fashionable shopping area of the town. There were no signs here of hardship; well-dressed people, many accompanied by French officers, strolled the street, gazing into well-stocked shop windows. Mr. Austen shook his head in disbelief. "You would never think . . . Jane, I do not ask you of your activities, but do you put yourself in danger? What happened last night?"

"I cannot tell you, sir."

He nodded. A group of French officers with fashionably dressed women on their arms forced Jane and her father off the pavement and into the muck of the road.

At the top of the street they turned right onto George Street and onto Bladud Buildings. They passed Paragon Place, soldiers and crowds increasing as they neared the London Road, until they came to the crossroads at Walcot Church, where the French had set up a guard.

"I come here every day," her father said. "A group of us wait to see if anyone who comes through has word of what goes on in the country. We are quite an exclusive club." He raised his hat to some other men who stood waiting, and they returned his gesture. Some held letters in their hands, asking the drivers of the few vehicles allowed to leave if they would act as unofficial postmen. Jane saw a soldier dash a letter from a woman's hands into the dung on the road and laugh when she wept.

"There's no news, Mr. Austen," one of the men said. "Rumors, as always, and precious little food or anything else coming into the city, but they say the French and their whores—begging your pardon, miss—have plenty. They send food in, but we don't know when."

"Shame on them! People are hungry in this town," Mr. Austen exclaimed. "And the use to which they put this church . . ." He gazed at the entrance of Walcot Church. Soldiers lounged at its elegant classical façade. He said to Jane, "Your mother and I married here. She wore a red wool riding coat and she was full of courage and gaiety. And now it is a barracks, defiled."

An officer approached and the soldiers snapped to attention. "Garonne." Mr. Austen gave a brief nod of acknowledgment.

"Go home, Mr. Austen," Garonne said. "There is no point in staying here on such a cold day, particularly if Miss Jane is in poor health. I would assist if I can, but, alas—" he gave an expressive shrug.

Mr. Austen escorted Jane to Paragon Place, where he left her, saying he must attempt once more to obtain a pass for the family, but Mrs. Austen and Cassandra insisted on accompanying him. The housekeeper and footmen were also out, standing in line for whatever fresh foodstuffs were available, leaving Jane and Betty, the housemaid, alone in the house.

Jane wandered through the dim rooms, restless and hungry once more. In her room, she untied the ribbon that held her manuscript and looked at the pages of neat, even writing. The words clanged and echoed in her head as she read. Competently done, but they no longer had any hold over her, no urge to reorder and shuffle and improve. Going back downstairs, she stopped in the drawing room to play a few chords on the woefully out-of-tune pianoforte.

She heard the front door open and Betty greet someone— Garonne, who came up the stairs and into the drawing room, a parcel beneath one arm.

"Ma'amselle, are you not cold?" Without waiting for a reply, he called to Betty to light the fire.

"We are a little concerned for our stock of coals, Captain."

"Oh, that? Bah, do not worry. We shall have coals." He laid his parcel on a small table. "This is for you. Or rather, I return what you were good enough to give to me."

Betty entered the room with a taper in her hand, and looked at them with curiosity before kneeling at the hearth.

"If you please, ma'amselle, open it."

"I cannot accept a gift from you, Captain."

"So. Betty, will you open this for your mistress?"

"If you wish, sir." Betty stood and wiped her hands on her

apron. She removed the brown paper and string. "Oh, Miss Jane. How fine it looks, to be sure!"

Jane's sketch of Cassandra now resided in a gilt frame.

"Captain, this sketch was a moment's work. It does not deserve this splendid setting."

He made a comical face. "Well, I cannot take it back, for it is yours, and it is also of your sister." He grinned. "My joke does not work in English. I wish you to have it, Miss Jane. Besides, I give the framer a leg of pork for this, and doubtless he has eaten it already; he cannot return my money, for there is none."

"I see."

"I shall hang it on the wall for you, Miss Jane. Tell me where."

"This is not our house," Jane said. "I thank you for the gift, Captain. Cassandra will be most pleased. I shall take it upstairs for her."

"But, ma'amselle! Do you not wish Mr. and Mrs. Austen to enjoy it also? Let it sit here—see, on the mantelpiece, for all to enjoy." His face became theatrically woebegone. "I am sorry my gift does not please you."

"It pleases me well and I thank you for it. If I seem ungracious it is because I am surprised, that is all. I had quite forgotten the sketch with all that has happened."

"Ma'amselle Jane, it is small pleasures that make life bearable in difficult times. Betty, you bring us hot water, eh?" He produced a small packet from inside his coat and handed it to Jane. "Yes, I am full of gifts today. Some tea, for I know you English cannot live without it."

Betty, with an expression of delight, curtsied and then left the room, leaving Jane and the Captain alone.

He stood at the fireplace, hands beneath his coattails, and smiled at her as she turned the package of tea over in her hands, debating whether she should fling it into his face. "It is rare I see you alone, ma'amselle Jane. Where is your family?"

"They accompany Mr. Austen to obtain a pass."

"I regret he will not get one."

"You seem very sure of that." He stood near the tea caddy on the mantelpiece, and to reach it she would have to move close to him.

"Your father is not a rich man. He cannot afford the bribe the official expects. It is best to wait. I have said that before."

Jane nodded and absentmindedly snapped the string that held the tea in its brown paper wrapping.

Garonne's eyes widened.

In one swift step she was at his side. She opened the tea caddy, which held only a little dust in one of its glass containers and poured the tea inside. The tiny rattle of the leaves on the glass was loud in the silence of the room.

Garonne stared at the dark fall of the tea and then at her. She touched his wrist. His heart pounded and a torrent of French, words of desire and longing, poured from his mind into hers. She should not have revealed her strength to him, but since she had . . .

"Captain," she whispered and saw his dark eyes still and soften. "Captain, when does the food arrive? And how?"

"*Ce soir. Apres minuit.*" He gazed at her. "Carts come in on the London Road, where we met today. The food is taken to St. Michaels Church."

"And how many carts? How many men guard each?"

He told her in a mixture of English and French.

"You do not need to leave guards at the church tonight," she told him.

"Of course."

"And one more thing—you must leave Cassandra alone."

"Cassandra?" He sounded, even in his enchanted, drowsy state, a little surprised. "But of course."

She broke the connection between them as Betty entered the room with boiling water and tea things. Jane stepped away, the tea caddy in her hands, and spooned tea into the teapot. The front doorbell rang and Betty went to answer it.

Garonne blinked. "I beg your pardon, ma'amselle. I believe you were saying . . . ?"

"My family has returned. What excellent timing."

There was much admiration of the portrait in its handsome frame and the gift of tea. Both Cassandra and Mrs. Austen seemed in slightly better spirits.

"But so many people who seem to have nothing better to do than stand on the street!" Mrs. Austen commented to her husband. "We should do something for them, my dear. Some beg, while others seem to wait, although I do not know for what."

"They have no work," Mr. Austen replied. "So much of the town's commerce depends upon those who come here for pleasure or for their health, and those are either cured or have run out of money themselves. You saw for yourself how few visit the Pump Room."

"Can you not do something, Captain Garonne?" Mrs. Austen asked.

"Many will have nothing to do with us," Garonne replied, spreading his hands. "They do not see us as friends. It is too bad. The most sensible thing for these men would be for them to join us in some way. There is much work to do to bring peace and prosperity to this new republic."

"I don't believe we need your sort of peace, Captain." Jane managed to keep her fangs under control. "And you ask men to oppose those who are their neighbors or relatives. Are you surprised they will not join you?"

"Many have," Garonne said. "Understand, ma'amselle Jane, we are not your enemy. Why, here we sit like old friends, and I learn to like tea. It is well done, no?"

Jane glanced out of the window at the dimming light. Soon it would be curfew and she had important news to relate to the Damned. She slipped quietly from the room when Garonne and her family were deep in a discussion of a military parade to be held soon in front of the Royal Crescent. She penned a brief note to Luke, explaining what she had discovered, and dispatched it with a footman. She resigned herself to another evening with her family: dinner, tea, sewing, her father reading aloud from Smollett in an attempt to cheer the family, and then her true life would begin again.

She retired early, claiming fatigue from the day's activities, changed into her men's clothes, and swiftly made her way to the house on Queen's Square.

William ran down the stairs to meet her, to her surprise. "My dearest Jane!"

She was thoroughly astonished, that one who had treated her with indifference should now show such warmth, and angry with herself that his words should fill her with painful pride.

"How is Luke?" she asked.

"Much recovered. He has the appetite of a lion. Come, we shall join the others. I am most pleased at your intelligence. But first if you wish, you may visit Luke and the others upstairs."

Luke lolled at a card table in the drawing room with James and George. "I have a prodigious hunger," he commented. "Is it not dark yet? George, what is your play?"

"Damnation, I suppose I shall have to offer the Royal Pavilion. I've precious little else. I suppose you would not accept Caroline?"

Luke stood as Jane entered the room and took her hands, raising them to his lips. "I have you to thank for my life."

"You are my Bearleader."

His lips skimmed her hands, pausing at the sensitive inner wrist where his fangs touched and pressed.

"You called me lover. Is that your wish? I am of you now. We are more deeply connected than ever." He lowered their joined hands and gazed into her eyes. "You deny your true nature, Jane, and thus you deny me and my love."

"I am not sure this is my true nature." How easy it would be to fall under his spell; how hard it was to resist him, with his scent and passion thrilling through her, urging her to yield to him.

"You are so stubborn, so determined. I can wait."

"For all eternity? Besides is there not some business with another lady to conclude?"

William observed them with a cynical twist to his lips. "If I may interrupt this most tender of scenes, we have work to do, and we shall dine late tonight after we've destroyed those wagons and their escort."

"Destroy the food?" Jane turned on him. "I must insist, William, we do no such thing. People go hungry; I have seen it with my own eyes. We must give the food to the city."

"And have the French hang anyone with a full belly? A ridiculous idea." William took George's cards from him. "You're ruined, as usual. I suggest you stop playing immediately."

"No, she is right," Luke said. "I believe the evidence will be disposed of before Renard discovers the loss."

"I trust you are right," William said.

James, Clarissa, and Margaret, who joined them soon after, were vociferous in their agreement that the food should be distributed to the hungry, and William, grumbling, was finally persuaded to join the plan. As they talked, the doorbell rang frequently and others joined them; a few, from their easy elegance and fine manners, appeared to be gentlemen, but most of them were men in simple clothes who viewed the others, particularly the Damned, with caution and curiosity.

"Why, Miss Austen!" One of the men, spectacles gleaming, stepped forward to take Jane's hand.

"Mr. Thomas!" She was delighted to meet the apothecary again and wrung his hand. "How do you do, sir?"

He winced.

"I beg your pardon, sir. I'm stronger than I realize."

"You have decided against the cure, then, ma'am?"

"Yes, it did not seem appropriate in these troubled times."

"Excellent. My neighbors still boast that they fought with a she-vampire when the French invaded."

A handful of vampires whom Jane had not seen before also crowded into the dining room, where a large wooden chest, lid flung open, revealed muskets and other weaponry.

"I suppose you have neglected to teach your fledgling how to handle firearms," William said to Luke.

He looked up from inspecting a musket. "I beg your pardon. I've been somewhat busy being dead. She'll help with ammunition."

"Madness," muttered William, "to bring a fledgling on such a mission."

"How else shall I learn?" Jane asked.

"Damnation, come if you will. Do as Luke tells you and you may be of some use." He pulled another musket from the chest and handed it to one of the townsmen.

"He's in a foul temper. He does not like to consort with those he considers below him," Luke murmured in Jane's ear. "It is a hard pill for him to swallow, that we vampires must join forces with mortals, and baseborn ones at that."

"But they have more to lose," Jane said.

"They'll be happy enough in heaven. From a theological point of view, we have more to lose than they. But enough of philosophy." Luke handed her a large canvas bag. "You'll carry this over your shoulder. It holds extra ammunition."

The Damned did not partake of the simple meal of bread and mutton that followed, although some joined their guests in drinking ale. Jane was amused to find several of the men staring at her legs, both intrigued and embarrassed by her men's dress.

Clarissa, typically, was more forthright in her interest with the men, attempting to engage them in conversation and asking if they had wives or sweethearts.

"It's not right, ladies fighting," one of the men burst out, staring at Clarissa's hand on his sleeve.

"Oh, I'm hardly a lady," Clarissa said.

"Beg pardon, ma'am," said the man, confused. "But I thought you were. As well as being a—being what you are."

"I can be very ladylike," Clarissa said. "I can be many things." Her fangs extended.

"Jesus Christ!" The man scrambled away from her, his beer spilling onto the table.

"Behave, Clarissa." Luke mopped up the spill. "I apologize for my sister's manners. She forgets herself."

The man looked even more alarmed, backing up against the sideboard. "You—they hanged you yesterday! I saw it with my own eyes!"

"To be sure, they did. But a French hangman, my dear sir— well, need I say more?"

The table burst into easy laughter and the man cowering

against the sideboard was persuaded to take his place once more.

"Tell me, sir," Mr. Thomas said. "Will you, ah, gentlemen or ladies require my services as surgeon?" He hesitated and then burst out, "I should be most interested if I could but dissect a specimen. I have never had the opportunity, you see. I was rather hoping that after the hanging, I might . . . but I beg your pardon, I am being most untactful. My wife is forever saying I have the manners of a bull and I fear she is right."

"Regretfully, there would be little left for you to dissect should the opportunity present itself," Luke said. "Now, on the Continent, it is a different matter, with a free exchange of ideas between our kind and physicians."

"Indeed, yes, I have heard your blood has remarkable restorative powers!" Mr. Thomas cried, pushing his spectacles farther up his nose. "And do you use it for each other's injuries?"

"We do," Luke said, smiling.

"Have you not considered what a boon for mankind this would be?"

William interrupted. "England is unusual in that here we are not persecuted, but it is not the case elsewhere. Both the Inquisition and the Revolution in France sought to destroy us. Why should we share our life essence with those who might turn on us?"

"I assure you I mean no disrespect, sir." The apothecary raised his glass to William who, after a slight hesitation, raised his own back.

"Is it true you can't abide garlic?" one of the men asked.

"Can *you*?" Luke asked.

The man wrinkled his nose. "Nasty stuff. My brother's a farmer, spends half his time looking for garlic in his fields for it ruins the butter and cream."

"Reckon you're one of them, then, Jake," the man seated next to him said to general laughter.

"How about crucifixes? Not that I hold with papist trappings," another asked.

"Ah, I regret that is another myth," Luke replied. "You are more like us than you may think. We associate the crucifix with the Inquisition, so we have no great liking for the symbol."

Conversation moved on to news from other parts of the country, in particular from London and the whereabouts of the Royal Family, and the guests helped themselves to clay pipes and a jar of tobacco, both of which were met with great appreciation.

"I hope the old King's safe, even if he's mad half the time," one of the men said. "I reckon I'd be off my head with that Prince of Wales as my son."

George opened his mouth to make an indignant reply, but a stern look from William quelled him.

"Aye, he's a terrible rake," another replied, leaning to fetch a coal from the fire to light his pipe. "The Frenchies are welcome to him, if you ask me."

"We've heard the Royal Family is safe," William said. "There's unrest against the French in almost every town and city. We shall prevail, gentlemen."

There were murmurs of agreement and approval, but the man whose brother owned the garlic-loving cows shifted uncomfortably in his chair. "That's all very well, sir, but you see, we don't want things to go back to the way they have been. Say what you will about the French, and I don't hold with cutting off people's heads, but they'd give us common men the vote. Neither Whigs nor Tories nor King George will do that, or not any time soon. Not in my lifetime, I'll warrant."

"The Prince of Wales has long been a friend of reform," George said.

The man snorted. "A friend to anyone who'll pay his debts, if you ask me. But you do see, sirs, that England under French rule might be better for some of us."

"Then why are you here?" George asked.

"Well." The man tamped tobacco into his clay pipe. He reached for a candle to light his pipe and blew a cloud of fragrant smoke into the air. "I never thought I'd see the *tricouleur* fly from the Abbey or that I'd fight side by side with vampires—let alone female ones—but in a couple of hours we'll be doing just that. I don't trust you Damned, or Parliament or the King, but I trust the French less, and better the devils you know than the one you don't."

Chapter 14

The night was cold and damp, with a steady rain. The wide streets of Bath lent little cover to those who could not blend into shadows, and the mortals of the party took the precaution of smearing their faces with ashes before they left the house. With some of the vampires, they left for St. Michaels Church, only a few streets away where Broad Street and Walcot Street joined.

The remaining Damned continued north on Walcot Street, taking refuge in the dark shadows of the church's burial ground to the east. They waited until the sound of marching feet and creaks of heavily loaded vehicles announced that the carts had arrived. The guards offered a challenge and some conversation took place between the soldiers.

The French officer on horseback, who led the wagons and its accompanying guard, cursed as his mount scented the presence of the Damned, put back its ears and shied.

He turned in the saddle. *"Allons!"* he shouted, indicating that the wagons were to follow him onto Cornwall Street that would run into Walcot Street and thus directly to the church, which was their destination.

Some of the Damned ran ahead, invisible in the shadows, to find any guards stationed along the route and dispatch them before they could raise an alarm when the ambush took place, a scant quarter mile away. The rest of them, Jane included, followed silently behind, far enough away so they would not panic the horses.

The train of carts creaked down the road, accompanied by the soldiers, who had no idea that soon they were to be attacked from rear and fore, trapped in the road, and that their attackers would have superior, terrifying powers of strength and speed.

Jane and the others encountered a mass of panicked French soldiers, while the horses that led the wagons reared and fought the drivers. A French soldier aimed his musket at her, changed his mind, and used it as a club. The blow landed on her shoulder as she ducked, missing her head, and the musket fired, nearly deafening her. She stabbed up and under, and the soldier frothed blood and fell. She pushed him out of the way, kicking another soldier on the knee, and saw him go down beneath the hooves of a terrified horse—the mount of the officer who led the convoy.

The horse screamed and reared, steel-shod hooves waving over her head.

"Steady, steady!" The man who cared neither for the King, the French, or the Damned dodged between Jane and the horse, grabbing its reins, and tossing his coat over its head. Temporarily blinded, the horse calmed enough to stay on all four feet.

Jane fought her way to the front of the wagon and swung herself onto the seat next to the driver. To her surprise, it was not a Frenchman, but an English boy of about twelve.

"Don't kill me!" the child cried, cowering away from her.

"Drive forward!" Jane shouted, and grabbed the whip from his hand. She cracked it over the backs of the pair of horses drawing the wagon, and it lurched forward. "Follow the other wagons. You'll be safe and you shall have food. But keep your head down—these gentlemen will fire muskets."

She pressed his head down as Luke, James, and George clambered aboard the wagon, muskets in hand. She slipped the bag of ammunition from her shoulders and launched herself onto the back of a French soldier, stabbing down as she landed. Behind her, the officer's horse had broken free and galloped down the street away from them, stirrups swinging wildly.

The street beside the wagon was a tight mass of men and vampires, the air thick with the scents of blood and sweat and panic.

To me. Luke's command broke clear into her mind and she fought her way forward, her feet slipping on blood. A French soldier confronted her, sword at the ready, and she growled, fangs out, and dodged beneath his guard. His eyes widened with fear and shock as she stabbed and bit simultaneously, his blood astringent and strong with terror.

So now you fight like a vampire. Luke's amused drawl.

The wagon lurched forward and she ran after, smelling her own blood—she must have been wounded but could not tell where. Soon, she suspected, she would feel some pain before the wounds closed and healed.

The wagon swerved right, pulling up outside the church. Luke wrenched apart the heavy chain and padlock on the doors and pushed them open wide to admit the carts.

Inside the church a man labored over a flintbox, a lantern to hand. His hat and coat dripped water and his hands were pinched and red with cold. Of course, it must be near pitch dark here, and the horses were uneasy at the presence of the Damned. The vampires stood back as the horses were freed from the shafts of the wagons and led back outside. The townspeople began to unload the carts, exclaiming over the variety and quality of the food.

"What will happen to the horses and carts?" Jane asked Luke.

"Taken to the outskirts of the town—the horses, that is. The carts they'll leave here. Come with me." He swung himself into an emptied cart that still held a faint smell of cabbage and onions and held his hand to her. "We must wait for the town to rouse. When curfew ends, people will arrive to take these goods to the market. Let me see where you are hurt. You were brave but careless."

She pushed cabbage leaves aside and settled next to him. He peeled a glove from her hand.

"Ouch!"

"Yes, you've smashed a knuckle here. On a man's teeth, I trust."

"No, I think it was his musket." She watched, fascinated, as he breathed on the wound and it closed and disappeared. "Something is wrong with my side."

"You were stabbed?"

"No." She remembered the details now. "A cart swung and trapped me against the wall. I didn't think much of it then, but now I remember. It's odd."

"No, it's good. You're becoming stronger. Our perception is different from that of mortals, particularly when we fight or are in other situations where we are purely physical creatures. Then we do not think." He unbuttoned her coat and waistcoat as he spoke. "Afterward we may remember small details, a touch, a breath, a glance."

"Are you sure you speak of fighting?"

"What do you think?" He tugged at her shirt. "Undo the fall of your breeches, if you will, so I may loosen your shirt. Where are you injured?"

"Here." She pointed to her side.

His fingertips probed and pushed at her skin and she let out a yelp of pain.

"A broken rib. You'd be in pain for weeks with this as a

mortal." He bent his head to her side and the cold of his tongue and breath burned and seared. "Keep still and stop being such a vicar's daughter, Jane."

"But you—I want—I don't know what I want." With an effort she ceased babbling.

"I do. Whether I should be the one to provide you with what you need is another matter. Does that still hurt?"

"A little." But the feeling of unease, the unaccustomed burning heat of his touch remained. "Why does that feel hot? I didn't think I'd feel heat again."

"You can get a sensation of burning by touching ice with your tongue. Have you never done that? Bitten into an icicle?" His expression was far-off and dreamy. She had a vivid impression of a small child, dressed in outlandish embroidered clothes, reaching to snap an icicle that hung from a low eave, snow all around.

That is you?

I have told you, I will not reveal my past to you.

"But you just did," she said, confused.

His hand rested on her side, on her bare skin. "You have the capacity for great power. In a decade or so, we shall see what you are truly made of."

"We? You will be there with me still?"

"I have become your Bearleader." His finger moved, tracing the bumps of her ribs. "I will be there. Yet I do not know whether I can be all things to you."

"Why?"

"Because although you become stronger and more like one of us, I do not know whether you will stay. Do you intend still to return to your previous existence?"

"I don't know." She lay next to him, her head pillowed on his arm. "I cannot write. When I look at my novel it is as though I see only marks on paper. I can read the words, yet they make no sense to me, and as every day passes it becomes more extraordinary to me that once I was the slave to my fancy and the passions of imagined people. I have lost that which gave me the greatest joy and the greatest sorrow of my life. And I miss my sister. Will you and the others be more of a family to me than my mortal family? Maybe I shall regret it when my sister and brothers are dust."

"There are always regrets, Jane." He pulled her shirt down and tucked it inside her breeches. "We are at war. Do you think you would write if you were not one of the Damned under such circumstances?"

"I don't know. I think I would miss it more. As it is, I find I don't care, and that seems extraordinary to me."

"Beg your pardon, sirs. We must move this cart." The young driver whom Jane had met briefly during the ambush stood staring at her and Luke. "They made me come and tell you."

If she could have, Jane would have blushed at the discovery. She sat and hastily buttoned her waistcoat and coat, and pushed herself from the cart, feeling only a slight twinge in her ribs and a sudden, huge hunger.

"When do we dine?" she muttered to Luke.

"Not until after dawn," he said. "Did you not partake during the fighting?"

She shook her head. "As much as I could, but there was not much time." She couldn't understand this hunger. Normally she would have found herself eyeing the nearby mortals, scenting their blood, discovering the rhythm of their heartbeats. But this was different. She was vaguely aware of the presence of those from whom she might feed, but it was Luke who occupied her senses and whose every gesture and movement roused a response in her own blood and bone.

Luke gazed at her, shaking his head, with a faint smile on his face.

"And what does that supercilious smile portend?" She wanted to fight him, caress him, savage him and soothe him all at once. She wanted his blood, his breath, his strength to subdue her own. Her fangs extended.

"I shall have to ask William's permission."

"Why? Ask William what?" She caught his hand, bewildered, as they walked away from the wagon, but the contact was too great, sending her into a spin of desire. She snatched her hand back before he could sense it, although his continued quiet amusement suggested he was very much aware of her mood.

"It's rather awkward, you see. I've become your Bearleader, but if I am to be your lover I must request permission from the one who created you, and that's William. Normally Creator and Bearleader would be one and the same and it would be a great breach of propriety."

"How about asking *me*? And what about Margaret?" Jane cried, and stamped away from him, furious and disappointed.

Her fangs ached and for the first time in days she had trouble subduing them. She kicked viciously at a turnip that lay in her path. It sailed in a graceful arc across the church and smashed on the floor.

"You and I must talk," said a calm voice from behind her. She turned to see Margaret with a large sharp knife in her hand.

Jane found herself assuming a fighting stance, light on the balls of her feet, knees slightly bent. She reached for her knife but it was gone—now she remembered removing it as she lay in the cart with Luke.

"I am not a fool," Margaret said. "You brought him back from the dead where I failed. Others in the household talk, but what I hear is impossible. All say that you are to be Luke's Consort."

"If that is true," Jane said, "you should be the last person to whom I would confess it."

"He was my Consort for near twenty years. I am entitled to know all his dearest concerns."

"But you are not entitled to know mine."

Margaret's fangs extended. "Obstinate, headstrong girl! He is descended from kings, as am I. He will never become connected with such a one as you. Tell me, Jane, is he your lover yet?"

Jane, herself *en sanglant*, braced herself for Margaret's attack. "You have declared it to be impossible. I would not dare contradict you."

Margaret leaped with the strength of a seasoned vampire, forcing Jane against the wall of the church, the knife against her throat. "Tell me, damn you, are you his Consort?"

"Oh, don't be such fools." Clarissa strolled up to them and lifted Margaret's blade aside with one finger. "No gentleman is worth such passion. Come with me and help me cut up some meat. I rather think you both need to clear your heads."

Jane followed Clarissa, reminded briefly of fighting with Cassandra over a doll when she was quite little, and her amazement at how angry they both became; of later, when they were halfway to becoming women, great passionate arguments over books or ribbons that left them weeping or in helpless giggles. As then, the world had become an unpredictable place of seesawing emotions and urges.

Obediently she joined some of the other vampires and a nervous, flustered townsman who was a butcher, and who winced as they hacked sides of meat into manageable lumps. The man looked wretched, torn between fear and fascination, afraid to interfere with the efforts of creatures of superior strength. Jane smiled at him in an attempt to set him at ease. "Where should I cut, sir?"

He crossed himself and backed away, his blush flooding his

face and matching his nose, red with cold. "Wherever you wish, ma'am. It is of no consequence. But at the joint of the leg, yes, that is good—" He stared as Jane wrenched the meat apart. "There is a knife for that if you wish."

Clarissa smiled, *en sanglant*, and the butcher's face took on a sickly hue.

"Pray do not tease him," Jane said.

"Why not? I am bored. I wish to dine." Clarissa's gaze raked the occupants of the church. "These are poor, skinny creatures. Don't you find excessive fear spoils the appetite?"

"They can't help it." Margaret drove her knife into a large piece of meat and ripped it in two.

Hushed voices outside indicated the presence of more people from the town; curfew was over, and a swarm of people carrying baskets and handcarts entered the church, loading them with food.

A child carrying a basket almost as big as himself sidled toward them, his eyes wide with fascination. "If you want this, pray come and take it," Margaret said with surprising gentleness.

"That child shows no fear," Jane said.

"He is too young to be frightened, but he knows we are different." Margaret looked at the child, her face soft. She steadied the child's basket and tipped the meat into it. "Eat well, little one."

A woman ran forward and put a protective arm around her son. "Thank you, kindly, sir—milady."

"I do not dine on children," Margaret said. "You need have no fear."

But the woman pulled the child and his basket away, scolding him in a loud and angry voice for some trivial offense. Margaret stared at the child, longing on her face.

"Would it have been worth it?" Clarissa asked.

"I ask myself that every day. Apparently I have all eternity to ponder my decision." She grimaced and stuck her knife into another side of meat. "Come, let us get this business out of the way, and then we'll return home to dine."

In groups of two and three the townspeople slipped from the church. Bundled in cloaks, carrying baskets and bundles, they looked like servants and apprentices on their way to work or sent on errands, scurrying quietly in different directions through the dark town.

"A good night's work," Mr. Thomas said as he passed by, a large sack slung over one shoulder. "A very good night's work, Miss Austen, but I suggest you all leave soon before the French change guard. I gather they do so in half an hour."

"An excellent suggestion." William nodded to Jane. "Will you come to the house?"

"No, I shall return to Paragon Place." How her father would grieve if he knew of this defiled church, scattered with debris, the altar smashed, tombstones on the wall defaced, and horse dung on the flagstone floor. Her hunger faded. The Damned had not been responsible for the defilement, but they seemed indifferent to the fate of the church.

Jane washed her bloody hands at a pump in the street, the water leaving a thin glaze of ice on the cobbles. It was considerably lighter now, the city waking. She slipped into the alley at the rear of the church, and joined the early-morning jostle of people in the street, breathing in their fear and hunger and anger. A group of French cavalry clattered up the street, ignoring the clods of frozen filth and insults that were thrown their way. As they neared the church she heard urgent shouts; they must have discovered the unlocked doors, the empty interior.

As she approached the house on Paragon Place, the front door swung open, to Jane's surprise and alarm. She pulled her hat over her eyes and continued to walk. Possibly their footman had opened the door for another reason, but she became aware that it was no servant who stood there.

"Jane!"

He had discovered her and she was too unsettled by the events of the night, and Luke's revelation and the discovery of her own desires, to attempt evasion.

She turned on her heel and faced him.

"You make a handsome boy," Garonne said.

Chapter 15

"Good day, Captain." She stood her ground and watched him take in her breeches, her disheveled, bloodstained appearance.

"What have you been about, Miss Jane?"

"I regret I cannot tell you." She walked past him and into the house.

"But of course not. You have been with your lover. You hide it so well from your family, but I—I have observed. I see you leave the house. You break curfew. I think you bribe the servants not to tell, eh? This is not good, Miss Jane."

"What do you want, Garonne?" She turned to confront him, but he opened the door to the dining room and gestured that she enter.

"Your lover must be a man of unusual tastes."

She shrugged and tossed her hat onto the table. "That has nothing to do with it. It is safer for me to walk the streets so. Your soldiers do not always respect a gentlewoman, I've heard."

"They would certainly not respect a woman dressed as you are."

"I'm tired, Garonne. I wish you good day. I shall change into my women's clothes now."

He stopped her with an arm across the doorway. She consid-

ered: she could take him easily enough with her fangs if she did
not have time to reach the knife in her boot. But she had scarcely
dined, and desire and hunger weakened her. If she revealed herself and failed, the consequences could be dire.

Even as she considered her course of action, the two French
soldiers who were also quartered in the house came running up
the stairs from the basement, talking loudly of the stolen supply
wagons. Garonne closed the door, leaving Jane alone in the
dining room, and she heard a brief conversation that ended with
the front door opening and closing, and silence. But Garonne
had not left; he came back into the dining room, leaning against
the door, one booted foot crossed over the other.

"You and I, we talk," he said. "Our supplies have been stolen,
many men killed. You know anything of this, ma'amselle?"

"I have little enough to say to you, sir, and I have no idea what
you are talking about."

"I have word from London," he said. "You have friends, relatives, there? Ah. There is a tribunal set up. We seek out the
enemies of the republic. Your mad King, he is still hiding somewhere, but we shall find him. And then—" He brought one hand
down in a sudden, eloquent gesture.

So it was happening.

"And then, in the provinces, tribunals set up, and here, soon,
in this city. Your father, Miss Jane, to us he is the enemy. He is a
man of the church."

"Even you can hardly make the claim that my father is a
member of the corrupt and powerful second estate. This is not
France, Captain."

"No." He cocked his head to one side and folded his arms
across his chest. "But it is not up to me to decide who is a threat,
who is not. I know Mr. Austen is a good man. But others . . . well,
they do not know that. A tribunal would not know."

"Then help my family get a pass so they may leave the city."

"You think your family will be safe in the country? For a little, maybe. Not for long."

Jane had a sudden urge for, if not some blood, at least a cup of tea. She strode to the bellpull and wrenched at it.

"You call for help?" Garonne said.

"I want tea!" she snapped.

"Of course. Your servant should not see you dressed like that." He opened the door and ordered Betty, who came in response to the bell, to bring tea.

"For a revolutionary, Garonne, you are quite a prude," Jane said as they waited for the tea things to arrive.

"Not at all. But Betty, she will be shocked. Me, I admire you greatly." His gaze was warm and appreciative.

"So you have said, sir. What do you suggest our family can do if you are indeed correct that a tribunal and the guillotine will be set up here?"

"I think you know, Jane."

Why did men so enjoy exasperating riddles?

In answer to the knock at the door, Garonne opened it long enough to receive the tray, which he brought over to the table, and stood aside for Jane to make tea. "We are wrong. It is tea that is the religion in this country."

"And beer. Gaming. Dogs." Jane spooned tea into the pot.

"You and I, we get on well," Garonne said.

"As well as an unwelcome guest and his hostess can."

"Ah, but this is not your house. You say so often."

She looked up. "You have word of my aunt and uncle?"

"Regrettably, no." He watched as she poured the hot water over the tea leaves.

She replaced the lid on the teapot and settled herself to wait while it brewed. She assessed him carefully and sensed nervousness, desire. "What were you about to suggest, Captain? I trust whatever you suggest has nothing to do with my sister." If he expected Jane to plead his cause with Cassandra she would kill him, and devil take the consequences.

"Your sister?" He threw up his hands. "Ah. No, it is nothing to do with your sister. But it is everything to do with you, *chère* Jane."

"But—but you have made your intentions toward Cassandra quite clear, sir, if not the nature of them."

"I have?"

"You showed a marked partiality in the matter of the picture that you had framed."

"Oh, the picture. No, the picture was of value to me only because you drew it."

"I see." She poured tea in a dreadful parody of polite behavior, wondering that she could have been so mistaken. "And now you suggest I become your mistress so I may save my family's heads."

"You are direct. I admire that." He nodded with great energy and stretched a hand across the table toward her. She pushed a cup of tea into his hand.

"I have not given my assent, Captain."

"But you will." His smile became knowing. "I think you will find your family gives you no choice. After all, you have eaten the food I bring into this house; you accept my protection as escort; why, even now you drink the tea I have brought. Already you are halfway to saying yes to me, and your family, they will not argue too much."

"You are mistaken." She pushed away her cup of tea and thought longingly of tearing into his throat. "You insult me, sir."

"Bah. These are unusual times, Jane. You, a respectable unmarried woman, take a lover beneath their noses. You think they do not know? Already you are dishonored. Naturally you will take another lover before long and it shall be me, and why not? Your family may pretend to object, but they will thank you."

"I doubt it very much, Captain." Her tea finished, she stood.

He lounged in his chair, eyeing her. "You had best consider what you do, Jane. Do not think too long. I think you and I, we shall do well. I like you, as a man likes a woman, eh? And I think you like me a little too."

"Good morning." She left the room. Thank God Cassandra was safe from his advances. She ran up the stairs, tore off her wet and dirty men's clothes, hid them beneath a loose floorboard in her bedchamber, and then changed quickly into shift and petticoats as though she had recently risen from her bed. Not a moment too soon. She heard Cassandra outside and her tentative tap at the door.

"Jane? May I enter?"

"Of course. I'm up."

Her sister, fully dressed and wrapped in a large shawl, ran across the room to the bed, kicked off her shoes and snuggled under the coverlet. "Ooh, I'm so cold, Jane, but it doesn't seem to affect you. I wish we could have fires in our bedchambers, but we have to be careful of our use of coal. Captain Garonne does not know whether he can help us get any more."

"I pray you will not ask the captain for help. He is our enemy," Jane said.

Cassandra frowned. "You smell strange."

Sure enough, she reeked of bacon and animal fat. "Yes, I woke early and went to the kitchen to make sure the meat in the larder was still fresh."

Cassandra gave her an odd look. "We have no meat."

"Then it must be the rushlight. I think I held it too close to my hair." For someone who was Damned her ability to tell lies was quite dreadful.

"Will you visit your friend Miss Venning again today? How does she do, poor thing? She must miss her brother dreadfully."

Jane thought of Clarissa *en sanglant* prowling around the mortals in the church. "Oh, she bears up remarkably well." She hesitated. "Cassandra, I must confide in you. Pray do not tell Mama or Papa, for it will only distress them. Garonne has told me that in London a tribunal has been set up to try those who are against the French and that they will put to death any they consider guilty."

"The guillotine!" Cassandra covered her mouth.

"Indeed, and as in France, tribunals will be set up in other cities and towns—here, for instance—and as you know, this revolutionary French government has no great love for the church."

"What shall we do?" Cassandra was almost as pale as Jane. "And Papa—he will not be safe. Oh, I do wish we could leave this place!"

"I too. Our only hope is that the French will be driven out."

"Garonne told you of this? Then it must be true, although we have heard all sorts of wild rumors. But there is something else—what is it?"

Jane poured water from the ewer on the washstand into the bowl. It gushed out with a thin layer of ice. She splashed it onto her face and attempted to raise a lather with the tablet of soap. "Garonne asked me to become his mistress. He said he could protect us against a tribunal and thinks, because we have accepted his gifts of food and tea, that already I am inclined to accept his offer."

"Oh, Jane!" Cassandra burst into loud sobs, huddled beneath the bedclothes.

Jane took the few steps between them and hugged her fiercely, making Cassandra squeal with alarm. She lessened her grip and held her sister, who wept as though her heart were broken, the pent-up tears of the past few days, of the last year, all the sorrow rushing out of her like blood. After a while Jane pulled the ribbon from Cassandra's hair and reached for her hairbrush. She drew it through the waves of Cassandra's rich brown hair, darker than her own, knowing this would soothe her sister.

Cassandra quieted, her sobs turning to the occasional sniffle, and blew her nose on the sheet. "Oh, I beg your pardon," she muttered, mortified. "These are your sheets."

"I would rather have you than anyone else in the world blow their nose on my sheets," Jane replied, which made her sister give a weak giggle.

"What shall we do?" Cassandra asked.

Jane continued to brush her hair in slow, regular strokes. "We must impress upon Mama and Papa that we should accept no more favors from him or allow him to escort us anywhere. I did not tell you this before, but the evening we were at Sydney Gardens his uncle the general suggested I should sell myself for a pass to leave the city. He suggested other women had done as much."

"Good God! I pity any woman who would do so. But—but you cannot stay in the house." Cassandra took the ribbon from Jane and tied her hair up again. "Not after this."

Jane's breath caught. It was what she wanted, to be with the Damned, to no longer have to lie to her family. But if she left this house, would it break the last, weakening tie with her family?

"You must go downstairs and warm yourself. Yes, I know my hands are colder than yours, but I'm not yet dressed. We shall ask our mother for advice."

When Jane arrived downstairs, she found Cassandra and her mother in the morning room, sitting close to the fire, their needlework on their laps and the remains of breakfast on the table. They looked up as she entered.

"What is this, Jane? What have you done to upset poor Captain Garonne?" her mother inquired.

"Poor Captain Garonne? Surely, ma'am, you are mistaken." She glanced at Cassandra, who now seemed to be intent only on her embroidery. "The truth of the matter, ma'am, however much Cassandra may have tried to protect your feelings, is that he asked that I become his mistress and I refused him."

"I am sure you are mistaken, Jane. Why, I saw him this morning and he was quite civil, although I could see he was distressed. When I questioned him he said you and he had fallen out, and he was disappointed since you were such good friends."

"Good friends, ma'am! I assure you I have never given him the slightest encouragement. Besides, we do not talk of a proposal of marriage."

"Cassandra and I think you are mistaken."

"No, I do not think so, ma'am," Cassandra said in a small, defeated voice. "How could any woman be mistaken by what the captain suggested to Jane? Pray do not attempt to put a good face on it, ma'am, it will not do."

Her mother laid her sewing aside. "My dear, we should not rush to hasty conclusions. We have thought Garonne to be very gentlemanly and generous, but perhaps we have been mistaken. You must take great care not to be alone with him anymore, Jane."

Jane sighed. "Does Papa know of this?"

Cassandra looked up. "Papa is out. I expect he will not be back until later."

"I see." Jane crossed to the window. A light layer of frost lay on the panes in fantastic, curling patterns. When she pressed her fingertip against them, they did not melt and she did not wince at the cold. She heard the small popping sound of a needle penetrating fabric, the whisper of thread pulled through, the crackle of the fire—small familiar sounds, or rather, the sounds she would barely have heard in her former existence, a time when the two women sewing were dearer to her than anything in the world.

She turned back and regarded her mother and sister with the dispassionate gaze of a stranger: a middle-aged woman, worn down by the demands of a large family and never having quite enough money; a young woman with the lines of disappointment already showing on her face.

They're tired and I am part of their burden.

"Ma'am, Cassandra. You know that several days ago Miss Venning offered me the position of companion and I have delayed the decision in deference to my own family's needs." They both looked up from their sewing.

"I have never intended that a daughter of mine should leave to go into service," Mrs. Austen said. "Frankly, I was surprised at the offer."

"It is a very genteel, superior sort of position, ma'am. I would not be a servant."

"Consider how the poor thing lost her brother, ma'am. She is all alone in the world," Cassandra said. "And you would come to visit us, Jane, would you not?"

"Of course."

"I think it might be for the better," Mrs. Austen said. "She does seem quite a superior sort of young lady."

Jane had hoped they would agree, but she was saddened by her mother's ready approval. On the other hand, if her mother and sister had begged she stay, she could only guess at their motivation.

"I shall write Papa a note. I think it best I leave as soon as possible."

As she left, Cassandra rose and accompanied her. "You have not been the same since your illness."

"I'm well enough, now." Jane walked ahead of her down the passage to her uncle's study. She heard the coldness in her voice and hated herself for it. This was Cassandra, her beloved sister.

"I thought you harbored a tendresse for Mr. Venning."

"He was a very pleasant young gentleman." Jane opened the study door. To her annoyance, Cassandra followed.

"Brr, it's cold in here. A pity indeed that he was persuaded to act so rashly against the French."

Jane sat at the desk and chose a small piece of paper. Aware that Cassandra lurked nearby and might well read over her shoulder, she penned a brief note to her father, explaining that she had gone to stay at Miss Venning's house as her companion. It was the last note she might ever write to him, one that might be passed around, analyzed, pondered over. Would he finally tell her mother and sister the truth when she was gone and lost to them?

Tears rose to her eyes. She brushed them away, fearing she would weep and howl as Cassandra had done before breakfast.

She folded and sealed the note. Cassandra followed her up the stairs and into her bedchamber like a woebegone puppy, offering to help her pack. Jane was touched and felt tears rise again, but she needed to get Cassandra out of the way so she could pack her men's clothes. Finally, she hit upon the idea of asking to borrow Cassandra's gray pelisse, since Miss Venning was in mourning for her brother.

"Of course!" Cassandra darted out of the room, giving Jane a chance to pull her men's clothing from its hiding place and fold it at the bottom of her trunk.

Cassandra returned, the gray pelisse folded in her arms. "You will come back, won't you, Jane?" Cassandra asked in a small voice. She smoothed the sleeves of the pelisse.

"I assure you, I shall be a frequent visitor; in fact I shall be here so often you will beg me to leave. And in between visits I shall bombard you with so many notes that our footman's shoe leather will be thoroughly ruined."

Cassandra laid the pelisse in the trunk. "Mama and I are both worried about your lack of appetite and how thin you are. Will you not take some breakfast before you leave?"

"I believe some lingering effects from my illness are common still. My appetite will return, I am sure. Cassandra, I shall be perfectly well. Come, smile for me. That long face does not suit you."

"No, it is more than that." Cassandra took a pair of stockings from Jane and folded them more neatly than she ever would. "I feel you still have a part of you missing. I miss my sister, my most beloved sister. When will you come back to me, Jane?"

Jane took her sister's hands. Fear, worry, deep sadness, bewilderment. She knew she should look deep into her sister's eyes and tell her to stop worrying and assure her that everything would be well. And Cassandra, her eyes soft and dazed, would agree with her.

But she could not do it. She could not bear to deceive her sister further, but neither could she tell her the truth and see Cassandra's repulsion and shame.

Cassandra, however, saved them both by assuming a resolutely cheerful air that made Jane love her all the more for her fine show of courage. "Do you have everything? Well, then. We shall send the footman to carry your box. Pray do not let him linger at Miss Venning's house. Poor thing, I expect she longs to leave Bath as much as we do. Where does the family come from?"

"Surrey, I believe," Jane said vaguely. She accompanied her sister downstairs and gave her an affectionate kiss farewell, holding her tightly as Cassandra's confusion and sadness overwhelmed her. "I love you so much, Cassandra."

Cassandra giggled. "You will be a mile away, Jane. Do not be such a sentimental creature."

Jane wanted to pick up her skirts and run down the street of elegantly proportioned houses, past the lounging French soldiers who eyed her with lust and contempt, run home to her own kind. But she walked with eyes modestly downcast, a gentlewoman accompanied by her servant, ignoring the swirl of scents and emotions that swirled around the street. Her façade would have to be maintained only a short while longer, and there was a sweet pleasure in the delay and anticipation. Each step brought her closer to the house in Queens Square and those who waited for her there—the community of the Damned to which she now belonged.

She would not think of Cassandra's brave cheerfulness at her departure or the grief her sister would inevitably experience as she waited all her life for Jane to return.

As usual, since it was so early in the day, it took some time for the footman to answer the door. "They're all asleep, ma'am," he said, scratching his head beneath the powdered wig.

"It doesn't matter." Jane dismissed the manservant from Paragon Place who had carried her box and walked into the quiet house that was now her home.

"So you've come to us." Clarissa, wearing an elegant, filmy gown, ran downstairs and embraced her. "You have left them. Have we not told you this is what you should do? I am so glad. Now you are truly one of us."

Chapter 16

"Another one, miss?"

Jane, her mouth full, nodded eagerly as Mr. Jacques Brown the cook placed another delectable profiterole onto her plate.

Whatever else she had expected with her arrival at Queens Square, it was not to end up in the kitchen being fed treats by the staff.

Clarissa, after her enthusiastic welcome, had yawned and apologized, and retired to her room. Every other one of the Damned was asleep, or taking whatever sort of rest they required after the long night. With some timidity she had tried to announce her arrival to Luke, who had sent a distinctly grumpy reply into her mind that he would be available later in the day. Disconcerted, reluctant to stay in the dining room (gloomy and with gossiping footmen cleaning the furniture), and equally reluctant to view the squalid aftermath of the usual drawing-room debauchery, she had wandered into the kitchen in search of company and sustenance. It might not be the sort of sustenance she really wanted, but Mr. Brown was so pleased to feed someone who appreciated his cooking that his enthusiasm was quite as satisfying as his pastries.

"A little apple tart, next?" Mr. Brown dipped a spoon into a bowl of clotted cream, rich and heavy. "Very nice, miss, with cream. You will like it."

"Thank you. I'm sure I will." She held her plate out yet again.

A couple of men, Jack and another she did not recognize, and a woman came down to the kitchen as she finished her slice of tart. From their careful gait—she imagined their descent of the steep kitchen stairs must have been exceedingly cautious—and their satisfied, sleepy smiles, she gathered they had entertained in the drawing room.

Her offer to revive them was met with bright smiles and Mr. Brown grumbled as he drew them off glasses of ale and set the visitors to toasting bread on the kitchen fire. She bit into her finger and dripped a little blood into each glass.

"You will burn your toast," Mr. Brown chided them—for they watched her bloodletting with avid, greedy eyes. "Thank the lady now, if you please."

Footfalls pattered down the stairs, and Ann entered the kitchen. "Your bedchamber is ready for you, Miss Jane."

She wasn't ready to sleep, but she thought she might as well get some rest. Her plate scraped clean, she followed Ann upstairs—right up to the top of the house, where normally servants would sleep. But servants' bedchambers would not be as richly appointed as this, with a curtained bed, expensive mahogany furniture decorated with a tasteful ivory inlay, and a fire lit in the small fireplace. Her box of possessions, looking distinctly shabby, stood on the intricately patterned carpet.

"Where do you sleep, Ann?" Then, seeing a knowing smile spread over the girl's face, she added, "Don't any of the servants sleep in?"

"Mr. Brown has a room off the kitchen, and I generally sleep with Miss Clarissa. She likes to have me close to hand. All the others come in by the day or by the night. It's best that way, for when we move."

"A move is planned? Where to?"

"Oh, yes. Sometime, that is, but I don't know where or when. They don't usually tell me until the same day. It's their way, for they are used to not staying in one place for too long." She bent to unfasten Jane's box. "I can help you unpack, miss. Why, what's this writing?"

"Nothing!" Jane snatched the manuscript from her hands. Cassandra must have slipped it into the box when Jane wasn't looking.

"You wrote all that, miss?"

"Yes. It's a novel."

"Goodness." Ann bent over the box. "They're not much for reading although George has a few books. He's next door to you, miss. You may want to lock your door. Or not." She giggled and pulled out one of Jane's gowns. "This needs ironing. Is this your best?"

"I'm afraid so." Her best gown, the same muslin she had worn when she had been created, looked sadly drab.

"Miss Clarissa will lend you hers. She has lots of gowns." Ann made a face as she shook out one of Jane's morning gowns, a striped cotton. "If there's cloth to be had in the town, I daresay you'll order some new ones."

"I regret I can't afford it."

"Mr. Luke will pay."

"Oh."

"It's what a Bearleader does." Ann rummaged in the box again. "Or a protector."

"Where does he sleep?"

"Oh, he doesn't, miss. Not much. Neither he nor Mr. William. They're old, you see. They usually rest a little after they dine, but they don't go to bed like others."

Jane, aware that she clutched her abandoned manuscript to her chest, walked the few paces over to the dressing table and laid it down carefully. "Could you bring me a pen and ink, when you've finished with my clothes?"

"Certainly, miss. I'll darn these stockings for you too."

Ann left with her arms full of clothes, and Jane paced the small room and peered out of the window at the gray day and the stark, bare trees of Queens Square. The surrounding elegant, beautifully proportioned houses that on a sunny day would appear the color of Mr. Brown's clotted cream today looked merely drab and brownish. She lay on the bed, wondering if she could sleep, but was too restless. And hungry, but she could wait until nightfall.

A footman brought her pen and ink, and she drew a chair up to a small folding table and gritted her teeth. She would write. She had to write.

But this was dreadful stuff. Why, her sentences barely made sense—they were clumsy and ugly but she could not see how to improve them. She turned the page and read on until she realized she had lost the narrative thread entirely. Was it her or was it what she had written?

She considered. Maybe she was thinking like one of the Damned, contemplating eternity and the knowledge that nothing needed to make sense; that there was no form or structure because life continued, whatever sort of pattern you attempted to apply. She thought back over the events of the last several days.

She had been created.

She came to Bath.

The French took the city.

She fell in love with Luke—no, that was nonsense, particularly falling in love with Luke. If she had not become one of the Damned, she would not have come to Bath. If Margaret had not come to Bath, Luke and the others would not have come here. There were no connections, no patterns. She might as well argue that the French invaded England because Jane Austen attended an assembly in a country town.

As for Luke, he would not allow her to read his mind or give any sign that her regard was returned, although he would flirt with any pretty woman, she suspected—and then there was his earlier attachment to Margaret. Well, she had all eternity to sigh over him, a thought that did not appeal overmuch.

Better to think that there was this brief day to get through, after which the others would awake, and they would dine and dance, and possibly kill some Frenchmen.

"So you are here."

Jane whirled around. Margaret stood in the doorway of the room. Despite the earliness of the hour she appeared elegant in a morning gown of a soft blue, her hair held with a matching fillet. A subtle perfume wafted from her. She had completely recovered her strength and beauty, her red hair striking against her white skin, a far cry from the frail, half-dead creature Jane had met in the Pump Room.

"Will you not come in?" Jane asked, but Margaret had already entered and sunk gracefully onto the bed.

"What is it that you do?" Margaret asked.

"I'm writing." Jane tapped her manuscript into a neat pile, and tied the ribbon around it—how like Cassandra to replace the workaday string with one of her own ribbons. As she knotted the ribbon, a faint scent, a memory of her sister, arose.

"I did not mean that. I mean, why are you in this house? Why have you joined us?"

"I thought it was time," Jane said.

"I see." Margaret toyed with a lock of her hair that had fallen over one shoulder, like a streak of blood on her skin. "It is usual for the company of the house to decide among themselves who shall live with them. I am surprised Luke or William has not told you this. You see, not everyone wants you here."

"You mean you do not."

"I was not consulted. Neither was William, to whom you can only be an embarrassment."

"But Luke is my Bearleader. Where else should I go?"

Margaret shrugged. "He is your Bearleader because he pities you and because your Creator has more important concerns. Do not flatter yourself that it is anything more." She rose to her feet in one long, sinuous movement. "Be careful, Miss Jane Austen. You have no power here. You should go."

"Go where?" Jane produced the words with difficulty. She was so tired. It would be easier to just agree with Margaret, to leave the house, to . . . "Stop!" she said, gathering the last of her strength, and it was as though she took a long, refreshing draught of clear, cold water.

Margaret briefly showed her fangs and left the bedchamber in a swirl of drapery and a waft of perfume that now seemed rank and bitter.

Jane must have fallen asleep, for in the next moment, it seemed, Clarissa was shaking her awake. The fire had burned down and the daylight was fading, the room filled with shadows. Jane's former self would have found the room gloomy, but now the shadows were friendly and warm, an invitation to the night and its pleasures.

"More hunting tonight," Clarissa said with relish. "Up with you, sleepyhead."

Yawning, Jane sat up and reached for the men's clothes, now cleaned and pressed and accompanied by clean linen, that Clarissa had laid on the bed.

"What do we hunt?"

"You'll find out. I can promise you better fireworks than anything Sydney Gardens can produce."

Downstairs, where they gathered in the dining room, Jane was aware of a subtle shift in regard toward her; Margaret, who stood quietly to one side, was silent but showed none of her earlier venom.

William bowed, one gentleman to another. Luke stepped forward and retied her neckcloth for her. "Much better," he said, and turned her toward the mirror over the fireplace.

"Much better," Luke said again, although this time he referred to her fuzzy and faded reflection. George's reflection was barely visible and Margaret's showed only as a faint shimmer.

William poured wine and handed glasses to them all. "To Jane, who is now one of us, and to good hunting tonight."

Luke touched her wrist. *You're making nearly as much noise as that great oaf George.*

I heard that, came a petulant reply in the dark.

She was tempted to giggle.

I'm hungry.

George's complaint startled her into a breath of nervous laughter.

Hold your tongue, said several silent voices at once.

She was hungry too. Luke had smiled with his usual charm and assured her she would dine after the night's mission had been accomplished. They would work better hungry than if they were stupidly sated. She had to admit there was a definite logic to it, but was disappointed. Under other circumstances her stomach would have growled, but as she was now she experienced a nervous alertness, senses magnified and highly tuned, aware of the unspoken currents that passed among the Damned as they quietly made their way through the dark streets.

William, leading the way, made a small gesture with one hand, and they melted into the shadows, into doorways, and down a dark alley as a troop of French cavalry passed them, clattering down the street. Several of the horses seemed to be aware of their presence, sidling and showing the whites of their eyes before their riders took charge, gathering the reins and collecting their mounts.

The sound of the hooves died away.

Luke moved forward and conferred with William in a series of gestures, then waved the company back into the shadows.

The streets here were unfamiliar to Jane but she could smell the river close by, and the scents of tobacco and coal. She knew they must be near the Methodist chapel the French used to stable their horses, and to the west of that lay their destination, the quay on the Avon.

Sure enough, the troops gathered outside the chapel, the breath of men and horses steaming in the night air. Most of the cavalrymen had dismounted, some gathering around a brazier, hands held out to the warmth, making conversation.

Luke led them down another narrow dark alley and the smell of the river became stronger, the stars bright overhead despite the city smoke. They had reached the quay, which was scattered with barrels, a small crane, and piles of rope. Fragments of ice floated gray and crackled on the river. He made a small gesture with one hand and the vampires sank into the shadows. He and Jane settled into a space between two barrels.

A rat nearby stopped and raised itself on its hind legs, snuffing the air, then dropped to run in a panicked circle before darting away.

They sense us, Luke said.

Why are we waiting?

You'll see. A guard came into view, beating his arms against his sides. He passed within a foot of the concealed vampires, bringing with him a scent of tobacco, sweat, and blood. *Count. One, two, three . . .*

The guard reached the end of the quay, turned, stamping his feet against the cold, and passed them again. Another guard approached, and they passed, pausing to nod and exchange a few words. Jane couldn't understand what they said.

I wouldn't expect a lady, however educated, to understand that. They speak in vulgar terms of the weather. Keep counting.

As she counted, the guards passed and each turned to march down the side of a small stone building. In all, four men kept guard, their paths crossing every few seconds.

What is in that building?

Powder. Luke laid his fingers on Jane's wrist and conferred with the others, mainly William. His touch dulled the others' comments—they both knew she was too inexperienced to interpret all the voices.

He nodded. *We wait until William gives the signal before we take them.*

They watched as the soldiers circled, disappeared, returned, passed, creating an uneven, lumbering pattern.

He laid a hand on hers again. *It is time.* Luke slipped away from her into the shadows, moving closer to the padlocked door. For a moment he was exposed as he ripped the hasp and padlock apart, fangs extended, before slipping into the warehouse.

Two of the soldiers reappeared, marching toward each other.

They would cross at the doorway and they might notice the broken fastening and the slightly open door. They paused as they approached each other, and stopped to exchange a few words. One of them became alert. He pointed to the door but before he had a chance to speak, the dark figures of Margaret and William emerged from the shadows. The struggle was brief and insignificant, but left the two men broken and limp on the ground.

Now, Jane and George. At William's order she slipped through the shadows the way they had come. At this point, the two other guards would notice a break in their rhythm and hurry back to see what had happened to the other two.

Sure enough, a soldier, bayonet fixed, ran toward her.

She leaped from the shadows, knife at the ready, and slid the blade up and through his ribs, her other hand over his mouth. Her vampire strength and speed proved true. Blood spilled, hot and steaming, and the soldier staggered and then fell, his weapon clattering on the ground, hands clutching at her and then at nothing. She licked a little warm blood from her hand and ran on to join Clarissa and James, who had been sent to deal with the sentries who kept guard in front of the stable. There were only two of them, and they were dead by the time she arrived, the brazier felled and bright coals fading on the cobbles.

They retreated back into the shadows. This was the dangerous moment; if any more soldiers arrived, William and Luke could be trapped in the explosion.

Then she heard the sound of approaching hooves, the jingle of harness and soldiers.

We should take them, Margaret said.

Too many, James responded. *They'll run us down. A dozen, at least.*

We'll run, draw them off. Clarissa glanced down the street.

No use, they'll know something's afoot, Jane said. She remembered the response of the rat, and of how animals sensed and feared the Damned. *The horses. We must show ourselves to the horses.*

The cavalry approached, the horses at a canter approaching their stable, reins loose, and then the group tightened and became an orderly group once more at the sight of the corpses. They slowed, tightened, and at a command from their leader, drew their swords.

Jane, from the shadows, revealed herself to the leading horse, delving deep into the creature's mind, her fangs lengthening. The horse squealed and shied away from her, while the rider cursed and tried to get his mount under control once more. The efforts of the other vampires turned the group of cavalry into a roiling disorder, hooves sliding on the icy cobblestones.

Go. Are we all together? As Luke and William joined them, a great whoomph of sound arose and for a moment the street became as bright as day, and then they were running as flaming debris rained down, running back into the shadows and darkness.

The journey back to Queens Square took some time, the streets crowded with French soldiers. Luke led them on a twisting, complex route through mews and alleys and narrow streets in the older part of the town, choosing always the darkest and quietest places.

In the drawing room of the house on Queens Square a group of guests clustered at the window, exclaiming at the lurid orange of the sky. The others from the night's mission stood in a cluster, still carrying the scent of smoke on their clothes. Footmen served glasses of champagne.

"To our fledglings!" William raised his glass to Jane and George. "Well done, both of you. Tonight you were assigned tasks that, had you failed, would have threatened our whole enterprise, yet you triumphed. Jane, your quick thinking with the cavalry was well done indeed."

"Now may we dine?" George asked. He eyed a pretty woman, who blushed and giggled behind her fan.

William smiled and raised a hand. "Not so fast, George. As a reward, you and Jane may choose your dining partner for the night, Damned or mortal."

There was a murmur of surprise in the room, followed by applause; an invitation to dine from a fellow member of the Damned was a high honor, particularly for a fledgling.

"Most obliged," George said. "Clarissa, will you have me?"

Clarissa smiled and held out a hand to him. They retired to one of the curtained alcoves.

Across the room Jane received waves of hatred and resentment from Margaret and an attempt to once more plant seeds of doubt and divisiveness in her mind. Elated by praise from her Creator, Jane pushed Margaret's jealousy away.

"I choose Luke."

Chapter 17

A silence fell on the room at Jane's request. She discerned rapid reactions of shock, amusement, and anger, most of the latter from Margaret.

"This is a somewhat unusual request." William spoke quietly to Jane. "He is your Bearleader."

"My Bearleader by adoption, sir, as you well know."

"There is also the matter of a former association with another of our company." William's gaze shifted from Luke to Margaret.

Despite the formality and the careful avoidance of names, all of the Damned present, and possibly some of the mortals, would pick up on the undercurrent, the unspoken. Jane felt for Margaret: how dreadful to have your humiliation revealed to all, to see your affections spurned. On the other hand, it could be Jane's own humiliation that was to follow. She waited.

"The lady in question and I no longer have an understanding," Luke said. "I have renounced her as my Consort."

"Margaret?" William addressed her directly.

Margaret let out her breath in a long hiss. "Vows were made, sir."

"Ah, yes. Your vow to Mr. Cole." Luke's lips parted slightly to reveal his fangs.

"We have long accepted that the rules of mortals do not apply to us, Luke. Margaret, what say you?"

She bowed her head. "I defer to the gentleman. If he wishes to make a lowborn and bastard fledgling his Consort, I shall not stand in his way." With one last, venomous glance at Jane, she left the room.

Luke bowed to Jane. "I'm honored."

She had thought his affections engaged when they first met at the Pump Room—certainly he had admitted to an attachment, but now, with a greater knowledge of the Damned, Jane recognized that his wish for a reconciliation with Mrs. Cole was for her to be with the others as much as with him. For the Damned must cleave to one another, their bonds as strong as love or death.

It is true. He reached for her hand. *We were Consorts, but that is a lesser loyalty among us.*

"You mean I cannot expect constancy from you?"

"Certainly. As much as I can give and so long as love lasts. Maybe our love shall prove immortal." He drew her toward a curtained alcove where a low divan stood, heaped with velvet and satin pillows. "But our greater loyalty—yours and mine—is to all of the Damned."

She surprised herself with a delighted giggle. "And so I am your Consort!"

"And I yours." He knelt on the pillows and extended his hand to draw her down to him.

"Like royalty."

He shrugged. "Some of us are royalty. Or rather, we were."

"Were you?"

"Jane. Dear Jane, I have all of eternity to tell you of myself." He raised his hand to his neckcloth and untied it.

"Yes, and you have all of eternity to distract me when I ask." And she was distracted, watching the slow uncurl of the cotton cloth, its fall and spill onto the dark blue of his coat, and the gradual unveiling of the tender skin of his throat.

"Your trouble, Jane, is that you speculate upon what will or may be." He paused, the neckcloth half loosened, to unbutton his coat. "You observe, you weave stories."

"Once I did," she said. "No longer."

He traced her neck with one finger. "It is the mortal in you still that experiences regret. It shall pass."

Hurry up! I'm hungry!

His actions slowed, his fingers stilled on a coat button, and he gave a slow, satisfied smile. Mortified, she realized he had overheard her thoughts.

"I beg your pardon," she muttered.

"On the contrary, I am most flattered by your ardor."

"I regret it's mostly hunger."

"So you may like to think." He slid the coat from his shoulders and began, with excruciating slowness, on the buttons of his waistcoat.

She, meanwhile, dispatched her own coat, waistcoat, and neckcloth in short order, fangs aching, and toed her boots off. "I should like to wear something pretty for you," she said with a sudden burst of sadness that came from a place that was now far distant. Once she and her sister pored over fashion papers and labored at endless small adaptations to their gowns, for when they found love at a provincial assembly, they would want to remember every detail, every ribbon and trim and embellishment, of what they wore at the moment their lives changed.

"You're dressed as prettily as I am," Luke said, "although my waistcoat is finer, I think. Is that not enough? I suppose you could ask Ann to dress you up. Or maybe not."

Jane followed his gaze to another alcove, where George and Clarissa now tangled with Ann, down to her stockings and garters and little else. "I think quite definitely not," she said. "I shall manage as I am."

She pulled at one end of his neckcloth and drew it from his neck, tossing it aside, where it lay abandoned in creamy loops on the bloodred velvet pillows.

She woke to a tinny, clinking, repetitive sound and rolled over and stretched, well pleased and her hunger sated. Luke was gone; she remembered him slipping away some time in the night. By the light it must be afternoon, at least. She pulled on breeches and shirt and stepped out, ready to investigate the strange noise.

The Prince of Wales sat at the pianoforte, slumped and dejected, wearing only a shirt. One finger tapped a key, over and over.

"George?"

"Beg your pardon, did I wake you?"

"What's wrong?"

He shook his head. "It's foolish. I'm having the time of my life, all this debauchery and blood and fighting, but . . ."

She sat on the bench beside him and slipped an arm around his shoulders. "Don't be sad, George."

"It's gone, Jane." He tapped the note again. "It's not music. It's just a sound."

She reached for a book of music that lay on the lid of the instrument. "Have you tried . . . ?"

He flipped the pages. "Ah, I think I used to play this one." He set the book on the music stand and smoothed the pages flat. He placed his hands on the keyboard and shook his head as he produced the opening phrase of the sonata.

"No good. It's strange, there's something missing; it's all

empty noise. I remember you said something similar about your writing. Is it the same?"

"I fear so."

He closed the book and laid it on the instrument again. "It will come back, I suppose, when I . . . you know. I hope so. It's foolish of me to be so downhearted. And you? Now you've taken up with Luke, do you still plan to take the cure?"

"Let's go downstairs for a cup of tea." She was not ready to consider that question, not after last night.

He brightened. "Excellent idea. I wonder how long we'll enjoy tea." He stood and offered her his arm. "If you do, ah, return, Jane, I trust we'll remain friends."

"I'd like to think we will, but we'll be vastly separated. And we may not like each other so much."

"I suppose you're right." He sighed again as he opened the drawing room door. "You mean you won't like me."

She was about to ask him if he really believed the Prince of Wales would care to associate with an obscure country parson's daughter, when something crashed through the window and bounced on the carpet.

"Good God, a stone! Is there a riot?" George asked.

"I trust you won't call upon the French to subdue it—" She pulled him out of the way as another missile followed the first.

"Damned fornicating blasphemers!" someone shouted from the street. "Go to hell, where you belong!"

Jane picked her way across the broken glass and, flattening herself against the drawn-back shutters, peered out of the window. A group of people, mostly men, were gathered in the street below, preparing to throw more stones.

She heard the front door open, and saw the crowd scatter and then run.

The front door slammed shut and footfalls thudded on the stairs.

William rushed into the drawing room. "Are you hurt?"

"No," Jane replied, before realizing that all his attention was directed at George, and felt foolish.

"What the devil's going on?" George asked.

"Bad news." William tugged at the bellpull. "The French arrested and hung seven men this morning in retaliation for the destruction of the powder store."

"They confessed to it?" George asked.

"Of course not. The French chose seven at random. They didn't care about the food wagons being captured, but this is another matter." There was a touch of impatience in William's voice. "Before we know it, the French will be on our doorstep, for they've started arresting citizens on trumped-up charges. Put your breeches on, George. We'll move at nightfall. Where the devil are the footmen?"

Luke entered the drawing room. "I sent them to inquire if the other houses are safe. This changes things entirely."

"Can we trust the footmen?" George asked.

"Why, certainly. They know we shall hunt them down and rip their throats out if they betray us. But this is what comes of involving mortals in our affairs, Luke. We have always regretted it. Always."

The door slammed as William left.

" 'Pon my word, he's a sympathetic fellow," George said.

Luke shook his head. "Jane, pack your things and then come with me. We'll take a walk around the town and see what the mood is." He added with a wink: "Pray put on a pretty gown if you so wish."

Jane went upstairs to the room that she had not even slept in yet, and packed the clothes that she had unpacked the day before. She hesitated as she picked up her manuscript. At this point it was only so much ballast, fit only for converting to spills or cutting into strips to curl her hair. But she put it in with her other possessions, if only to remind herself of her former life and of Cassandra.

Ann, dark shadows under her eyes, arrived yawning to help her with stays and gown, and repacked some of the clothes, complaining that Jane would make yet more ironing for her. Finally, bonnet on, with a muff and gloves she did not need but had to wear so as not to attract attention to herself, Jane arrived downstairs to find Luke giving directions to a group of roughly dressed men who had dragged some boxes and chests into the hall.

"Where will we go?" she asked.

"You'll find out tonight." He raised a hand to her cheek. "But how do you do this day, Miss Austen? You have a certain sleek, satisfied air I've not seen before."

"I do very well. You look much the same."

"Our blood is well matched." He raised her hand, pushing the glove back to kiss the bare skin of her wrist, a sensitive spot that made her shiver with delight. So she had discovered last night, when other mysteries were revealed to her.

"Oh, do go out and do something useful." William pushed the dining-room door open and viewed them with distaste. "And be careful. Luke, remember you are supposed to be dead, and Jane, keep your wits about you."

Luke fitted a pair of gold-rimmed spectacles on his nose as disguise and took his swordstick from the stand in the hallway. Arm in arm, he and Jane left the house.

"I should like to walk with you and not feel that I must guard myself so," Jane said.

"I regret it is how things are for us, even when the country is at peace. We have always had our enemies. Tell me what you can sense."

She concentrated. "I feel . . . I feel a little anger. It's strange, there was even less when the French invaded, for then people were mostly sullen and shocked. But also hope and excitement, and some relief. And there's food again—look how many people carry baskets as though they have been to the market."

Luke stopped to view the wares of a woman who sold gingerbread on the street.

"Go on, sir," she said. "Buy a piece for your sweetheart—look how hollow her cheeks are, poor thing. The waters will set you up right away, miss—that and my gingerbread."

Luke smiled and handed the woman a sixpence. "Is trade good, mistress?"

"Surely it is, just as the Frenchies said it would be." She handed Luke a handful of gingerbread molded into fantastic, twisted shapes, sprinkled with sugar. "Why, yesterday the market was as full of goods as I've ever seen. Of course, the town is always cheered by a hanging, but it's a pity they blamed honest men for what those wicked Damned did." Her fingers, freed of the gingerbread, formed the ancient sign against evil, forefinger and pinky extended, the others tucked under.

Jane, her mouth full of gingerbread, swallowed and would have said something, but Luke flashed her a warning to be silent.

"Indeed!" Luke said. "How extraordinary the Damned should be here, when everyone knows the waters are poison to their kind."

"Oh, not for long." The woman nodded at a poster stuck to the side of a building. "They'll round them up and cut off their heads, to be sure, and good riddance to them. Why, that storehouse of grain they blew up last night was to have been given to the poor."

"Quite an extraordinary explosion that 'grain' made," Luke said.

"Yes, that's what my man said, but doubtless, they have their wicked ways." The woman dipped a curtsy and approached another customer on the street.

Luke pinched off a piece of gingerbread before Jane devoured it all and led her over to view the poster on the wall. In unevenly set type, it announced that a tribunal led by General Renard was to seek out enemies of the city. Citizens who reported suspicious activities would be given rewards.

"So it has begun," Jane said. The gingerbread turned dry and tasteless in her mouth.

"So it has, but it will not last long." Luke did not sound overly concerned.

"How do you know?"

"Oh, things are going well elsewhere."

"What things? Where?"

"Patience. May I have another piece of gingerbread?"

She handed him a very small fragment. "Mmm, delicious," she said to provoke him as she chewed the last mouthful.

"What next? Would you like to see the hanged men? I believe they're outside the Abbey where I met my most recent end."

"Oh, stop it." She pulled her gloves back on. "What a dreadful thing to say. That was horrible."

"It wasn't very pleasant for me, either." He linked her arm in his and they strolled on.

As they turned into Westgate Street, the door of a house flew open and a number of French soldiers pulled a struggling man, coatless and with a spoon in one hand, into the street.

"But I haven't done anything! I was eating my dinner!"

"You are to be questioned. Come with us."

"But—"

One of the soldiers hit the man with the butt of his musket. He dropped to his knees, one hand at his bloodied face, and they dragged him away, his feet slithering on the paving stones.

Is he one of us? Jane asked in horror.

No. The French seek to take advantage of people's fears. They hand out food, yet arrest or hang the innocent. They seek to divide us.

"Sir!" A voice came from behind them. "Miss Austen, I have a message for you."

They turned to see one of the footmen from the house, out of breath, who must have run after them.

"Miss Austen, a message came from Paragon Place just after you left and Mr. William told me which way you'd gone. Mr. Austen is ill."

"Oh no!" She turned to Luke. "I must go to him."

"As you wish."

"He is my father! Do not be so cold, Luke."

He drew her aside, her hand in his. "Do you wish me to accompany you?"

"No, of course you cannot! It would be exceedingly awkward to have a dead man sit in the drawing room and make conversation over tea. Pray tell me where the new house is and I shall make my way there when I can."

He shook his head. "No, it is too dangerous for you to know. One of us shall come for you. You will be safe enough with your family, but you will need to dine."

Memories flooded back into her mind, pricked at her skin and tantalized her fangs. "Of course."

"You should go." He raised her gloved hand to his lips and sought the small gap where his fangs could graze her wrist. *There is so much I would say to you, yet I fear you will surrender to your family's influence. Come back to me.*

"As soon as I can I shall return." *Despise me for it if you will, but I cannot surrender my former loyalties as easily as you expect me to.*

He straightened and clasped her gloved hand briefly between his. "Go, then. Simon shall escort you. Be careful."

She set off with the footman, turning back for one last look at Luke, and then chided herself for being overly dramatic. Now she had to think of her father and her family, and not agitate herself with thoughts that this might be her final duty as Jane Austen.

"What did the footman from Paragon Place say?" she asked.

"Very little, miss, only that you must come home."

They continued through streets that still showed signs of recent battle, and Jane was surprised to see several people, mostly young men, wearing revolutionary cockades, strutting about and ostentatiously addressing one another as "Citizen." But they were regarded with cynical tolerance by most of their neighbors; and altogether there was the feel of a community trying to establish some sort of normalcy.

When they reached Paragon Place, Jane ran ahead and the front door opened. A footman must have been watching out for her arrival, but the hall was deserted. There was no sign of either Cassandra or her mother.

Garonne stepped forward. "Citizeness Austen, I arrest you in the name of the Republic."

Chapter 18

"What!" Jane shook his hand from her arm. "How dare you! I am not subject to you."

"On the contrary, Citizeness, I have every right to exercise my authority over one who is the enemy of the Republic." He nodded to a pair of soldiers who stepped forward and gripped her arms.

"What on earth do you think I have done?" Rapidly she assessed her situation. She could break away, but it was still daylight, too early for her to seek refuge in the shadows. *Luke, help me.* But there was no response.

"Where are my parents and Cassandra?"

"Not here," Garonne said. He gave her an unpleasant smile. "If you were to escape, ma'amselle Jane, even if you were able to, I should be obliged to arrest them in your stead. They are at church. They are safe enough for the moment. Or for as long as you comply with the authorities and tell them all they wish to know."

He led her into the street. A cart stood there, with half a dozen other prisoners, their hands bound, their faces showing varying degrees of shock and bewilderment.

"If I may, Miss Austen." Garonne held out a length of rope.

She could snap the rope with very little effort, lunge forward and tear out Garonne's throat and probably take the two soldiers as well, but she did not dare risk her family's safety. She held out her wrists. "So this is how you repay my family's hospitality, Captain."

"Most grudging hospitality, as you have said many times." He let her bound hands drop and helped her into the cart in a mockery of civility. "Tell the tribunal the truth and you shall be home again soon enough, ma'amselle Jane. Or back in your lover's bed, whichever it is you prefer." He gave her an insolent salute as the cart bumped forward.

Jane apologized to the other people in the cart and squeezed herself down into the straw that covered its floor. This might even have been one of the food carts she and the others had captured—it held a faint scent of blood but a stronger sense of terror from the people already aboard.

"I was having my dinner!" complained a familiar voice, coming from a man whose face was now covered in drying blood. He still clutched his spoon in one hand and, despite the violence of his arrest, which Jane had witnessed only a short time before, his napkin remained tucked into his waistcoat.

"There has to be a mistake," another man muttered. "I am a very respected member of the city. I own three shops."

A young woman wearing an unseasonably flimsy gown and with the remains of rouge on her face gave a cynical smile and leaned forward to stroke Jane's fur tippet. "Very nice. My advice is, sell it once we're inside, and buy yourself some comfort."

"Inside where?"

She shrugged. "Oh, they'll imprison us I should think for a

time. But we're not headed for the prison. This is the fashionable part of town. What did a nice young lady like you do to fall afoul of the Frenchies?"

"Hold your tongue," said the respectable shopkeeper. "You've no cause to address your betters."

"My betters? We're all the same in this cart, sir. Liable to lose our heads."

Another woman gave a frightened whimper. She held a basket with a lid on her lap, her hands clenched tight on the handle.

"They say they've beheaded over fifty in London so far," said a pale-faced young man with shaky hands. Jane could scent his fear and wondered what he had to hide.

"You are misinformed, sir. I heard only thirty-two." The gentleman whose dinner had been interrupted removed his napkin and dabbed at his face. "But they say the Prince of Wales was among them."

"No, I have it on good authority that he is in Scotland, where one of the most noble families in the land has the privilege and honor of protecting him," said the shopkeeper.

"And they're welcome to him," said the painted woman.

Jane, who had last seen the Prince standing bewildered among shards of broken glass, wearing only his shirt, did not bother to argue with them.

"What's in your basket, mistress?" the painted woman asked.

The older woman whimpered and clutched the basket even tighter. The cart jolted, bumping the riders in the cart together, and the basket flew open to reveal a chicken that squawked and flapped among them.

One of the soldiers guarding the prisoners darted forward, grabbed the bird, and wrung its neck, making a cheerful comment about dinner, while the chicken's owner wept, her apron held to her face.

"That's a pity, we could have eaten it," said the painted woman.

"It's *my* chicken," the other woman said between sobs. "But I can tell a slut such as you will have no trouble getting a full belly."

"Of any sort." The owner of the spoon waggled it suggestively at her.

"Business is business," the girl said. "You won't be so proud in a day or two." She was younger than Jane had thought, not more than sixteen, but her cynicism and worldly bravado made her seem older.

"Aren't you cold?" Jane said.

"I'm used to it."

Jane handed over her muff.

"What do you want for it?" The girl's eyes were hard and suspicious.

Jane had thought to offer it as a gift but realized to do so would insult her. Everything in this girl's world had a price. "Very well. You owe me a favor. I may call upon you later."

The girl nodded and held out a hand, bare and reddened with the cold. "My name is Polly."

Jane removed her glove and took Polly's hand. "I am Jane."

The contact of the girl's skin sent a flurry of disjointed images into her mind—a lover gone away, a French officer or two, possibly three (much brandy and rumpled sheets and lasciviousness), and a tangled mess of jealousy and anger.

Polly released Jane's hand to delve deep within the silk-lined fur of the muff and shiver with pleasure, not cold. "I may have to sell it. I hope you won't be offended."

"Not at all," Jane said.

The cart turned onto Brunswick Place.

"This is the Riding School," Polly said. "They're going to keep us here, I think."

A group of people who had been waiting outside ran forward, shouting to the occupants of the cart and thrusting letters and baskets into their hands, begging for them to be delivered to prisoners.

The soldiers shoved the supplicants away, but grabbed the baskets which Jane was sure would never reach those for whom they were intended. Jane tried to gather some letters that had been thrown into the cart, but a soldier snatched them from her.

"Give those to me!" he said and ripped one open. "They write dangerous words."

"Particularly when read upside down," Jane said in French.

He snarled and slapped her, a casual, heavy blow with the back of his hand. She tumbled over in the cart, blood trickling from her lip. Her fangs extended in anger as she thought of how she could burst her bonds and rip the life from the soldier, how she would have no mercy on him. She fought to control her fangs and assured her neighbors she was not badly hurt as she struggled to sit upright again.

"Really, it is very little," she said, trying to sound shocked and ladylike. "Thank you, sir, I am sure it appears far worse than it is. It hardly pains me at all." As the wound would heal in a matter of an hour or so, it was politic to make light of it.

Large gates creaked open and the cart lumbered into a cobbled stable yard. Soldiers lounged around, eyeing the new arrivals, particularly the women, made clumsy by their bound wrists as they clambered from the cart. Jane offered to hold the basket for the woman whose chicken had escaped, but she clutched it to her, shaking her head in terror.

"My good man," the respectable shopkeeper said to the nearest soldier, "there has been a mistake. Take me to your commanding officer, if you please."

The soldier grinned. "Yes, milord, of course, milord." He

aimed a vicious punch at the shopkeeper's considerable belly, and laughed as the man sank to his knees, retching.

Polly, meanwhile, smiled at a soldier who produced a knife and cut her bonds, gazing into her bosom with great appreciation. Jane snapped the rope binding her wrists and looked about her. There were too many soldiers at the gate for her to attempt an escape, even at night. A large iron cooking pot, tended by a hefty woman in an elaborate hat, steamed on a fire in the center of the courtyard. More soldiers leaned on the stable doors that opened into the yard, looking out at the activity. A wide doorway opposite led into the large building that housed a riding ring, an area where prisoners walked and others had claimed favored spots, wrapped in their cloaks.

Polly tapped her on the shoulder. "I have sold the muff for two blankets. This one is for you."

"Thank you." Although Jane did not need it, she draped the large, rough fabric over her shoulders. A dozen or so fleas, panicked by her presence, leaped out and away.

"Ooh! Do that for me, if you please!" Polly handed her the second blanket. "How do you do it?"

Jane shrugged. "Fleas don't like me. I'm lucky, I suppose." She handed a blanket, free of vermin, back to Polly. "I fear they will return. After all, they must hop somewhere."

"You could do that for money or food." Polly's thoughtful expression suggested that she might offer herself as Jane's handler. "So, why did they arrest you?"

"There was this French officer . . ." Jane let her voice trail away. She sighed.

"A respectable girl like you! Well, any woman may fall." Polly sounded quite cheerful. She wrapped her blanket around herself. "Let us see what is going on here and how we may best settle in."

There must have been fifty people, arrested that day, men and women and a few children, roaming around the Riding School. Some sat huddled and wretched, refusing to talk, some weeping. One group had acquired some bottles of spirits and were busy getting drunk, playing dice on the uneven surface of the cobbled stable yard.

The woman with the feathered hat looked up from her cooking pot, flapping one arm to drive away smoke. "Sixpence a day to eat, ladies. The Frenchies will bring in bread but you may be sure it's poor stuff." She eyed Jane with interest. "I'm Mrs. Glimm. I'll take your gloves for food for seven days. 'Course, if they cut off your head before the week is out, I'll have the better part of the bargain." She roared with laughter and stirred the contents of the pot with a piece of wood.

"Has the tribunal tried anyone yet?"

"They'll start tomorrow, so Pierre says." Mrs. Glimm nodded at a soldier, a skinny fellow half her girth who gazed at her with adoring eyes. He burst into a torrent of French that Jane recognized as a declaration of passion.

"Can't understand a word he says. It don't matter." The woman's mottled face softened as she looked at him. "What he has between his legs does well enough for all it's a French one. Just like an English one, eh?" This last was addressed to Polly, who nodded in agreement.

"But he could not save you from arrest?" Jane asked.

"Lord love you, no, he didn't arrest me. He pays me to cook." And to spy on others too, Jane thought, but she smiled politely and told Mrs. Glimm she would consider the trade of the gloves. Her hands were smaller than Mrs. Glimm's, but she had no doubt the gloves would be sold for something else.

"Miss Austen!" She turned at the sound of a familiar voice to see Mr. Thomas, the apothecary.

She gave him a polite nod, the condescending greeting of a lady to an inferior, for the benefit of Mrs. Glimm, who, feathers nodding on her hat, threw a handful of dirty potatoes into the pot.

He understood; he bowed and backed away. After a few minutes, during which Polly helped put more wood on the fire, Jane strolled into the indoor Riding School and sought him out.

"How long have you been here, Mr. Thomas?"

"Since this morning, ma'am." He glanced around. "We must be careful. I daresay they do not know you for what you are?"

"I don't believe so. What do they intend to do with us?"

"The tribunal will try us soon. I've heard rumors that they expect a guillotine to be delivered to the city any day."

"And who is on the tribunal?"

"Renard, but as for the others, I don't know. I trust there will be men of integrity with him. But what happened to the rest of your household?"

"I believe they're safe, but I am concerned for my family."

"Ah." He looked at her with sympathy. "I am most sorry, Miss Austen."

Overcome with emotion, she shook her head. Until now, the enormity of Luke's silence had not made any real impact on her. Maybe he thought that she had abandoned him and returned to her family. Once again she tried to call to him, and then to William. A faint echo of a response came to her, and then silence. For the first time she understood the immense importance the Damned placed on loyalty to one's fellows; to be a solitary vampire was dangerous and lonely.

She listened to the swirling emotions and thoughts of those around her. She was the only one of the Damned among mortals who did not understand her and would fear and hate her when they discovered her identity. She was not safe from the French and neither was she safe from her companions, not after the rumors spread about the explosion.

"Mr. Thomas, I know you mean well, but I beg of you, do not seem overly familiar with me. I believe there are spies all around. These are desperate times and people will do anything to save their skins."

"I regret you're right, Miss Austen." He gave a friendly nod and bow, that of one casual acquaintance to another, and strolled away.

She looked through the open door into the courtyard to see Polly, in the gathering dusk, talking to a French soldier. Jane hesitated, wondering if Polly was being threatened, but as she strained to hear their conversation, she realized that she was negotiating with him.

"Eh, *jolie fille*, I give you food, good food, the time you are here."

Polly, even with a rough blanket around her, managed a seductive sway toward him. "Very well. You pay me a shilling first."

"A shilling? Then I take a little taste, so." The soldier grinned and put his hand into Polly's bosom.

She slapped him away. "A shilling or nothing."

The man fumbled in his pockets and pulled out some coins.

"A shilling." Polly swiped a half-crown from his hand and tucked it away in a pocket in the side seam of her gown. "And food for every time after."

She led him inside the stable.

Mrs. Glimm banged on her cooking pot with a discarded stirrup, and the prisoners streamed out to be fed. A large basket of bread stood nearby and was emptied within a few seconds by those who could not afford her dubious cooking.

Jane waited until Polly and her soldier emerged from the stables, he buttoning up his breeches and whistling loudly, she with a large piece of bread, of much better quality than the prisoners', wrapped around a slice of bacon. Polly offered Jane a bite.

She took a small mouthful as a gesture of good will. "Polly, I'll give you my gloves if you can find me pen and ink and a way to send a letter out of here."

Polly fingered the leather of Jane's gloves. "I'll see what I can do."

"You may take them now."

Polly swallowed the last of her bread and bacon. "He says we'll be tried tomorrow." She jerked her head toward the soldier. "I don't know how much longer we'll have."

Jane considered her situation. She would need all her strength and wits and for that she needed to dine, and to dine soon. "I've changed my mind, then. I don't think I will have time for a letter. But there is something I need and maybe you can help."

Polly blinked as she saw Jane's canines emerge. "Lord love us, you're one of them?"

"Yes. I need to dine. I won't take much. Are you willing?"

She grinned. "Willing? Could be the best thing that's happened all day. All week, even." She held out her wrist. "If you please."

Jane bit into her wrist and tasted both the first surge of blood and Polly's shiver of pleasure. And then she tasted hostility and outrage, a small, resentful presence that made a violent protest. She drew back, breathed on the wound and licked it clean.

"Polly!"

The girl smiled, drowsy with pleasure. "Well, go on. You'll take more than a mouthful."

"I can't. You're with child."

"What!" Polly drew back. "I thought—you're sure?"

"Quite sure. Your child was not at all pleased that you give away the blood you share."

"Oh, Lord. Nothing but trouble," Polly said. "I'm sorry I couldn't oblige. I can ask—"

"I beg you do not mention my nature to anyone. The towns-people have turned against us for the most part."

Polly nodded and held out Jane's gloves.

"No, keep them. I don't feel the cold. I wear them only for propriety."

As darkness fell, the prisoners retreated into the riding ring, huddled together for warmth. A few squabbles broke out over particularly prime spots, free of drafts, and some of the children and several of the adults sobbed or cried out in fear in their sleep. Polly retreated into the stables to sleep with her Frenchman ("He may smell, but at least he's warm").

Jane crept into the riding ring and laid her blanket over a family who slept near the door, in the coldest spot. She did not feel in the least sleepy, but desired solitude and quiet. In the stable yard the soldiers on guard gathered around Mrs. Glimm's fire, talking softly of their homes and the families they might never see again. Jane melted into the shadows and listened to them and the small sounds of the night.

I will not forget you.

The thought came to her so distinctly she jumped as if some-one had shouted in her ear.

Luke, where are you?

There was no reply. Was Luke's message a farewell, a promise, a reproach? She had no way of knowing.

Ice glazed the muddy cobbles. Overhead, on this rare, clear night, the stars glittered, cold and remote, and Jane stood mo-tionless, watching their stately progress across the heavens until they faded with the dawn.

"Why, you're up early, miss." Mrs. Glimm stirred an unpleasant-looking porridge over her cooking fire. "Sixpence if you've changed your mind. Or the gloves."

"Thank you, ma'am. I'll take the offer under consideration."

A commotion broke out at the gates and for one moment Jane hoped that it was a rescue. The soldiers, who had been lounging around the courtyard, sprang into action, keeping the prisoners back, as the gate swung open to admit another cartload of prisoners, terrified people, some of whom were only partly dressed and must have been hauled from their beds. They climbed out and stood looking around in disbelief and fear.

An officer on horseback accompanied the cart. His horse shied and steam rose from its damp flanks as it caught Jane's scent, making the carthorse in turn shift nervously in its traces.

"Citizens!" the officer called out. "If I read your name, you come here." He pulled a list from inside his coat and read out some half dozen names.

Jane's was among them, as was that of the very respectable shopkeeper, who looked somewhat the worse for wear after his ill treatment and a cold night in the Riding School, and the woman who still clutched the basket that had once held her chicken.

"It must be a mistake," the very respectable shopkeeper said to Jane as they were chained together. "A mistake, I assure you. I shall send for my lawyer as soon as I am able. And character witnesses, yes. They will see that they should not have arrested me."

"It is more than likely we shall be tried under the laws of the French Republic," Jane said. "I believe that French law does not allow for a presumption of innocence."

"But—but this is England!" the shopkeeper cried in bewilderment. "I have done nothing wrong. As I told the officers, I must make a profit, for it is my livelihood and how was I to know that . . ."

Jane put a finger to her lips, chains clanking, to warn him that silence might be the wiser course, but the gentleman continued to bemoan his fate and declare his innocence.

Surrounded by soldiers, they were marched out of the Riding School and a short distance down Russell Street to the New Assembly Rooms.

Jane thought of when she had last roamed these streets, learning to use the darkness, hunting with Luke. She remembered the soft pressure and taste of his mouth, sweeter than the fresh blood on his lips, that surprising first embrace, her fear at her own boldness.

Jane gazed at the portico of the building, where, formerly, sedan chairs had plied their trade. Now soldiers stood on guard. They were escorted into the foyer of the building, where, to Jane's relief, the chains that bound them together were removed, although the shackles on their wrists remained.

The first time Jane had been to the New Assembly Rooms she had clutched Cassandra's hand so tightly she feared she might split her glove, overwhelmed by the fashionable elegance of the crowd and the brightness of the many wax candles. Through the doors there, flung open to admit newcomers, a large crowd had danced with an elegance far surpassing similar gatherings in Basingstoke or Portsmouth.

But now the doors were closed and a French soldier stood on guard. The air was dim and cold, the stone floor clammy.

"You wait," a soldier told them. "You do not talk."

Jane was relieved, knowing that otherwise the respectable shopkeeper would once again run through his usual complaints and denials. She sank to the floor, leaning against a pillar, and observed her fellow prisoners; in addition to the ones she already knew there was an elderly man with an unmistakably arrogant, aristocratic bearing, and a young, well-dressed couple who held hands and whispered together.

The door to the ballroom opened a crack and the soldier on guard held a whispered conversation with whoever was inside.

"Citizen Green."

"That is I," said the respectable shopkeeper. "And it is Mr. Green, if you please."

The soldier at the door sniggered and made a chopping motion with one hand. With the butt of the soldier's musket, the respectable shopkeeper was shoved through the door.

They waited. The young couple whispered together while the elderly gentleman folded his hands, eyes closed as though in prayer; the other woman continued to clutch her basket as though it represented safety and normalcy.

Jane closed her eyes. She imagined attending an assembly here. What sort of gown would she wear? Possibly something like Clarissa's, white with silver net, and with a few silk flowers in her hair. She would like to have sandals that laced in the classical style and showed off her narrow feet and slender ankles. As she moved into the brightly lit room where a dance was already under way, a handsome gentleman—Luke, of course—would approach her and ask for the next dance, bowing low. Walking around the ballroom, greeting friends and acquaintances, she would hear whispered comments on the elegance of her gown and what a handsome couple they made.

She hoped Luke did not overhear her daydream; how embarrassing to have one's fantasies, however innocent, known. And it certainly was an innocent fantasy—as one of the Damned, should she not be daydreaming of spurting blood and athletic carnal relations with the gentleman? But she would be willing to undergo any amount of ridicule from him if he would send her word again.

Mr. Green, the emphatically innocent shopkeeper, had not returned. She could hear, very faintly, a murmur of voices, but even her keen hearing could not distinguish words.

The door cracked open again and a whispered consultation took place between whoever was inside and the soldier on duty.

"Citizeness Austen."

She stood, straightening her skirts and bonnet as best she could and walked forward. The soldier opened the door a little more and pushed her inside.

"You may approach, Citizeness Austen."

The main room of the Assembly Rooms had a dingy, dim appearance and a strong scent of blood. She saw it now, a large puddle on the wooden floor, straight ahead of her. A little weak winter sunlight came through the elegant arched windows. A dozen or so soldiers lined the walls. They stared at her with curiosity. At the end of the room, on the small stage where the musicians played, a table was set up. Three men sat there; one was Renard, who had commanded her to approach, and the other wore the uniform of a high-ranking French officer.

And the third man—oh, thank God. Everything would be well now.

Chapter 19

Colonel John Poulett left the table and stepped down from the stage.

He took her bare hand in his gloved one and spoke softly. "Miss Austen, pray have no fear. I regret deeply that you have been inconvenienced."

"Thank you, sir. Or should I address you as Citizen?"

He grimaced. "It might be best."

He turned to the other men at the table and addressed them. "General, Citizen, I assure you Citizeness Austen is of no threat to the Republic or any of you. You should release her immediately."

"Ah." General Renard winked at her. "So, you break my nephew's heart, eh, Citiziness?"

"That is my offense, General? It seems rather a hard price to pay, if every woman who refused a gentleman's attentions were to be arrested and flung into prison. It certainly does not endear the captain to me."

"Ah, you English, you joke under bad circumstances; it is admirable." He called to a soldier to bring Jane a chair. "In prison, you say?"

"Yes, General."

"But—but when I heard of your arrest, I gave orders that you were to be placed in the very best accommodation, Citizeness, since I could not free you without many papers and the formality of this trial. Surely they did not put you in with the common traitors and criminals!"

"I have been at the Riding School."

"This is unconscionable!" Poulett rose and addressed the other officers at the table. "Miss Austen is a gentlewoman."

"A thousand apologies!" Renard gave a wild wave of both hands. "I am desolated. Sit, sit, Poulett. But you shall go free soon, Citizeness. Now, just a very few questions. I must fill out these papers, you see . . ." He perched a pair of spectacles on his nose, which gave him the appearance of a short, kindly cleric, and rummaged among the papers on the table.

"Ah!" A document in his hand, he peered over the lenses at her. "Now, I see you are acquainted with Citizeness Venning. How is the lady?"

"She was quite well when last I saw her."

The third man at the table took notes, the scratch of his pen loud in the room.

"*Bien!*" he beamed at her, all friendliness and ease. "Poor young lady, to lose her brother so. Yet justice had to be done. You knew him too, I believe?"

"I was acquainted with him, yes."

"And?"

"What else can I tell you, General?"

"Ah. This is delicate. You became Citizeness Venning's companion, for I know my nephew was to blame for your hasty departure from the house on Paragon Place. He is too hot in the blood, you know."

"Yes, I was her companion."

"*La pauvre,* she was sad." He smiled again. "No, do not fear, Citizeness Austen, we shall not arrest Citizeness Venning. She pays the price with her tears and the shame of an assassin brother."

Poulett leaned forward, elbows on the table. "Miss—that is, Citizeness Austen—I have a slight acquaintance with Citizeness Venning. As the colonel says, it is a delicate situation. I really feel I should pay a call on her, if you think that appropriate."

So that was why they wanted her, and why they showed such charm and friendliness. They wanted to find Luke and the others, and Poulett was in deep with the French. She hoped the shock of her discovery did not show on her face. "Why, certainly, Citizen. I am sure she would be glad to receive you."

"Later, Citizen," Renard said, with some annoyance. "You English and your morning calls. Let us continue with this business."

"Pardon me, Renard, but maybe Miss Austen knows her address, for she appears to have left the house on Queens Square."

"Bah, you can find her at the Pump Room, I daresay. Or at church." Renard searched his papers again. "Your father, Citizen Austen, seeks to leave the city, still, I believe."

"That is correct, sir."

Poulett looked confused. "Citizeness Austen, you do not know where your employer lives?"

"No, she spoke of moving, but I do not believe firm plans were made."

"And why did your family come to Bath, Citizeness?" Renard continued.

"For my health, and that of my mother, who was also unwell."

"Ah. You look pale, Citizeness. I trust your health improves soon. Well, we are finished here. A thousand apologies for your ill treatment. You may give Colonel Poulett Miss Venning's address, and then you go home."

Jane smiled. "I regret I cannot help you, sir."

"You are sure?" Renard took his spectacles off and closed them with a snap. "Well, that is too bad." He shrugged. "And how is Citizen Venning?"

Jane feigned confusion. "She is unmarried."

"No, I mean her brother. He lives, does he not?"

"But—but he was hanged on your orders, sir."

Renard nodded. He was no longer the affable, slightly comic Frenchman. He beckoned over the soldier who had provided Jane with a chair, and whispered to him. The soldier left the room.

He returned with another prisoner, a bloody, frightened man in chains, who was flung to the floor in front of Jane.

"Yes, sirs, that's her. She is one of them."

She did not recognize him but she recognized the voice. On the night the French invaded and she had fought on the London Road barricade, there had been one of that group of men who had recognized her as one of the Damned. Her heart sank. Almost certainly it was he who had betrayed Mr. Thomas, and probably the others who had been with them that night.

"Now, Citizen, look at her carefully. It was dark, you say. Maybe you take your bonnet off, Citizeness? She wore a bonnet, then?"

"No, no, she wore only a cap, like ladies wear indoors. But I knew right away she was—"

Renard stepped down from the stage and tore at Jane's bonnet strings, flinging her bonnet aside. There was little good humor or civility about him now. "So?"

"Yes, 'tis her." He spat at Jane. "You'll burn in hell, you bloody whore."

Renard nodded at the soldier, who hauled the prisoner to his feet and escorted him from the room.

Jane feigned confusion. "I beg your pardon, sirs. Of what am I accused?"

"Your family must be concerned about you, Miss Austen." Again, Poulett playing the role of the concerned English gentleman. He had rested in her arms and offered his blood to her, taking comfort and pleasure in the act, but now he betrayed her. She was shocked at how painful the realization was.

"I am grateful for your concern, sir."

"Where are they?" Renard shouted, his spittle flying in her face.

"They are at Paragon Place, sir."

"Not them!" Renard grabbed her shoulders. "You think I am a fool? The others of your kind. *Les Damnés.*"

"Now, Renard, calm yourself." Poulett grasped Renard's arm and drew him away. "Miss Austen is gently bred. Why, see how distressed you make her. Ma'am, he is but a rough soldier and he needs your help. Tell us the address and you may go."

"I fear I do not know, sir."

"She fools you, Citizen Poulett. She denies what she is." He turned to the soldier on duty and shouted an order. Jane caught the word *miroir.* Now there could be no escape for her. If only she had been able to dine last night, she might be able to fight her way out, but she could feel her strength fading.

Poulett knelt at her side. "Jane, tell them what they need to know and we will let you go. Quickly, before they bring the mirror."

"You, sir," she replied in an equally quiet, polite voice, "may go to the devil."

"I shall do my best to guarantee the safety of your family, but I can only do so if you tell him what he needs to know. I beg of you, Jane, consider what you do."

"You think I would trust your word after this?"

He fell silent.

The soldier returned with a small, silver-backed mirror, the sort a lady might have on her dressing table. Renard held it in front of Jane's face and gave a crow of triumph, yelling at the officer at the table to write down the evidence.

"So, Citizeness, you know what we do to your kind. You think you live forever, but Madame la Guillotine will send you to hell. Where are the others?"

"I don't know."

He drew back his hand and slapped her face with enough force to knock her from the chair onto the floor. "Tell us!"

"I don't know," she repeated, "and if I did, I would not tell you."

Poulett offered Jane his hand. She ignored it and rose to her feet. Her weakness alarmed her. She knew it was not merely that last night she had barely fed; she was enervated by her isolation from her own kind.

"So. It is almost noon," Renard said. "Tonight you wish to drink blood, I think. It is unfortunate that you are our prisoner and there will be no blood. Perhaps later, in a day or so, you will change your mind about telling us. Or we shall find them, and you suffer for nothing when you could so easily tell us and save yourself. And then, we take your head. That is all. Take her away."

She turned her head to Poulett and showed her fangs, snarling.

He stepped back, fear on his face.

"If ever I have the opportunity, I shall kill you," she said softly. "I may be bound for hell, but I believe you shall be in a greater lake of fire than I, for I have not betrayed my friends."

* * *

Cassandra, I have a fearful headache. Something clanked as she woke, on a hard surface that was surely not any sort of bed, and neither was she in any sort of bedchamber. The ring on the wall that secured her chains and the cobbles on which she lay indicated that this room might once have been built onto the outside of an existing building. Sure enough, the wall behind her was of elegant Bath stone, marred by dripping dampness. Had she been able to feel the cold she would not survive long here.

They must have knocked her unconscious to chain her, once she had been revealed as one of the Damned; in truth she wondered why they had bothered, as weak as she felt. A very little daylight, the heavy, golden light that came just before dusk, filtered through a small high window. She listened. *Luke, where are you? Help me. I am held prisoner, in the Assembly Rooms, I believe.*

From far away she heard a muffled series of thumps. Fireworks? Surely not in daylight. They must be artillery, which meant that the English resurgence, aided by the efforts of the Damned, was under way, as Luke had predicted. She wished she could tell how far off the guns were, for time surely ran out for her.

She was hungry but she would not think of how she longed to dine, or yearned for the flavor of Luke's blood, full of power and joy. Now she wished she had taken more from him, instead of indulging in the nips and bites of amorous play.

The door rattled. She drew her legs beneath her and sat, exploring the back of her head with one hand. Sure enough, there was a large lump there. The door opened and two French soldiers sidled in, one with a pitcher in his hand and a large bundle of straw beneath one arm.

The other kept guard as the first one took a few steps toward her, dropped the straw, and, to her amazement, thrust a crucifix at her.

She giggled. "Put the pitcher down, if you please, so you may cross yourself," she said in French. For good measure she displayed her fangs.

He placed the pitcher on the floor and they both dashed from the room, slamming the door behind them. She heard the rattle of the key in the lock and their footfalls in a rapid and unmilitary retreat.

Encumbered by her chains she crawled toward the pitcher of water but found she could not reach it, even with outstretched arms. Using her feet, she pulled straw toward herself, made herself as comfortable as she could, and waited. She was fairly sure either Poulett or Renard would be here to tempt or bully her, or worse.

The light faded to darkness. The far-off artillery fire continued, and inside, small noises of the night, rustles and rapid heartbeats, emerged. If she must, she could capture a mouse or rat for its blood. She followed the comings and goings of small furred creatures, hoping her stillness would accustom them to her presence.

Luke, protect my family if you will not protect me.

She saw the light first, the bobbing golden light of someone carrying a lantern, and recognized the scent of Poulett, accompanied by another man she did not recognize. For a brief moment she considered attacking Poulett—she was fairly sure she could—dining on him until he was too weak to move, for she wanted his humiliation as much as his death. She rearranged herself on the straw, ready to spring in the faint chance that he might come close to her.

The door opened and Poulett stood inside, the lantern held high. He bent, retrieved the pitcher, and placed it closer to her, stepping back out of her reach.

"I have done all I can, Jane," he said. "There is a warrant for the Austens' arrest but I have delayed it until noon tomorrow. Time is running out."

"I can hear the guns," Jane said. "Time is running out for a traitor such as you."

He ignored her and unbuttoned his coat, removing it to hang on the door.

Her fangs extended, painful and sensitive, as he loosened his shirt cuff and rolled back the sleeve.

"You must be very hungry," he said.

"Not hungry enough to want you." But her fangs betrayed her.

He took a small penknife from his waistcoat pocket and nicked the skin of his wrist. His blood welled and dripped.

"Can you smell it, Jane?"

"Do not flatter yourself, Poulett. Your blood is quite pleasant but nothing extraordinary. I'd rather dine from the rat that runs along the wall behind you."

As she hoped, he turned with a curse and lifted the lantern, peering at the bottom of the wall.

When he faced her again he was all sympathy and concern and she hated him. "Jane, my dear, let us be sensible. Think of your family, for most assuredly they will now be executed for your folly and misplaced loyalty and I can do nothing to help them. Do you think Miss Venning and the rest have even given you a moment's thought since your disappearance? The Damned are beautiful and seductive but faithless; they will use you and toss you aside, and that, I fear, is what has happened." He shrugged. "But of course, that is what you are now you have become one of them. You have lost all Christian feeling; you do not care for Mr. and Mrs. Austen or your sister."

"Why did you turn traitor, Poulett?"

He held his wrist out and blood dripped onto the cobbled

floor. "Come, Jane, I hate to think you will try to crawl here when I have left and lick this blood from the floor. You hunger for my blood. You shall have it. You know what you must do."

She rolled over away from him and stared at the stone wall. She listened to his breathing (and his heartbeat, damn him), the rustle of cotton as he blotted the small cut closed, the slither of the silk lining of his coat as he dressed again.

"Does your new friend Renard know of your weakness for being dined upon?"

His palm caressed embroidered velvet as he straightened his coat. "I doubt whether he even cares, my dear. I'll bid you good night."

She would not think of that drop of blood on the cobblestones. Instead she rinsed her mouth and washed her face, trying not to dwell on her hunger or give in to her despair.

Luke, why have you forsaken me?

"One hour, Citizeness!" Renard shouted.

Jane blinked at him in the morning light. She had slept a little since dawn, worn out by hunger and sorrow. She suspected the sounds from outside throughout the night, shouting and random loud noises, had been created specifically to unsettle her and wear down her resistance. Several times Renard, heavily guarded, had arrived to bully and threaten her.

"I beg your pardon, sir." She had discovered that a bland, slightly stupid, ladylike air enraged him.

His bodyguard watched Jane with great attention as he bent toward her. "In one hour, Citizeness, I arrest your family. They like that, to know you *une Damnée*? And you are here, alone with all these soldiers. You are shamed! It is your fault that your family suffer and die."

"Your soldiers fear me," she said. "As you, General, should."

"Silence!"

He stood breathing heavily.

She yawned.

"Well?" he said.

"I beg your pardon, I believe you told me not to speak."

"Tell me where the Damned are." He reached for her arm and shook her.

The soldiers closed in, ready to protect him if Jane attacked.

One hour. She could at least give her family a little time and hope that somehow they had heard rumors of her arrest and go into hiding. It was a very faint hope, but possibly she should try.

She sank back with a sigh, eyes closed.

"Ah! You swoon." Renard kicked her. "Or you pretend. Tell us and you may drink from someone."

She opened her eyes to see the soldiers stare at their commander in horror; doubtless they expected to be ordered to succumb to her.

Poulett had now entered the cell.

"Do not fear, gentlemen," she said. "You will find it a most pleasant experience. Ask Citizen Poulett, who enjoys having the Damned drink his blood."

Poulett glared at her. "She deceives you, Renard."

"Tell me, then," Renard said to her. "It will go badly with you, if you lie."

"Lansdown Crescent. They mentioned it. I—"

"She lies," Poulett repeated, but already Renard was striding from the cell, shouting out orders. Poulett paused in the doorway. "You will regret this deception."

"Oh, I don't think things could be much worse for me. But as for you, I believe the artillery is closer to the city, and if the English take the city, I think things could go very badly for you."

Jane knew the fashionable crescent high on Lansdown Hill was a good half hour on horseback from the center of the city. By the time Renard's men had arrived and searched the houses, then returned to report that the Damned had not been found, it would be mid-afternoon or later.

She sank back onto her straw and made yet another effort to call out to Luke, but he gave no reply. The light at the window dulled and the sky became the color of pewter before Renard returned, again with a retinue of soldiers.

He was icy calm. "You lie to us, Citizeness. You know what happens now."

He nodded to the soldiers, who hauled her to her feet and slammed her face forward against the wall. The rough stone scratched her face and she was immobilized by the hands holding her at shoulders and wrists. So, what now? Were they going to dishonor her? She heard the sound of steel behind her—not the sound of a sword pulled from its sheath, but some other implement.

Hands fumbled at her hair, pulled it free of the pins, and grabbed a handful. She felt a tug, followed by a sudden lightness at her neck as shears clacked. And again. Hanks of hair slithered against her shoulder.

"Why, you make me fashionable," Jane said. "I am much obliged."

"Madame la Guillotine requires a smooth surface to do her work," Renard said. He ripped away the fichu tucked into the top of her gown, revealing her shoulders and swell of her bosom, and tossed it aside. "This also will get in the way. You are greatly honored, Citizeness Austen. You will be one of the first in the town to enjoy her embrace."

They released her, the soldiers stepping away before she could turn.

"So now you are prepared. Make your peace with the devil, Citizeness, for tomorrow you die."

She turned away from the wall and raised her hands to her newly shorn head. Locks of hair fell down her gown, tickling her skin, and onto the straw at her feet.

"My family . . ."

Renard shrugged. "We arrested them. Good night, Citizeness."

She supposed it was hunger and weakness that made her dream so. It was night, the time for hunting and gratification and pleasure, but she dozed while outside, the wind murmured to the intermittent background of stuttering artillery, and occasional gusts of sleet pattered onto the floor.

She dreamed she was back in Steventon, with Cassandra in the upstairs sitting room between their bedchambers. Cassandra trimmed a hat, a scattering of silk flowers and ribbon on the table between them. She picked the hat up to view it in the light that streamed through the window, turned it, frowned, and added another flower.

Jane bent over her sheet of paper. Her pen scratched out an entire paragraph with supreme confidence. It was time for the creation of another character. Someone handsome and untrustworthy who would charm and entice for his own amusement. A man who would prey upon innocence and generosity, yet provide pleasure and delight. Now she understood the significance of the touch of fingertips, the intimacy of a glance, a touch; how it was possible for the greatest propriety to mask passion and desire.

She wrote, smiling, the words flowing as the white sheet filled with her regular, elegant handwriting. Time dissolved. When she laid her pen down, Cassandra had put the finished hat aside and was hemming a petticoat with small, regular stitches, sitting close to the window to catch the rays of the late afternoon sun. Jane stretched and flexed her stiff fingers.

Her father entered the parlor. "So, you're hard at work, then, Jenny."

"Indeed, yes. Papa, Cassandra, pray listen to this. Tell me what you think . . ."

She woke on what was to be her last day on earth with the realization that now she had become, in her dreams, at least, a writer. What a pity. It was all such a great pity.

I wish you could have known, Cassandra. Papa, you would be so proud of me.

And I wish I could have bidden you all farewell.

Chapter 20

"They say it's fast." Mr. Thomas took her hand, partly for balance, as they stood in the cart, but mostly for comfort. He looked somewhat the worse for wear, the lenses of his spectacles cracked, bruises fading on his face.

From his touch she knew he was afraid, desperately worried for the wife and children he would leave behind, for his business had been seized, and there was no one to support them or protect them from arrest. Jane squeezed his hand back, sympathizing with his distress.

"Are you ill?" he asked. "I thought your kind did not sicken. I remember the first time you shook my hand, you had a grip like a vise."

"I have not dined for some time. I am weak. Help me stand, Mr. Thomas. I do not want to appear frightened."

The other occupants of the cart, a woman Jane had not seen before and the elderly aristocratic gentleman, stood in shocked silence. As she had guessed, she had been imprisoned at the Assembly Rooms, along with the other condemned prisoners, but she had no idea what had happened to the very respectable shopkeeper or the woman with the basket. She wondered what would happen to Polly and the other prisoners at the Riding School, how soon they would stand trial. She tipped her head back to look at the sky, full of scudding dark clouds driven by a biting wind.

"The guns are closer now," she said. "Have you heard any news?"

"I doubt English troops will gallop in to rescue us as the blade is about to fall," Mr. Thomas said. "That is the stuff of novels and fantasy."

"Some novels, sir." How odd to have a literary discussion in the cart that was about to take them to their death, surrounded by French troops. "It would be an excellent scene in a play, do you not agree? For in the novels I should like to read, mostly the characters talk of such things, for they are the ones who are left at home, remaining steadfast, while others seek adventure and bold deeds."

"Ah, the sort of book a lady would read."

"Or write," Jane said. "Sir, if you wish to pray, I shall stop my chatter."

He squeezed her hand again and bowed his head.

One of the soldiers clambered aboard the cart and picked up the reins, making a clucking noise with his tongue to encourage the horse forward. Ahead of them, General Renard sat astride a spirited black horse that sidled and pranced as they moved forward, away from the Assembly Rooms and down Bartlet Street, making their way to the Pump Yard, where the executions were to take place.

People lined the street—some curious, most excited and shouting. Clods of filth and stones rained down on the cart.

"Why do they do this?" the woman standing next to Jane demanded. She had a French accent and a ravaged beauty despite her chopped-off hair. "I come here to escape, I think it is safe here. Now it is not."

On the horizon Jane saw a puff of smoke and heard the crash of artillery fire coming from the direction of the London Road. She could not allow herself to hope that she might be saved, but if the fighting lasted another day, and the French were defeated, maybe her family would live.

"I never liked you English," the Frenchwoman said to Jane. Her face was bleeding from a cut.

"We've never liked the French much, particularly now," Jane said, distracted by the scent of blood, the woman's fear and vulnerability. What difference would it make if she were to dine on this stranger now? Yet it seemed absurd to quarrel with someone when they were both about to die. She raised a hand to ward off a particularly loathsome missile that flew toward the cart and bounced it off onto the head of one of the soldiers.

"What the devil is going on ahead?" The other occupant of the cart, the stooped, elderly man, who had coronets embroidered on the cuffs of his shirt, directed Jane's gaze. A great cloud of smoke hung in the sky over the city and Jane caught the scents of gunpowder and fear and panic.

"Our troops are here!" she shouted. "*A bas les français!*"

"They're coming in on the Bristol Road!" someone called from the bystanders.

Renard reined in his horse and ordered his men to silence the prisoners, for the crowd now surged around the cart, their disdain and missiles directed toward the French soldiers. The cart slowed almost to a halt as people surrounded it, packed so closely the French could not pull their weapons.

The driver cursed and wielded his whip on the crowd and the horse's back, so that they set off again at a lurch, the escort running to keep up as Renard urged his horse to a canter. The crowd fell back to let Renard and the cart pass, but then followed behind, a mob that was now becoming ugly. Filth and cobblestones showered onto the heads of the French troops; those who fell were trampled underfoot.

They turned into the Pump Yard, now a battlefield, the air thick with smoke and filled with men fighting hand to hand. A platform was erected outside the Abbey again, but this time it held the guillotine, the wooden structure twice the height of a man, looming out of the smoke. A pale winter sunlight illuminated the huge, deadly blade suspended above.

Renard, sword in hand, rallied his troops, leaving the cart unguarded but in danger from flying shot. Jane shouted to her companions to get down, and as she pushed the Frenchwoman to her knees, the woman cursed at her, screaming that she wanted to go home to Paris, away from these barbarous English. Jane supposed that the woman might look back on it, were she to live, and appreciate the irony.

Jane raised her bound hands and bit through the rope, then jumped from the cart, snatching a sword from a wounded soldier. As she did so a flash of red fire and a deafening explosion lifted the guillotine and blew it into fragments in a great cloud of smoke. Jane found herself on the ground in a singing silence.

Someone stood over her. She groped for the sword but it was not there.

The man's mouth moved but all she heard was the ringing in her ears.

He dropped to his knees beside her.

Jane. Jane, I am here. Jane, my love.

"You—you bastard. Where have you been?" She struggled to her feet, Luke holding her arm. He looked tired, his face dirty and covered with stubble.

Look.

He pointed to the top of the Abbey, where the *tricouleur* slid down the flagpole and the Union Jack was raised in its place, flapping in the wind. The sound returned to her, a great outcry of cheers and shouts, and hats flew into the air.

"We did it, by God, we did it!" Mr. Thomas, his ruined spectacles discarded or lost and blood spatters on his shirt, waved a sword in the air. "Miss Austen, I'd best get back to my shop, to see my family and find my spare pair of spectacles. It has been an honor and a privilege. Ma'am, sir." He bowed to them and left.

The discarded French flag floated from the top of the Abbey in a leisurely, graceful descent, coming to rest on the body of Renard, who lay dead, eyes staring blankly at the city he had lost.

A British officer rode up, a weary young man with a great beak of a nose, his uniform stained and torn. "Venning, get that woman out of here."

"She's one of us. Miss Austen, may I introduce Colonel Wellesley."

"Your servant, ma'am. Venning, you'll dine with the other officers tonight."

"I don't believe so, Wellesley."

"You damned Damned—pardon me, ma'am. No discipline at all." The colonel saluted Jane and wheeled his horse away.

"My family has been arrested—"

"No, they're safe. William persuaded them to move to other lodgings under a false name."

Jane shook her head. "I thought you had abandoned me."

"I know. I am sorry for it, but that you were able to hear me at all was remarkable for a fledgling. When we have put thoughts into each other's minds we have been closer to each other, and with other senses involved. William feared more knowledge would endanger you or possibly all of us."

"*William?* What of *you*, Luke? Are you so easily persuaded?"

"He is your Creator and mine, and has authority. There were other reasons too. You will understand, Jane."

"No. I do not understand." A sob burst from her. She turned her head aside, ashamed that she wept in front of him.

"When did you dine last?"

"With you." She rubbed her face, aware that she smeared smoke and grit into her skin.

Without a word he led her to the shelter of a nearby doorway and offered her his wrist, safe in the circle of his arms while the citizens of Bath picked over the battlefield, searching for their dead, and Wellington's victorious regiment marched through the city. "Odd that you drink from me so close to the poisonous waters. So it happened the first time too." His fingers traced her face. "This? Any other hurts?"

She winced, gulped greedily, and swallowed. "A stone. That was before they started throwing them at the French."

"That's enough. I don't want you falling asleep."

He frowned as she left a trail of blood on his cuff and presumably on her chin, for he wiped it with his thumb. "No manners. Have you forgotten everything I taught you?"

"Not everything." She met his gaze and held it, amorous from fatigue and shock and the richness of his blood.

"Ah. We'll go home."

"And home is . . . ?"

"The splendor of the Royal Crescent, with some very elegant French officers and their doxies as neighbors. Their soirees lasted almost as long as ours. I imagine they will have left by now."

"Right under their noses!" She laughed in delight.

She would have liked a leisurely stroll across town arm in arm, talking lovers' nonsense. In reality, it was a stroll through the margins of a battlefield, although most of the French soldiers they encountered were frightened and demoralized and more inclined to run away. When they entered the Circus, a woebegone group of the enemy approached with a white flag, and Luke told them in no uncertain terms to find someone else to accept their surrender. His fearsome *en sanglant* drove his point home and they scattered.

They continued along Brock Street with some caution. The architects of the city intended this modest street to emphasize the sudden space and elegant proportions of the Crescent, but who knew what surprises might await them. Happily, the Royal Crescent showed no signs of fighting, although many houses showed signs of a hasty retreat: front doors flung open, and looters carrying out furniture and bottles of wine. Now Luke and Jane's progress was impeded by an impromptu celebration as men and women stopped them to demand that they drink toasts to the army and to the King.

Luke led Jane into one of the houses that was full of the Damned drinking champagne, most of them battle-stained and weary—after all, this was the time of day when generally their kind would rest. Many of them greeted Luke, in a variety of languages, and regarded Jane with curiosity.

A woman smiled at her. "I trust you remember me, Miss Jane Austen, who tastes of ripe apricots. I am delighted to see you again, and William tells me you have played a major part in the protection of His Highness."

Smeared in dirt and blood, and wearing torn men's clothes, Sybil was worlds away from the elegant creature who had dazzled Jane at the Basingstoke Assembly. Jane offered her hand, gratified that her Creator had spoken well of her. "Indeed, yes, I'm very fond of George."

Sybil raised her eyebrows at Jane's familiarity, smiled, and moved away to talk to other members of the Damned.

Jane reached for a glass of champagne from a tray offered by a waiter, all of whom, she had noticed, were extremely good-looking and would probably be available for more intimate forms of refreshments later in the evening.

"They tell me you were there when the cannons got the guillotine, miss," the footman said with a shy smile. "And that you fought like a lion."

"Why, Jack! I didn't recognize you in livery," Jane said. "I think that's something of an exaggeration. But you'll be pleased to know that quite a bit of damage was done to the Abbey. I expect you'll have to repair your angel again."

William pushed his way through the crowd. To Jane's surprise he bowed and bent over her hand (which she noticed, to her embarrassment, was filthy with dust and dried blood). "Welcome back," he said. "The fledgling has proved her worth."

"Lord, your hair's a mess, miss," Ann said as she brandished a pair of scissors and a comb. "But then I wouldn't expect French soldiers to do much of a job. I'll tidy it up for you. You can't go to see Mr. William looking like that."

"I have to see William?"

"Yes, and it's time to get dressed, if you please, ma'am."

So it was; it was already dark, but there was a glow outside. Jane got out of bed, for she had fallen into an exhausted sleep, and crossed to the window. Outside a great bonfire blazed on the field that gave the occupants of the Royal Crescent the illusion of pastoral life with the pleasures of the town a short chair's ride away. Dark figures danced around the fire, singing and brandishing bottles.

"So we've won, miss," Ann continued. "All the Royal Family safe, and the Frenchies on the run all through the country, so

I heard. I expect George will go back; 'tis a pity, he gave me a guinea every time."

"I shall miss him too," Jane said. Despite the triumph of the day and the knowledge that her family was safe, she felt a weary sadness. Part of it, she knew, was that her abandonment by Luke was not fully explained, and her dream about writing lingered still. Of course George would return; she felt a pang that the man she had grown to like so much would become once again a plump, spoiled, dissolute figure of fun.

She listened to Ann chatter while her hair was dressed—a few combs and a spray of silk flowers hid much of the damage— she supposed it would grow again, for did not the male Damned shave? Clarissa had lent her a gown of gorgeous gray and gold silk that slithered and shimmered as she moved and a sumptuous pair of clocked stockings. Fan in hand, she descended to the drawing room, where Luke and William, handsome in their silk coats and breeches, greeted her with formal bows.

There was one other in the room: Margaret, who inclined her head to Jane with a look of scorn.

"You were betrayed," William said.

"I know," Jane said. "Poulett—"

"No, not Poulett. Or rather, not Poulett alone." He turned his head to Margaret, who was blatantly *en sanglant*.

Luke came to Jane's side. "As your Bearleader, allow me to advise you. You may call for her death or banishment."

"Her death?" Jane echoed.

"To be immortal does not mean you are invulnerable. I think you have learned something of that today and we are most distraught that it came to this pass. You see, I could not speak freely to you during your imprisonment without running the risk of Margaret overhearing. We did not wish her to know she was discovered until you and your family were safe. I am most sorry."

"As am I," William said.

Jane stood, silent, considering. "If—if I choose she should be banished, what then?"

William shrugged. "She will have to find other companions, if she can. She will have no reputation, no letters of introduction. Death might be preferable."

Jane hesitated. "I told Poulett I would kill him if I could. I took his blood. I trusted him. But . . ." She and Margaret had never trusted each other, bound in rivalry for Luke, but even now she could not countenance a killing in cold blood.

"Poulett is dead," Luke said. "By his own hand, earlier today, for the shame of becoming a traitor."

William crossed to the mantelpiece, where an elaborately carved wooden box stood. He opened it and removed a knife in the shape of a sickle, a curved blade that shone gray in the firelight. "This is what you will use, Jane."

She went to his side and took the knife in her hand. It was of stone, ancient and deathly cold even to her touch. "No," she said. "No, I can't."

"So you are not only lowborn but a coward also," Margaret said.

"Hold your tongue!" Luke snapped at her.

"No," Jane said. "I would hear what she has to say." She could not bear to hold the evil little knife anymore. She placed it carefully back inside the box, where it rested on a bed of dark red velvet, and felt a great relief as the lid snapped closed.

"You will leave us," Margaret said. "You will destroy what we have, what Luke has given you. You know it is the truth. It makes little difference whether I cease to exist or not, but you will leave knowing more than any mortal should of the Damned and you may destroy us all. That is why I wished you to die."

"Yet you took the risk of handing me over to the French. What if I had betrayed you all then?"

"I knew you would not. Not then. You have greater strength under duress than you know." Margaret shrugged. "It is when you choose to leave us that I fear for the Damned. Let us get this over with, if you please. Banish me if you will; William underestimates my power to survive. I may emerge from this better than you think."

"Very well. I choose to banish her." Jane looked at Luke for guidance.

William recited a formal phrase in a language that sounded familiar to Jane. Greek, yes, that was it—she remembered her brothers reciting their lessons, long evenings in the vicarage while her mother sewed, smiling at their accomplishments. Their youngest sister had watched and listened, and longed to know as much as her brothers.

She would never see that drawing room again, or her family.

William leaned to kiss Margaret on one cheek and then the other. "Go," he said.

She inclined her head and left the room.

Luke drew Jane's arm through his and led her to the window that looked out over the meadow where the dark figures cavorted around the bonfire. They did not have to wait long. A tall figure, swathed in a long, hooded cloak emerged from the house. She strode off into the shadows and disappeared from view without looking back.

"I shall not leave," Jane said.

Luke made no reply but linked her fingers in his.

* * *

"I assure you, it's been an honor, Miss Austen." George, His Highness the Prince of Wales, flanked by members of his own regiment, all jingling fashionable military splendor, took her hand as they stood outside the Royal Crescent house the next morning.

"Shall you take the cure here, sir?"

"Yes, but I'll be staying at a house outside the town. My physician says that, well, it's best to not be around you and the others while I recover. I might come back and beg you to bite me. Or the other way around, I'm not sure which."

"I wish you a speedy return to good health, sir. I'm sure you'll enjoy playing the piano again."

"I shall. But damnation, I'll have to see Caroline again. Family obligations, you know, Miss Austen. I suppose you don't have any of those anymore."

She shook her head. No family, no obligations, no Cassandra . . .

The handsome young George Brummell held the carriage door open, murmuring that possibly it was time for His Highness to leave.

"We've had some fine times, haven't we? William says I won't remember much, but it's probably just as well." George sighed and squeezed her hand. "You'll dedicate a book to me, I hope, Jane."

She smiled and curtsied as the Prince of Wales stepped into the carriage and drove away with his regiment as escort.

William stood in the doorway of the house. He brushed the back of his hand over his eyes. "I hate to see my fledglings leave."

Jane followed him back inside the silent house. It was early in the day for them, and most of the household and their guests were still asleep.

She trudged up the stairs—once again her bedchamber was at the top of the house—picking her way around guests who had fallen asleep on the stairs and landings. At the back of her mind a profound uneasiness stirred, a yearning for something or someone. Certainly it was not hunger, for she had dined well and often last night, until Luke had chastised her for her greed. In her former life she would have put pen to paper or played the pianoforte, or taken a long walk with Cassandra . . .

"Jane?" One of the women had awoken and sat blinking at her, shoving one of the visiting vampires from her lap.

"Polly! I am so glad you are well."

"What happened to you? Lord, look at your hair. Did the Frenchies do that?"

Jane smiled, relieved to see that Polly was alive. "Would you like to come to the kitchen for some tea? Or ale?"

Polly rose to her feet, swaying a little, and giggled. She started as Jane steadied her with a hand at her elbow. "Your hands are so cold. What an adventure, eh, Jane?"

Jane led her down to the kitchen where she revived her with a drop of blood in a cup of tea. Polly sat, her elbows at her table, accepting slices of buttered toast from Mr. Brown, and telling him of a connection she had with a most superior farm nearby that would supply the household with all the vegetables it needed. Jane slipped out again.

This time Jane reached her bedchamber, a small haven of quiet in the crowded house. Ann had unpacked her belongings, and her manuscript sat on a small table with pen and ink at the ready. Jane smiled at the maid's thoughtfulness and sat down. She pulled the ribbon undone and Cassandra's scent rose, a little fainter now, but still with the power to conjure poignant, loving memories of their life together. As that scent faded, so would her recollections of Cassandra.

She must write to her family, for she knew they would be concerned, her father most of all, since he alone knew that she fought. She took the last page of her manuscript and on the blank side wrote a short note assuring them that she was still in Miss Venning's employ and well. She hesitated and then laid the sheet down.

Her family should have not only the note, but the entire manuscript. Possibly Cassandra could send it to another publisher and make herself a little pin money; yes, she liked that idea, Cassandra picking through trims and fabrics with an endearingly serious look on her face, the most fashionable woman in Steventon, thanks to her sister's book. She retied the ribbon around the manuscript that was part of her former life.

She picked out a long, hooded cloak that someone had left in the bedchamber and went downstairs, the manuscript tucked safely beneath one arm, and out of the house. The formerly elegant Royal Crescent was a mess of empty bottles and discarded wine casks; a large black mound on the green pasture opposite still gave off a little smoke. On her walk through the town, she passed townspeople still celebrating, drinking and dancing in the streets. Several times she was obliged to turn down the offers of gentlemen who wished her to join in the celebrations or who invited her to more private revels indoors.

As she turned into Paragon Place, a troop of British soldiers escorting a handful of French prisoners passed her.

Her knock at the front door was not answered and the sense of unease that had plagued her since waking that day grew stronger. She stepped back into the street and observed that smoke rose from the chimneys, so undoubtedly someone was home. She listened carefully. From inside came a muffled whimper and a creaking sound, and a strong sense of fear and panic. Things were not right here.

With a silent apology to her aunt and uncle, she wrapped her fist in the folds of her cloak and prepared to ruin their fine solid mahogany door and its brass lock. One solid blow that left her knuckles aching, and the door swung open. She stepped into the foyer and then into the dining room, where Betty, gagged and bound to a chair, let out a crescendo of squeaks and whimpers.

"Sssh." Jane bit through the ropes. She whispered, "Tell me what is happening here, but quietly."

Betty nodded, tears streaking down her face.

Jane untied the gag.

"Miss Cassandra, upstairs—Garonne is there—"

Jane didn't wait to hear any more but flew up the stairs. She could smell them, Cassandra's beloved scent soured by fear and Garonne's potent blend of exhaustion and despair.

She flung open the drawing-room door.

Chapter 21

"Do what I say or Miss Cassandra dies." Garonne was filthy and exhausted, stubble on his face, his eyes red-rimmed. The hand that held the pistol to her sister's head shook.

Cassandra sat on a chair, wrists bound, tears spilling down her cheeks. She gave a tiny shake of her head.

"Be still!" Garonne's voice rose to a shriek.

"Let her go," Jane said.

Garonne watched her every move, his finger on the trigger, and Jane feared his shaking hand would accidentally fire the pistol.

"I must have a letter for a safe permit to return to France. I will not be a prisoner here. She will die if you do not."

"Certainly, I shall help however I can." Clearly he was mad. What influence did he think she possibly might have? "But—"

"You lie!" he screamed. "You write to Wellesley. I saw him with you yesterday."

She hadn't seen Garonne in the chaos of the battle. "Very well. Pray uncock your pistol."

"You think I am a fool? No. You write." He swayed as if about to fall asleep on his feet. "Or we wait for Mr. Austen to come home for his dinner and find his daughter dead, and then he writes the letter so I do not shoot you also, Miss Jane."

"Very well. I have a package beneath my arm. I shall put it down now. Pray do not be alarmed." Wishing she had thought to arm herself, she slowly drew her cloak back to reveal the manuscript. Clearly, this was a situation where the pen was not mightier than the sword; or was it?

"*Vite!*"

She had hoped her slow actions might calm him but he radiated fear and lethal tension, a man close to madness. When she attacked, it would have to be fast. Her movement had taken her closer to him and she shifted a little to choose the angle at which she would attack. She must strike the pistol away in the split second before it fired.

The clock on the mantelpiece whirred and began to strike the chimes before the hour of four o'clock.

Downstairs the door opened and Jane heard her father and mother exclaim over the broken lock and splintered wood. She pulled the ribbon free of the manuscript and threw it at Garonne.

The manuscript, several hundred sheets of paper, burst into its individual pages in midair, falling onto and around Garonne's head as she leaped for his throat. The pistol exploded in her ear, the smell of powder mingling with Garonne's blood, bitter with madness and terror. His body convulsed under hers as he fought her and she ripped with her canines as his breath let out in a last, frantic gurgle.

She let him drop onto the carpet soaked with his blood.

Someone was screaming.

"Cassandra!"

But her sister had flung herself from the chair and was stumbling away from her, weeping with terror.

"Cassandra, it's over. He's dead. You're safe."

Cassandra's eyes rolled up and she dropped to the floor in a swoon.

Jane looked up to see her mother and father standing in the doorway clinging to each other, regarding her and the bloody room with horror. No wonder, she was still *en sanglant*, and covered with blood.

She reversed her canines.

"You're looking very well, ma'am." Jane gave a giggle of shock at her ridiculous words, but it was true. Mrs. Austen wore a coarse linen apron with bloodsmears and worse on it, but she had a sense of purpose and energy that Jane could not ever remember seeing before.

Mrs. Austen ran to Cassandra and cradled her in her arms.

Her father blinked at her. "We—we have been at the hospital. With the wounded. Your mother . . . I . . . ." He held up a copy of the New Testament and looked helplessly at Jane's mother and sister, both of them on the floor, weeping.

"I've rarely seen a messier kill." Luke stood in the doorway.

Cassandra looked up. She screamed. "He—he's dead!" She swooned again.

It was Luke who took charge, escorting them downstairs into the dining room, where he poured large glasses of brandy. There would be no dinner for hours, if at all, for the servants had only recently returned from celebrating the victory, somewhat worse for wear for drink; and the family had little appetite. Garonne, it appeared, had hidden in the house and revealed himself only an hour previously, when the house was empty except for Cassandra and Betty, and when he knew that the Austens would return soon for their dinner, at four o'clock.

"And that very kind Mr. Fitzwilliam—I believe you are acquainted with him, Jane, for he is a friend of Miss Venning's—

had found us lodgings for the past couple of days for he feared the French might arrest us. We thought it was safe to return," Mr. Austen said. "Cassandra had the headache and stayed here today while we went to the hospital. But Mr. Venning, I thought you had been hanged. And why are you here?"

I knew you were in danger, Jane. "A case of mistaken identity," Luke said. "Some more brandy, sir?"

"I regret I have deceived you all," Jane said. She had intended to add that she must say farewell, but the words would not come.

"Not all of us, my dear," her father said.

Mrs. Austen shrugged. "Who gives a damn? Both my girls are safe. I beg your pardon, I have just spent the better part of the day with cursing soldiers and I fear I picked up their foul language. Cassandra, come upstairs with me, if you please." Murmuring comforting words about hot water—if the fire was not out—and soap (if there was any left) she led Cassandra out.

Jane watched her leave, heart heavy. She could not bear that Cassandra would remember her like this, covered with blood, an unnatural creature. Tears rose to her eyes as she relived that terrible moment, Cassandra cowering from her in terror and shock among the pages of her ruined, bloody manuscript.

"I am most obliged to you for returning my daughter, sir," Mr. Austen said.

"I assure you, sir, you have nothing to thank me for," Luke said. "If I may, I would speak to Jane alone."

"Very well." Mr. Austen bowed and left the room.

"It is always a mistake, to come back," Luke said. He swirled the brandy in his glass. "I am sorry you felt compelled to do so, even though you have saved your sister. Do you not see how they fear you?"

"They do. But they love me too."

"No." He shook his head. "They love the Jane who is dead to

them now, their daughter and sister. That is the Jane they will remember, not the monstrous creature who has ripped out a man's throat in front of them. That, they will want to forget, if they can." He stood and held out his hand. "Let us return home."

"No." She had not meant to say it as bluntly, if indeed she had meant to say it at all. "No, I cannot."

"Ah." He sat at the table again, shaking his head, a great wash of sadness enveloping them both. "Margaret warned me of this, William also. I trusted you, Jane."

She made no reply.

"It is not enough to tell you that I love you passionately, more than I have ever loved before, and that I can give you an eternity of happiness? I suppose not. And I suppose it is no good to remind you that my love is returned, for you love me, Jane. I dare you to say you do not."

She wanted to tell him that she loved him, that she would never love anyone as much, but the words would not come.

"Tell me." He seized her hands. "I know you better than I know myself, or so I thought. I will give you everything, anything your heart desires. But if you will not stay with me, I must know why."

"Because I must write again and I must be with my sister and my family. There—it is the truth I have denied myself as one of the Damned. You may give me all the pleasures of the world, sir, you may be all things as my lover, but you cannot restore what I shall lose. I have struggled in vain to deny my heart's desire; I can do so no longer."

"Your writing. And your sister. And you do not even know whether this—this *experiment* among the Damned will leave you with your talent for writing as it was."

She flinched at the contempt in his voice but held his hands still, for she could not bear this last touch to end, even though his pain and humiliation burned through her. "On the contrary, sir, it leaves me stronger. You told me once I listened and observed, and while I could not write I remembered and I learned. I will write again, sir."

He released her hands and stood. "Consider, Jane. You'll marry some bore of a country gentleman who'll kill you in childbed and who won't want a bookish wife anyway. Perhaps you'll stay a spinster and lose your bloom and die young of some disease they'll find an easy cure for in a hundred years or so. Or you'll see your sister die first."

"Now you're cruel."

"No, it is the truth. But let us paint a happier picture for Miss Jane Austen. You write a few books that entertain your family and you win a little fame, perhaps even some money, while you live. And after, what then? Your books languish forgotten on dusty bookshelves and you are but a name on a binding that disappears with decay and time. You think your books offer you a chance at immortality? Oh, Jane, do not delude yourself. Come back to me. To us."

"No. No, I cannot."

"You break my heart. And it's an old heart, and a tough one. That is your final answer?"

"Yes."

"I will regret it forever. I hope you shall not."

She stood and blundered from the room as though all the strength and grace of the Damned had deserted her. Her father stood at the top of the stairs, waiting for her, so she thought, but he gave her a sorrowful look and continued up the next flight of stairs to the bedchambers.

She went back into the drawing room, still splattered with blood, although a sheet had been thrown over Garonne's corpse. From the window, she watched Luke walk away and wept. Her

Bearleader, her love: a slender man whose step was usually jaunty and graceful. But now she saw one who faced an eternity of sorrow, for despite years, centuries, in which he had played at love, she was the one who had broken his heart.

She wiped the tears from her eyes and bent to pick up a page of her book. And another, where the ink had run with blood. Jane waved it dry and reached for another, speckled with blood. And another; so many pages to collect and sort and cleanse.

It was a beginning.

The vampire stood at the doorway of the Pump Room. He did not want to go further inside, for the vapors of the poison water made him uneasy, but he had to see her for the last time before she took the cure. It was crowded today, with wounded officers and townspeople thick at the counter where glasses of steaming mineral water were dispensed. He searched the crowd for her; he knew she was here but he could not yet see her for the throng of people.

He stepped back and bowed as a woman, a pug running at her heels, entered the Pump Room. The pug showed its teeth and growled, but its owner glanced at him with a flirtatious smile; not recognizing him for what he was, but seeing a man who excited her desire. Later, she might blush at her brazen invitation.

He was not interested. There was only one woman he wished to see here, and he had failed her.

And there she was, taller than most of the women in the room, and to him, the most beautiful; bright hazel eyes, cheekbones too sharp for fashion, glossy chestnut hair, pale skin which some might envy and others might consider a sign of ill health. Others were interested in her too, young bucks ogling her through quizzing glasses, people wondering who she was because there was something different and exotic about her, even though her dress was modest and her companions seemed to be middling sort of people. The aunt and uncle, returned from their enforced country visit; her parents, tired and anxious; and her sister hovered protectively around her.

Her father handed her a glass of water. She made a face, wrinkling her nose for comic effect, and her companions laughed, but with some anxiety, he could tell.

She walked, no, she strode—for the moment, she still had that grace and wondrous flow of movement their kind possessed—into a patch of sunlight that streamed through one of the tall glass doors and inspected her glass, as one might contemplate a fine wine, as the steam rose into the air.

She looked straight at him, smiling faintly, and raised the glass in a gallant, ironic toast.

Artemis Photo Studio

Janet Mullany

Raised in England on a diet of Georgette Heyer and Jane Austen, **JANET MULLANY** has worked as an archaeologist, a classical music radio announcer, a performing arts administrator, a bookseller, and a proofreader and editor for a small press. Her first book, *Dedication* (2005), the only Signet Regency with two bondage scenes, was followed by the award-winning *The Rules of Gentility*, published by HarperCollins in 2007 and by Little Black Dress (Headline, UK) the following year. She has gone on to write more Regency chicklit for Little Black Dress and is at work on the next encounter between Jane Austen and the Damned. She lives near Washington, D.C., where she drinks a lot of tea and gives etiquette lessons to a cat.